WILL TO KILL

ROBERT M. DAVIS

Will to Kill

© 2014 Robert M. Davis

ISBN: 978-1-61170-181-4

Cover designed and illustrated by Bob Archibald

Printed in the USA and UK on acid-free paper.

 Robertson Publishing™
www.RobertsonPublishing.com

To purchase additional copies of this book go to:
amazon.com
barnesandnoble.com
www.rp–author.com/robertdavis

DEDICATION

FOR ROBIN BROOKS
Magic words from a courageous lady
made this book become a reality.

"A GOOD WRITER IS BASICALLY A STORY-TELLER,
NOT A SCHOLAR OR A REDEEMER OF MANKIND."
—Isaac Bashevis Singer

CHAPTER ONE

The early morning knocking on Dean's motel room door stopped after four sharp raps. He turned off the water flowing into the bathroom sink, placed his Gillette safety razor on the porcelain and flexed his throwing arm. A mask of shaving cream covering his light brown stubble held fast to his cheeks and jaw. More often than not, door-banging at this hour was a harbinger of bad news. Dean knew full well who pounded on his door and why. If he was quiet, maybe Rowdy would go away. Hope wasn't much of a strategy, but it was all he had left.

A mosquito buzzed Dean's ear. Sighting the little vampire fly was difficult under the bathroom's low-wattage bulb. The mosquito droned past him again before landing on the cracked mirror. One flick from a towel squished the annoying little sucker onto the glass. Not all of Dean's hand-eye coordination skills had abandoned him.

Another series of knocks rattled the door. If nothing else, Rowdy persisted. In silence Dean counted to sixty then expelled a relieved breath. Maybe he had bought himself a little more time. Maybe, once he arrived at the ballpark, he could talk them into letting him take batting practice. And maybe, just maybe, a pre-game home run barrage would change their minds about cutting him from the team.

Dean moved into the bedroom with a subtle limp wearing only the shaving cream. A soft dragon-fire belch reminded him of last night's drinking binge. His friend for the last nine years, Jack Daniel's, had taken advantage of him again. Jack had become Dean's pain killer when he tore knee ligaments his rookie year after chasing a pop fly and colliding with an infielder. Jack was the kind of friend parents warned their kids not to play with, but the always-present ache was less severe under Jack's influence. A hard swallow did nothing to lubricate the dryness in Dean's mouth and throat. He was in desperate need of water, antacid tablets, aspirin, and an elixir shot of Jack.

The clock radio clicked into action from the nightstand. Jerry Lee Lewis belted out his hit song, "Great Balls of Fire." The pounding in Dean's head kept time to The Killer's frenetic singing and piano performance. Jerry Lee had the talent to crank out one hit after another. Dean had once performed the same way on a kind of stage between the white chalked lines of a baseball diamond. But hits were hard to come by nowadays.

"Hey, cool cats," a gravelly-voiced radio disc jockey announced. "The hits keep on coming so groovy and so fine in our year of 1959. Let's simmer down The Killer's ivories a few degrees with Johnny Mathis' new hit single called '*Misty*.'"

A delicate piano introduction filled the room. Background strings broadened the melody. Dean went to the nightstand and twisted the Motorola's knob to the Off position." Portions of striped, multicolored wallpaper were peeling from the sheet rock. The musty-smelling carpet was lumpier than a minor league dirt infield. Six months of each year, for nine years, he had lived in similar cheap digs throughout the continental United States.

Jesus, what city was he in? He glanced up at the gross ceiling. It would be easier to remember the team he was playing for. The Mustangs. He was in Montana, home of the Billings Mustangs. Proof he hadn't destroyed all of his brain cells. Yet.

The woman in his bed lit a cigarette and exhaled a stream of smoke. Long fiery-red fingernails sifted through her strawberry blond hair. She sat up, exposing small breasts.

"Come back to bed, Dean the Dream Mason, before someone else knocks on your door?"

"Listen, ah. . ."

"Babs," she said, flicking an ash onto the floor. "My name is Babs. Honey, I've seen some heavy hitters in my time, but you was beltin' 'em down in the bar last night like a hall of famer. No wonder you got anemia."

Babs probably meant amnesia, unless she wasn't referring to his weakened brain. Once again, the previous night's events had been deleted from his memory bank, including the aftermath of meeting her in a bar. Most people referred to booze-induced memory loss as a blackout. His Aunt Maddy always used the term liquor-shock. If anyone would know, Aunt Maddy would. Until a stroke disabled her, his only living relative had been a pro's pro at drinking away a night's recollection. Now she resided in a nursing home room, partially paralyzed and sober.

"Look, Babs," he said, his voice raspy. "As you so eloquently pointed out, I had too much to drink last night. Sometimes I don't know when to stop."

Had he taken advantage of her? Or vice versa? Either way, he wasn't proud of himself.

"Ever been told your eyes are the same color of blue as Mickey Mantle's?" she asked, after blowing out a series of smoke rings.

"More than a few times," he said. In what seemed like a lifetime ago, his abilities as a ballplayer, not the color of his eyes, were compared to The Mick.

Dean stooped to search through his suitcase on the floor near the bed. Relief was in there somewhere. Drifting from league to league and team to team had prompted him to live out of his traveling bag. He snatched a handful of aspirin and Rolaids.

"About last night, Babs, I apologize if I said or did anything disrespectful."

"Well at least you've got some class." Babs mashed her cigarette to death in an ashtray on the nightstand. "More than most of the players I, ah . . . meet. How about disrespecting me one more time?" Babs stripped the sheet from her waist and punched his pillow. "With the slump you're in, this may be the only chance you get to run the bases today. Besides, I never had anyone who looked like Santa Claus before."

"Nothing personal, Babs," Dean said, touching the foam on his face. "But I need a session in the batting cage more than—"

Three hard knocks turned his attention to the front door. He slid into a pair of Jockey underwear. Babs jerked the sheet up to her chin.

"Open the damn door, Dream," Rowdy Morgan's gruff voice demanded. "I need to talk to you."

Dean turned to Babs and pressed a forefinger to his lips. The only time he saw Rowdy away from the ballpark was in a bar. He opened the door a few inches. His craggy-faced manager stood in the entryway, his cheek bulging from a chaw of tobacco.

"Mr. Finley wants to see you right after batting practice." Rowdy spit a stream of brown tobacco juice into an old beer cup. "Sorry, Dream. Wasn't my call."

Dean nodded to Rowdy before closing the door. Needles of anxiety pricked at his stomach walls. Loud tom-toms thumped in his chest. Sweat formed on his neck. How many times had he received a similar message during his minor league career? His body always reacted the same way. But this time, baseball's version of the Grim Reaper had just knocked on his door.

CHAPTER TWO

After K.A. pushed the floor length curtains aside, a twist on the French door handles proved futile. He jimmied a switchblade knife into the latch until the doors opened out onto a terrace scattered with leaves. The chill encompassing Twin Rose Nursing Home felt good against his layer of sweat. Why do they keep these places so damn hot? He sucked in mouthfuls of crisp air then spread several towels from the bathroom on the balcony floorboards near the railing.

Dawn was overtaking night, but the outside floodlights still beamed. Overcast filled the San Francisco sky. Bending at the waist, K.A. leaned over the wooden railing to peer three floors down. Rosebushes covered the grounds close to the building. A little further away, a cement walkway encircled the roses. Beyond that, a stone statue of a robed religious man, centered in a water fountain, provided tranquil sound. For some patients, Twin Rose was a place to recover. For others, their last stop at living.

He returned to the room leaving the doors open. An old woman stirred in bed, moaning in her sleep. He lifted a thickly cushioned easy chair from in front of the doors. His wiry build belied unnatural strength. The piece of furniture probably weighed more than the decrepit bag of bones lying in bed. He carried the chair to the balcony railing, setting the stubby legs down onto the towels so it would seem as if the chair had been dragged on the towels from inside the room.

When he returned to the room, the old woman was sitting up in her bed, stringy grey hair matted to her skull. One side of her face sagged, distorted from a disabling stroke. She stared in confusion then pointed a crooked finger at him and screeched like a frightened cat. How did she know he didn't belong here? His female nurse's dress fit well as did the dark wig.

He slapped the old woman's face hard to shut her up. Her

head conked against the headboard, terminating her ear-piercing squeals. She managed a pathetic groan.

Pounding on the wall came from next door. The unintelligible rants held a consistent tone of irritation.

Time was now an issue. K.A. would have to hurry. He lifted the old woman from the bed and charged out to the balcony. His unpredictable libido came alive, making him erect.

One of the woman's eyelids popped open, unveiling her inner fright. She battled back as best she could, hitting him with her one functional hand. He gave her an admiring nod. The old gal still had fight left in her.

He stepped up onto the chair next to the railing and heaved the old woman over the side with a violent grunt. Her white nightgown flapped with the whim of the air currents. She screamed. Then he heard a bone-cracking thud as her body hit the cement sidewalk.

A plump, dark complexioned man wearing a tool belt came into view. The man gaped down at the crumpled body and covered his mouth with a hand. A flood of blood spread to the man's work boot, causing him to stumble into a rosebush while wailing loud enough to wake the dead.

The killer backed away from the terrace then scurried through the room into the hallway. His pace slowed to a fast walk as he headed for the stairs. Most people hated their jobs. He loved his work. And why not? He'd been born with a God-given gift, like a great athlete or a musician who plays notes by ear. The old woman's death was another masterpiece performed by the Kill Artist, K.A. for short.

CHAPTER THREE

Dean entered the locker room carrying his mitt and spikes. Years of sweat and decay permeated the clubhouse. The rest of the team was still out on the field taking batting and fielding practice. When he had finished his first round of batting cage swings, manager Rowdy reminded him to see Mr. Finley.

Walter Finley sat on a wooden stool by Dean's locker. He wore his usual double-breasted suit and fedora. The owner of the Billings Mustangs exhaled a mouthful of smoke then spit out a loose piece of tobacco from his Chesterfield cigarette.

Dean removed his cap and considered the old man. Mr. Finley had been nothing but fair to him and generous to a fault, unlike most baseball management in Dean's experience. He had given Dean an opportunity to keep playing ball when other clubs showed no interest in a washed-up, twenty-seven-year-old ballplayer.

"Let me make this easy on you, Mr. Finley," Dean said. "I'm eighty-eight and out the gate. Nothing personal. You're just doing what's best for the club."

"It's the most difficult part of my job, you know?" Mr. Finley glanced down at his nicotine-stained fingers then up at Dean. "Turns my gut to tell a man who I like and respect that he's through. I hope your batting practice was a good one."

Dean ran a hand through his short-cropped, light brown hair. His batting practice had been anything but spectacular. He didn't hit one half-speed fastball out of the ballpark, but strength and skill were not the issue. Attempting to stay on balance with a lame limb had robbed Dean of his natural power swing, and made him a liability in the field.

"After the game I'm also cutting your young buddy Beals Becker," Mr. Finley said. "Maybe you can give the boy a ride to Nevada if you're heading back to San Francisco."

"Damn it, Mr. Finley." Dean slammed his glove and spikes into the locker. "Don't cut Beals because of me. I know the kid doesn't have much talent, but he hustles. Let him stay on the roster for the rest of the season."

"Becker doesn't have one ounce of your ability, even now." Mr. Finley wiped an ash off his brown suit jacket. "That lad couldn't catch the clap in a Toledo cat house, let alone a fly ball. I kept him on the team this long as a favor to you. But I'm getting a couple of players sent down from Single A. If I keep Becker on the roster, he'd be taking up a deserving player's spot."

Dean peered down at the cement floor. Mr. Finley was right, of course. Professional baseball was a game to Beals, not a business. The way it should be for a player. At least Beals had a job waiting for him working his father's ranch in Nevada.

"Do you mind if I tell him?" Dean asked. "He'll take it better coming from me."

"Good idea. Thanks, Dream."

Dean unbuttoned his Mustang jersey. His finger traced over the thick, navy blue wool letters sewn across the front. This would be the last time he'd be taking off a baseball uniform. He enjoyed the shabby, foul-smelling confines of a locker room almost as much as the ball field. Yet, no longer could he close his eyes and refuse to acknowledge the truth. He didn't quit the game. The game quit him. He had always imagined that if and when this moment came, the feeling would be a sense of relief. Just the opposite. He was embarrassed. Ashamed he could no longer play a game he once excelled at and still loved.

Mr. Finley coughed uncontrollably. Dean turned around. The gray-haired club owner's fragile body bent forward, his face wrinkled, and pain-racked. The old guy was in worse shape than Dean had thought.

"Jeez, are you all right?" Dean asked. "Can I get you some water or something?"

"It'll pass," Mr. Finley choked out. "Doc says I got something. Wants to do more tests. Hell, it's probably TB." He crushed the cigarette on the floor with a Buster Brown oxford and peered up at Dean. "You've got a good head for the game, Dream. The players respect your experience and knowledge. They often go to you instead of

Rowdy. You ever consider being a coach or a field manager? Even a general manager?"

"Never gave it much thought." Dean stepped out of his baggy pants. "In the third grade, a teacher asked us what we wanted to be when we grew up. I said I was going to be a professional baseball player, and the class laughed. In the seventh grade, same question – same response. In the tenth grade, they didn't laugh, they cheered. All I've ever wanted to do was play baseball."

"I could use a man like you to help me run this club," Mr. Finley wheezed. "Someone trustworthy who knows the game. If you come on board, it'll allow me the opportunity to tend to some business and tie up personal loose ends. My kids can't wait to get their greedy hands on this team and my money. No way will I leave the Mustangs to them. I'm serious about offering you a management position. Please give it some thought after you're settled."

Dean mustered a perfunctory nod. Standing in his jockstrap, stirrup socks, and dirty white sanitary stockings, his eyes searched for another stool. He glanced back and caught Mr. Finley grimacing at the four-inch skin-zipper decorating the inside of his left knee. The scar looked raunchy. Underneath, it felt worse.

"You could have been one of the best, Dream, if—"

"We'll never know, will we?" Dean kicked off his socks. "When you're young, you think you can play forever, invincible to age and injury. Trying to come back from a bum joint robs the natural from ability. You can still play, but it's just not the same. Maybe someday a sawbones will figure out a way of repairing bones, cartilage, and ligaments without ruining a player's career."

"Most men would've given up years ago. Have you been staying off the sauce?"

"Nothing holier than a reformed drunk, is there?" Dean smiled at the team owner. "I still have my moments. This could be one of them."

"Can't say that I blame you." Mr. Finley's Adam's apple flexed in and out. "You're still a young man, Dream. Hell, you still look like an idol, even if you can't play like one anymore. Don't wait as long as I did to slay the spirit monster."

Several coughs gripped Mr. Finley again. He covered his mouth with the top of a clenched fist. Dean patted the owner's bony shoulder, not knowing what else to do.

"You know I live vicariously through you ballplayers," Mr. Finley said. "Even a blind man could see that women swoon over your Jack Armstrong, All-American Boy looks. You've got to tell me, Dream: Is Ballpark Beddy as good as they say?"

Dean smiled again. Beddy was a platinum blonde who sat in the first row behind the Mustangs' dugout exposing her all star cleavage. Some players swore she had a Stearns and Foster mattress label imprinted on her back. Mr. Finley stared at him with pleading, watery eyes. To Dean's knowledge, he'd never been with Ballpark Beddy. Hell, if it would make Mr. Finley feel better, what difference would a little white lie make? No sense in spoiling the old man's dream.

"She's nails, Mr. Finley." Dean secured a towel around his waist.

"Hot damn." Mr. Finley slapped his knee. "I knew it." His expression turned serious. "I could make a few calls to some other teams if you want me to."

"Appreciate the offer." Dean extended his right hand to the Mustang owner. "If I can't play in this league and for you, my days as a ballplayer are over."

"This should keep you going for a few months." Mr. Finley stuffed a wad of green bills into Dean's hand. "Take some time. Clear your head. Then consider my offer."

"You're a good man, Mr. Finley. Someday I hope to repay your kindness."

Invisible pressure pushed against Dean. This was worse than being traded. It was even more deflating than being demoted to a lower class minor league team. He had just been given a one-way ticket to permanent off-season purgatory.

"Oh, Christ," Mr. Finley said. "Where's my head? I almost forgot. A telegram came for you this morning."

"Read it to me, will you?" Dean said, after eyeing the entrance. His former teammates were still out on the field.

Mr. Finley patted his coat then extracted a yellow Western

Union envelope from an inside pocket. He donned a pair of wire-rim glasses. His fingers tore at the flap. The paper message shook in his hand.

"It's from an attorney named Franklyn Edwards. It reads: Mr. Mason. Your Aunt, Madeline Principal, had a fatal accident at the nursing home this morning. Contact me ASAP regarding the reading of her will." Mr. Finley refolded the telegram and frowned. "I'm sorry, Dean. Some people just never get a break."

The telegram from Aunt Maddy's attorney had been cold and matter-of-fact. Emptiness enveloped Dean, like he'd been set adrift in an endless desert with a hole in his canteen. Aunt Maddy was his last surviving relative. She had a gold-digging goddaughter out there somewhere, but a goddaughter wasn't really family. He retreated to the shower room. In spite of his aunt's recent stroke, the news was hard to take. He would miss the cantankerous old woman as much as the game.

Dean leaned his forehead against the cold shower room tiles. Icy water spurted from the shower nozzle. He was too numb to care. He'd just lost his baseball career and Aunt Maddy, and it wasn't even noon.

CHAPTER FOUR

Dean inched his Ford Crestline Victoria forward in downtown San Francisco's late afternoon traffic. Towering commercial buildings gave him a sense of being at the bottom of a Canyon looking up. Cable car bells, bus whines, and police whistles were as present as The City's breeze.

Foot traffic jam-packed the sidewalks. People wearing military uniforms, business suits, and Bermuda shorts, commingled with prostitutes, panhandlers, hawkers, and down-and-outers. They all wanted something from somebody.

Dean's fingertips attacked the steering wheel like a bongo-beating beatnik. Wind-driven litter progressed better than the mass of metal that trapped him. The skinny hands on the clock embedded into the dashboard pointed to 4:12 p.m. He had eighteen minutes to get to the attorney's office or he would miss the reading of Aunt Maddy's will.

His penny loafer stomped down on the brake pedal. The car came to a screeching halt inches from a staggering Market Street jaywalker wearing a tattered green overcoat. Survival was an adventure for drivers and pedestrians alike.

The bum defiantly stood in front of the Ford. Dean retaliated by leaning long and hard on his horn. The bum placed two hands caked with layers of The City's back alley filth onto the Crestline's orange hood.

"Is your horn broken, buddy?" the bum shouted, glaring at Dean through a windshield encrusted with hundreds of miles of road grunge.

"Yeah," Dean fired back, tilting his head out the window. "You wanna fix it?"

"My pleasure." The bum kicked the front metal grill three times with Keds long past their prime. His head bobbed up and down after he inspected his efforts. "My work here is done." He wiggled a middle finger at Dean and moved on. A symphony of skidding tires and honking horns erupted from northbound traffic. "Is your horn broken, buddy?"

"Some things never change," Dean said, smiling. "Bumper to bumper traffic. No available parking spaces. A vagrant with an attitude. Nice to be home again."

Dean spotted familiar commercial signs and storefronts, some of them landmark businesses, but change was in the air. Before leaving for spring training, he had read an article in the Sunday *Examiner* about the new 1950s phenomenon transforming major cities: middle class families fleeing urban denseness to migrate to spacious suburbs, altering inner city demography. Even with changing neighborhoods, The City would always be his favorite place to live.

The wrinkles in his white shirt and tan pants appeared permanent. He had intended to make a pit stop at Aunt Maddy's house to clean up before his appointment with lawyer Franklyn Edwards. At this point, he would be fortunate to make the reading of the will on time.

He squeezed his car into the lane closest to the curb. Running late might be a blessing. In the baseball off-seasons he had lived with Aunt Maddy. If he entered his eccentric aunt's house, unreleased emotions would most likely surface.

Sweet and sour aromas from nearby Chinese restaurants prompted a rumble from Dean's stomach. His last meal had been over three hundred miles ago, an early morning breakfast at Beals Becker's parents' ranch in Nevada. Even grabbing a quick hotdog at Doggie Diner was now out of the question.

More honking with little movement. He was getting nowhere fast. Dean turned right then left onto Bush Street. The odds of his finding a vacant parking spot were about as good as the United States landing a man on the moon. A blue, red, and white parking sign appeared halfway down the block: two bits to park for an hour, the same cost as a gallon of ethyl gasoline.

Dean pulled up next to the lot's wooden hut. A thin attendant, wearing a black and orange Giant's hat and a blue vendor's smock leaned his upper body out the half door. From a transistor radio inside the shack Giants' announcer Russ Hodges' voice blared.

"How long you gonna be, young fella?" The attendant's eyebrows lifted in recognition then he grinned. "Say, aren't you Dean the Dream Mason?"

"Yes, sir," Dean said, with a nod.

"Thought so." The man opened the bottom half of the door with a shove and offered his hand. "My youngest son played high school ball against you. You were the best prep baseball player I've seen since Joltin' Joe played here."

They shook hands. Joe DiMaggio had played prep baseball in San Francisco many years before Dean. Being compared to the Yankee Clipper was a great compliment. Now, however, he was just another ballplayer who never lived up to his press clippings. Yet, being recognized still gave him a warm feeling.

"Thanks for the kind words," Dean said. "What's your son's name?"

"Joey. Joey Logan."

Dean had no memory of a Joey Logan, but his dad's eyes were moist with pride.

"Sure, I remember him." Dean smiled. "Real good ballplayer. Say hello to him for me, will you?"

Mr. Logan looked down at his Red Wing Boots. He took a deep breath before raising his head. Unabashed tears blinked from his eyes.

"Wish I could," Mr. Logan said in a shaky voice. "Joey never came back from Korea."

"Jesus, I-I didn't know." Dean felt a pang of guilt for being classified 4-F because of his knee. "I'm really sorry, Mr. Logan."

From the side mirror Dean saw a shabby blue car of late 40s vintage speed into the parking lot. The front end smashed into his Ford's rear bumper. Metal on metal sounded. Dean surged forward from the impact then hit the back of his head on the door's window frame. His sense of time idled for a sec. He jumped out of the car holding a hand on his sore noggin and scowled at the driver's obscure image.

The Studebaker's driver-side door creaked open. A petite, dark-haired young woman wearing a powder-blue skirt, matching jacket, and frilly white blouse removed herself from the car. Dean lifted his hand from his head to shield his eyes from the sun. He'd seen that pretty face somewhere before.

The young woman charged past Dean, grazing his elbow with her shoulder. She inspected the coupled bumpers then turned back to him.

"I apologize," she said. "The sun kind of blinded me. And my brakes are bad."

"One more excuse and you're out," Dean said, touching the bump on his head again.

Mr. Logan pulled on Dean's sleeve, his expression similar to when he had recognized Dean. He gestured at the young woman with a handful of flapping tickets.

"Aren't you that Hollywood gal, Bridget, in that beach movie?" Mr. Logan asked.

"Sorry to disappoint you, sir," she said. "You're thinking of Gidget. A lot of people mistake me for her, not that I mind."

Dean zoned in on her face. Damned if she didn't resemble Sandra Dee. Sandra Dee with black hair. Her button nose was a bit different, but the resemblance was quite remarkable. So was her figure.

Dean blinked several times to refocus on his car's chassis. The Ford's rusty metal back bumper looked crippled. So did the rest of his car. Nine years of hard driving had taken its toll. One more dent wouldn't make a difference.

"It's not too bad." She batted her eyelashes. "Your car still runs, right?"

Dean shook his head. What a bullshit thing to say. Her vibrant brown eyes emitted more signals than a third base coach with three hands. Some women think a pretty face is a license to get away with anything.

"Listen, Gadget, or whatever your name is," Dean said. "If you'll just tell me who you're insured by and—"

"Insurance?" She pulled off her white gloves. "I-I canceled my insurance two weeks ago. I said I was sorry. Can't we just leave it at that?"

"I must have a built-in magnet that attracts every lowlife around," Dean said. "Next thing you're going to tell me your dog died. Or you lost your job and you're down to your last buffalo nickel."

"I don't have a dog," she snapped. "And, hey, I'm not a low... whatever you called me, mister baseball star. From the appearance of your car and the cut of your clothes, you're certainly no Rockefeller."

He would have remembered that angelic face if they had met before. But she seemed to know him. Was she a big baseball fan?

"At least I'm responsible enough to carry auto insurance," he said.

"I am a responsible person. I've just had a couple of bad breaks lately."

Dean folded his arms across his chest. He just had his bell rung and his car devalued. She never even asked if he was injured. Nor had she offered to reimburse him for the damage, even as lip service.

"Bad breaks don't give you license to ram your uninsured car into anyone you damn well please."

"Is it the sourdough bread in this city that makes all the men here such bastards?" she said, putting both hands on her curved hips.

"Maybe you just bring out the worst in people." Dean glanced at his watch. "Look, lady. You're making me late for an appointment. If you promise not to run over me on your way to a parking space, I'll forget the whole thing."

"Now that's a novel thought," she said.

"What, finding a parking space?"

"No, running you over."

She snatched a ticket from Mr. Logan's hand and hurried back to her car. The Studebaker ground its way through reverse, uncoupling the bumpers, then into first. The attendant waved to her when the car chugged past them. No secret which side he was on.

"You sure have a way with the ladies, Dean." Mr. Logan handed Dean a ticket and disappeared into the hut.

Dean flipped the ticket onto the dashboard and slid behind the steering wheel to park his car. Under different circumstances, meeting that perplexing young lady might have netted better results. But now he had less than six minutes before his appointment. Would Franklyn Edwards start the reading of Aunt Maddy's will without him?

CHAPTER FIVE

In the elevator of Franklyn Edwards' office building the uniformed operator eyeballed the floor number dial above the door. Dean's 4:34 p.m. shadow of whiskers reflected in the mirrored walls. The stale smell of a crushed cigarette butt in the ashtray made Dean crave a shot of Jack Daniel's. He swallowed hard, tasting the pseudo warmth of an imaginary shot of Jack.

The elevator car stopped with a hop at the sixth floor. Nerve-driven adrenalin forced Dean to jog down the lavish hallway. He opened a glossy brown door with brass letters that read: "Franklyn Edwards – Attorney at Law."

Valerie Dotson had her back to the door doing seventy miles an hour on a Royal typewriter. She terminated the rhythmic pounding and swiveled her chair around. Her shoulder-length auburn curls swung from the motion.

"Hey, pretty lady, remember me?" Dean said, entering the office waiting room.

"How could I forget the man with the killer blue eyes?" Valerie rose from her chair with a radiant smile. "Hello, slugger. Long time no see."

Dean's lower jaw dropped. A maternity smock covered her bulging stomach. Valerie rose and waddled towards him.

"I see somebody hit a home run," he said. "I hope you've got yourself a good lawyer."

"Better." A smiling Valerie held out a diamond sparkler on her left hand.

"Congratulations, Val. I'm happy for you."

"I told my little brother Victor I'd be seeing you today," she said. "He still brags to the other kids about the mitt and batting tips you gave him. You'll always be his hero. Mine too."

Valerie furnished a clumsy hug. Heat oozed from Dean's face.

He'd never embraced a pregnant woman before.

"I'm sorry about your aunt," she said.

"Thanks, Val. Aunt Maddy never told me why she met with Mr. Edwards. How did he ever talk her into writing a will, let alone paying for one?"

"Oh, Mrs. Principal didn't pay for her will," Valerie said. "Mr. Edwards performs will and trust services *pro bono* for many of his aged clients. I believe Mrs. Principal referred to him as a fine humanitarian."

Dean rubbed his chin stubble. Aunt Maddy wouldn't have cared about Edwards being a compassionate man, but Valerie had just solved one of life's mysteries. What would his Aunt have called the attorney if his services weren't free?

Valerie emitted an uneasy sigh. She placed her hands on her stomach. Dean offered his arm, leading her back to her chair.

"Shouldn't you be lying down or resting?" he said.

"I only work half days now," she said. "Greet clients, answer the phone, make a few calls, type letters. Heck, I'm in better shape than most of the folks needing Mr. Edwards' services." She glanced past Dean into the waiting room. "You know Martha Cooper, don't you?"

"The name doesn't ring a bell," he said, shrugging his shoulders.

Valerie pointed to a corner. Dean's head shot back after receiving his second major surprise in less than a minute. Miss Congenial from the parking lot was throwing him eye darts that didn't need a drop of poison to be lethal.

"Matter of fact," Dean said, "Miss Cooper and I have bumped into each other before."

A short time later, Valerie rose again and led Dean into Franklyn Edwards' private suite. Footfalls behind him caught Dean's ear. A maple desk and matching credenza served as the hub of an impressive office. At the opposite end, the plush furniture would shame most family living rooms. In between, bookcases with sets of leather bound law books bordered the side walls. Dean looked over his shoulder. Martha Cooper stood behind him.

"Won't you both please sit down?" Valerie motioned a hand

at two chairs in front of the desk. "Mr. Edwards will be with you shortly." She winked at Dean before exiting the room.

"What are you doing in here?" Dean said, sitting next to the young woman. "Stalking me?"

"Allow me to answer that question, Miss Cooper," Franklyn Edwards said, hustling through the doorway carrying a handful of legal folders and a pricey-looking leather briefcase.

The dark blue suit covering Edwards' soft, portly body was probably worth more than Dean's whole wardrobe. His cologne gave off a prosperous scent. Brown bangs concealed most of his forehead. A wide nose supported black-framed glasses that aged him. He placed his briefcase next to a Dictaphone on the credenza behind the desk. Springs in his cushy executive chair groaned when he sat down.

"Mr. Mason," Edwards said. "Martha Jo Cooper was your aunt's goddaughter."

"You're Marti?" Dean gripped both sides of the chair. Now he knew how she had recognized him in the parking lot. He remembered seeing a picture of Marti as a young girl. Little Marti had grown up to be an eyeful of cute. His ex-wife Dede had been in Marti's league of looks before she spent all of his baseball Bonus Baby money then divorced him after the knee surgery. Obviously, the goddaughter was in Aunt Maddy's will. That didn't concern him. What mattered was that his aunt had been kind to this person who had never reciprocated.

"I find it interesting that you should show up now, Martha Jo Cooper," Dean said.

"Mr. Edwards sent me a telegram." She turned to Dean and pointed a finger at him. "Aunt Madeline wrote in her letters to me what a terrific guy you were. Boy, did she give me a false impression."

"Aunt Madeline? Where do you get off calling her Aunt Madeline? You're just her goddaughter."

Edwards coughed. "When I requested that both of you be here today for the reading of Madeline Principal's will," the lawyer said, "I didn't realize your relationship was so acrimonious."

"Neither did I," Marti said. "My godmother wanted me to call her Aunt Madeline."

20

"My aunt sent you birthday money every year. Not once did you repay her generosity with a visit. Or even a phone call."

"For your information," Marti said, straightening her back, "your aunt and I communicated by mail. That is the way she wanted it. Why, I don't know."

Dean's eyebrows knitted together. If Marti was telling the truth, Aunt Maddy must have been trying to spare Marti from experiencing her godmother in a drunken state. Often it wasn't pretty.

"Aunt Madeline wrote how my letters brightened her day," Marti continued. "My godmother was a wonderful, compassionate person. She was like a guardian angel to me. I went to college and got my teaching credential because of her benevolence." Marti nodded. "You're one to talk. Aunt Madeline took you into her home at a young age after your parents were killed in that train accident."

Franklyn Edwards slammed his hand down on the desk. Diamonds sparkled from his gold pinkie ring. His view shifted from Dean to Marti then back to Dean.

"I've known couples filing for divorce that got along better than the two of you," Edwards said. "Please settle your differences on your own time. We've established that Mrs. Principal was a good-hearted person. And, I might add, a most challenging client."

"Is that legalese for my aunt was a pain in the ass?" Dean said, smiling.

"Can't you show just one ounce of compassion, even for the dead?" Marti snapped, throwing both hands in the air.

"Aunt Maddy was a loner," Dean said. "She didn't trust many people, especially professionals. No offense, Mr. Edwards, but my aunt detested lawyers almost as much as she hated paying taxes. She made use of your service because you offered it free."

"No offense taken, Mr. Mason. I was well aware of your aunt's aversion towards my profession and taxes. Furnishing *pro bono* service isn't total altruism on my part. Many of my clients turn frugal as they age – probably from having experienced The Great Depression. Then I'm the first attorney they call for additional legal work."

Dean focused on the impressive Silver State University and Law School diplomas on the wall above the credenza. Next to the diplomas hung an enlarged black-and-white photo of a battered two-story rural house, a picture that seemed out of place from the rest of the office décor – like wearing white sweat socks at the prom.

With an effort, Edwards leaned his heavy torso across the desk and handed out two document packets, one to Dean and one to Marti. The front page of each packet shouted LAST WILL AND TESTAMENT OF MADELINE PRINCIPAL with the word COPY stamped in blue ink.

"Oh, before I forget," Edwards said, pushing a large tan envelope across the desk to Dean. "The nursing home sent your aunt's personal effects."

Dean eyed the envelope. The finality of his aunt being dead would hit him when he opened the container. He would face those demons at her house with his friend Jack Daniel's.

"Dean, I was heartbroken to hear about Aunt Madeline." Marti's features softened. "No one informed me she'd had a stroke or was put into a nursing home."

"Man, she hated that place," he said. "But I had no choice. Aunt Maddy despised doctors almost as much as lawyers. She wouldn't accept medical help in her own home. And spring training was only a few weeks away."

"I'm sure it was the right thing to do under the circumstances," she said.

Dean regarded the plush wool carpet. Marti's words, sincere or not, didn't diminish his stockpile of guilt. A few seconds ago, he had chewed her out for being an ingrate – which, as it turned out, was what he was. He had always intended to repay his aunt's kindness caring for him after his parents died. Now it was too late.

"If you turn to page two," Edwards said, glancing at his gold, Cartier wristwatch, "the first provision declares that Madeline Principal is a widow, unmarried, with no children, living or deceased, and her nephew Dean Arnold Mason is her only living relative. The second provision declares that Mrs. Principal wanted to be cremated when she passed."

"I'm learning more about my aunt after her death than when she was alive." Dean's eyes lifted from the page. "She never revealed her burial preferences to me."

"In provisions three through six," Edwards said, "Mrs. Principal bequeaths the sum of one thousand dollars to each of the following charities: Indian Orphans of America, Sister Sophie's Orphanage, Baker's Boy's Town, and The World Orphan's Fund."

Dean flexed his achy knee. Four thousand dollars was more than a man's average yearly salary. For some reason his aunt had a soft spot in her heart for orphans, including one named Dean Arnold Mason.

"The seventh provision," Edwards said, adjusting his glasses with a finger, "gives and bequeaths to Dean Arnold Mason, Madeline Principals' real property, meaning the house at 220 Desmond Street in San Francisco, California, and personal property including all furnishings and possessions therein." He lowered his copy of the will. "In other words, Mr. Mason, your aunt's house and everything in it belongs to you. There is no mortgage. She apparently paid for the house in full at the time of purchase."

"Wow," Dean said, shaking his head. "I never considered she'd leave me the house."

"You deserve it," Marti said. "Your aunt often described how much you helped her."

"However, Mr. Mason," Edwards continued, "in order to put the title of the property in your name per provision number seven, you will have to pay all the back property taxes that your aunt neglected to take care of, plus pay the penalties and interest, and—"

"Aunt Maddy didn't neglect anything." Dean chuckled. "She knew exactly what she was doing by not paying the taxes. How much are we talking about?"

"Over three thousand, a little less than half the value of the house," Edwards said. "In addition, subject to this provision is a codicil that you must personally take up all existing old carpeting in the house and refinish the hardwood floors as you had once promised. If this provision is not met within ten days after the reading of this will, I'm empowered to sell the house, payoff delinquent taxes, and send the remainder of the proceeds to any orphan charity of my choice."

"I was sixteen when she made me promise to refurbish the floors," Dean said. "It must have meant a lot to her."

"The eighth provision," Edwards said in an impatient tone, "bequeaths the remainder of Madeline Principal's estate to Dean Arnold Mason. This includes all liquid assets in the form of one bank account and one investment account."

"Investment?" Dean said, his eyebrows nearly reaching his hairline. "Aunt Maddy had little trust for banks. I can't imagine her investing in anything less secure than a savings account."

"Be that as it may," Edwards said, "this type of investment for an older person makes a great deal of sense. Many of my more affluent clients are vested this way."

Dean picked at his callused hand. Earlier, Edwards had used the term frugal. His aunt had lived her life by the sovereignty of one ruler: Cash was king. She could be penny-pinching with herself then she'd give a handful of cash to a complete stranger.

"When did Aunt Maddy turn investor?" Dean asked, squinting at the attorney.

"Let me see." Edwards turned pages in a file. "Here we go. September 14, 1958."

"Last year," Dean said, "near the end of my season playing for a team in Texas—about four months before she had her stroke."

"Shall we continue with the reading of the will," Edward's said, pointing a gold pen at a page. "Provision number eight has this stipulation. Once Mr. Mason takes title to the investment account, he is to pay an annual distribution of one thousand dollars to Martha Jo Cooper for as long as either party is alive."

Dean stared long and hard at Marti. She must think he was angry about the money. He wasn't. Neither one of them deserved an inheritance. It bothered him that he hadn't been privy to his aunt's secretive past, including how she became Marti's godmother.

"Dean, I didn't ask to be in Aunt Madeline's will. Why are you so upset? She just gave you a house and all of her money. Besides, you should be well-to-do. Don't all professional baseball players earn huge salaries?"

"Not much of a baseball fan, are you?" he said, leaning toward her.

"I was actually a big fan of one baseball player until today."

"Sports haven't caught up with middle class affluence," Dean said. "Most professional athletes work other jobs in the off season to make ends meet. Even at the major league level. I didn't play baseball for money. I played for the love of the game. Nor did I come here looking to get rich. It's too bad my aunt didn't confer with me first before writing her will."

"Whether you approve or not, Mr. Mason," Edwards said in a cold voice, "a will is designed to dispose of one's belongings and assets as one wishes."

"Don't get me wrong, Mr. Edwards," Dean said. "I don't disapprove. Aunt Maddy took pleasure in giving her money away, even to people she hardly knew."

"Then the rest of your aunt's will should greatly please you, Mr. Mason," Edwards said, turning to the next page.

CHAPTER SIX

Dean exchanged a quizzical glance with Marti then focused on Franklyn Edwards. The attorney swiped a hand under his forehead bangs exposing a portion of an ugly scar, then cleared his throat.

"With the exception of the house," Edwards said, "Mrs. Principal's estate consisted of the two asset accounts as I indicated. One of the accounts, the investment, reflects a substantial amount of money. The other is Mr. Mason's aunt's trust checking account managed by Mr. Mason as her designed trustee under a limited power of attorney to cover her expenses."

Dean removed a checkbook from his back pocket. His fingers tore through the register. The last entry was payment for a doctor visit at the nursing home.

"There's a balance of three thousand and change in this account," Dean said.

"That balance," Edwards said, "is now a part of your inheritance. However, three thousand dollars will hardly cover outstanding expenses like the house and inheritance taxes, interest penalties, attorney's fees, cremation, medical bills—"

"I get the picture." Dean slapped the checkbook cover against his thigh before returning it to his pocket. "The checking account I just inherited is in the red. Most likely I can cover the outstanding bills, with the exception of the back taxes. Does the investment account have enough money to cover the rest?"

"And then some," Edwards said. "Your aunt invested eight hundred and seventy-five thousand dollars."

"Oh my God, Dean," Marti gushed. "You're a millionaire."

"Mr. Edwards, you just said *eight hundred and seventy-five thousand dollars*, right?"

"That's correct, Mr. Mason."

Dean felt his heart beating against his ribs. It would take United States President Dwight D. Eisenhower seven years to earn the amount his aunt had left him. How did Aunt Maddy acquire that much money?

"What exactly did my aunt invest in?" Dean queried, attempting to appear calm.

"Mrs. Principal transferred the money from her bank savings account to a charity."

"A charity," Marti said. "I don't understand?"

"Dean's aunt invested in The Billy Orphan Foundation, a philanthropic organization."

"Is this some kind of sadistic joke?" Dean leaned forward and placed a hand on the attorney's desk. "Aunt Maddy would never invest that much money in any entity."

"I assure you this is no joke," Edwards said. "The Billy Orphan Foundation aids homeless children throughout the forty-nine states, soon to be fifty states when Hawaii joins the union."

Edwards turned a document entitled "Billy Orphan Foundation Annuity Trust Agreement" around so Dean could read. Dean memorized the phone number and post office box address in Charity, Nevada. Penned at the bottom of the page were the signatures of Madeline Principal and Billy Orphan. Billy Orphan was a real person?

"Please excuse my ignorance, Mr. Edwards," Marti said, relocating a few strands of hair back in place. "But none of this makes any sense. Why would Aunt Madeline invest such a large amount of money with a charity?"

"An investment in a charitable organization makes perfect sense, Miss Cooper. Using The Billy Orphan Foundation offered Mrs. Principal almost everything she was looking for." Edwards held the document upright and tapped the bottom of the page on the desktop. "In this agreement, The Billy Orphan Foundation agreed to manage the principal of your godmother's investment at a guaranteed interest rate that was twice what she received from the bank. The interest was then remitted to Mrs. Principal's trust checking account every month to pay her expenses."

"So that's how the checking account was replenished each month." Dean moved his head side to side to loosen building pressure. "Logically, it still doesn't add up. Higher interest revenue shouldn't have made a difference to my aunt. Based on the numbers in this will, she had enough money in the bank to survive ten lifetimes – twenty since she lived like a pauper. A down-and-out man residing in the alley behind this building pampers himself more than she ever did. And how the hell can a charity afford to pay such a high interest rate?"

"I can't answer the last question." Edwards said, picking up a silver letter opener. "But allow me to clear up the confusion I see registered on your faces. Under this agreement, your aunt would pay the government next to nothing on her annual income taxes, a fact that pleased her to no end. But here's the real kicker. When she passed, there would be no inheritance tax on the investment money. Obviously that was important to her. Inheritance tax in California is quite considerable."

Dean couldn't help but smile. His aunt had been shrewder than he thought. Aunt Maddy benefited financially and, at the same time, screwed the government. He would receive thousands of monthly interest dollars for the rest of his life due to her cleverness.

"Many of my wealthier clients are involved in this type of charitable investment," Edwards said. "However, had your aunt come to me first, I would have advised her against this venture."

"Why?" Dean and Marti blurted out at the same time.

"The day Madeline Principal died, all the money she invested with The Billy Orphan Foundation legally went to the charity."

Dean had trouble catching his breath. The golden carrot Edwards had dangled before him had just been removed without a single nibble.

"But all of the money in Aunt Madeline's will was left to Dean," Marti said.

"Correct." Edwards touched his forehead again. "Nevertheless, the contract your godmother signed with The Billy Orphan Foundation takes precedence over the provisions of the will."

"That hardly seems fair," Marti said, turning to Dean.

"How legal is that contract, Mr. Edwards?" Dean asked.

"In my opinion, this contract is binding, Mr. Mason." Edwards' eyes shifted to Marti. "In terms of what's legally fair, Miss Cooper, I can explain it this way: If Mrs. Principal had declared in her will that Dean was the beneficiary of a life insurance policy, but, in turn, she later named Martha Jo Cooper as the beneficiary on the policy itself, you, Miss Cooper, would receive the insurance money when she passed, not Mr. Mason."

"But that is not what Aunt Madeline intended when she made out her will. She wanted Dean to continue receiving interest money from the charity after she died."

"Supposition, Miss Cooper." Edwards waved her words away. "Allow me to play attorney's advocate here. You're assuming Mrs. Principal hadn't changed her mind about Mr. Mason receiving the investment interest posthumously. Perhaps she wanted the charity to keep the money."

Dean could feel stomach acid rising to his throat. It was possible Aunt Maddy had second thoughts. Maybe, in the end, she chose the charity over him.

"This isn't right," Marti said. "Dean should sue the charity."

"On what grounds, Miss Cooper?" Edwards leaned back in his chair. "There is no proof Mrs. Principal demonstrated any state of confusion or mental instability at the time she signed the agreement. Furthermore, The Billy Orphan Foundation honored their commitment in good faith by sending interest payments." He pulled on his earlobe. "Yes, a lawsuit is a consideration. But so are legal costs. And the potential of losing a court decision. Or winning then having the charity appeal to a higher court."

"Let's see if I've got this straight." Dean rolled up his copy of the will. "My aunt created a will leaving me the balance of her trust checking account, an investment account, and her house. But the trust checking is exceeded by outstanding expenses. I can't take ownership of the house until I refurbish the floors and pay off back taxes and interest penalties – money I don't have. And she left me an investment account with a balance exceeding that of the San Francisco mint, except not one dime is actually mine nor is the interest."

"Mr. Mason, I fully understand your disappointment. However—"

"With all due respect, Mr. Edwards, I don't think you do." Dean turned to Marti. "Sorry, looks like we both lose. I came in here broke and now I'm worth even less. With the exception of my baseball Bonus Baby windfall, I've never had much. Probably never will. The way I see it, I haven't lost anything I never really had." Dean pointed his will-baton at Edwards. "However, if indeed Aunt Maddy wanted me, and indirectly Marti, to have that investment account and she was somehow duped out of it then I'm mad as hell. If that's the case, I'll fight anything or anybody to get it back."

"Believe me, Mr. Mason, I'm sympathetic to your position." Beads of sweat appeared on Edwards' cheeks. "Perhaps negotiation would be prudent in this case. I could write The Billy Orphan Foundation a strongly worded letter requesting a settlement that could possibly satisfy both parties. We might ask for half the amount Mrs. Principal invested and maybe settle for a third."

"Thirty-three percent," Dean said. "Not counting your fee. Which one of us are you negotiating for, Mr. Edwards? Furthermore, letters take time. Time I don't have."

"Most people don't make three-hundred thousand dollars in a lifetime," Edwards said.

"You should consider Mr. Edwards' offer, Dean," Marti said. "With an attorney representing you, your chances of recovering some of the money are much greater."

"Miss Cooper's right," Edwards offered. "I assure you, any legal fee that you incur from this office will be a small price to pay if we can reach a settlement."

"You're both only interested in getting paid off. At my expense. Thanks for the offer. But no thanks." Dean rose to his feet and chucked the will onto Edwards' desk. "I need to see an old friend. You can reach me at my aunt's house." He moved towards the door then turned around. "One last question, Mr. Edwards. You never told me what kind of accident my aunt had. Was it caused by another stroke?"

"Not exactly. Mrs. Principal fell from the third floor balcony of her nursing home."

Dean flinched. Marti gasped her surprise. Why hadn't Edwards told him this earlier?

"I'm not trying to play Perry Mason here," Edwards said. "Your aunt's fall could have been accidental. There was no note. But, by all accounts, it looked like suicide. Not uncommon for an old, sick, lonely person. She probably just gave up."

"Aunt Maddy fell from the balcony?" Dean gripped the door handle. "Mr. Edwards, you may know a lot about the law, but you don't know jack shit about my aunt."

"What is your point, Mr. Mason?"

"Aunt Maddy didn't commit suicide." Dean opened the door. "Nor was her fall an accident. Someone murdered her."

CHAPTER SEVEN

San Francisco's swirling late afternoon wind greeted Dean. His shirt and pants flap-talked against his body. A distant voice called out his name. He was in no mood to talk to anyone after the drubbing he had taken in Franklyn Edwards' office minutes earlier.

Dean turned onto Samson Street and sidestepped a cane-aided man. How many times had he heard that bad things come in threes? In the last two days, he had lost Aunt Maddy, baseball, and now his inheritance. Lost? Or had they been stolen? The knee injury had cheated him out of having a long, successful career. Legalities had just deprived him of a fortune – two realities he could ignore. But someone had robbed what little life his aunt had left. Tomorrow he would begin his journey to find out who killed Aunt Maddy and why, starting with the nursing home. Tonight, however, he needed to regroup with a friend.

"Need a date, stud?" A short, frumpy woman posed in a doorway wearing skintight pedal pushers and two-ply make-up.

"You're too late," he said. "I just got screwed at the attorney's office."

Dean veered onto Pine Street. A red neon sign with a martini glass outline blinked "AST FREDDY'S." The first letter "F" burned out, unchanged from the first time he'd traipsed into Freddy's bar eight years ago. When he entered his eyes widened to adjust to the room's murkiness.

"Dean the Dream Mason," Fast Freddy announced, standing in his usual position behind the long, sculptured mahogany bar. He pounded his hard stomach with a fist and crouched into a boxing stance. "I can still whup your young ass."

"You'll have to stand in line, Freddy. Today everyone wants a piece of me."

Dean shook the former middleweight boxer's gnarled right hand, a hand decorated with long scars. Too many breaks. And one too many operations.

Dean slid onto a barstool, joining three regulars spaced apart down the bar. Hardcore drinkers. He inhaled the tavern's familiar musty scent. Several sharp snorts from the end of the bar caught Dean's ear. Old Edgar was in his usual spirit stupor after an afternoon of boozing. Dean swiped a stale pretzel from a bowl. Not much changed at Freddy's, except the 45s in the jukebox.

Freddy scooped a pile of ice cubes into a stubby glass. With a flip of his wrist, he poured from a black-labeled bottle until the chestnut-colored liquid reached just beneath the lip. Then he placed the glass of Jack Daniel's on a small napkin square in front of Dean.

"This one's on me, Dream," Freddy said in a low tone. "You look like you could use it." He lifted one foot onto the top shelf under the bar and reached into his sock for a red pack of Pall Mall's. Freddy rolled a cigarette to Dean, leaving the pack on the bar. "I'm assuming you haven't quit the habit of borrowing."

Dean tamped down one end of the cigarette on the bar top until tobacco receded into the paper. He only smoked when he drank. Freddy flicked him a quick light and fanned out the match. Dean inhaled and blew out a solid white stream. His brain seemed to expand from the nicotine bite. The smoke drifted upward, commingling with a ceiling haze created by other smokers.

The whiskey caused the ice cubes to crackle in the glass. After several drags, Dean crushed out the cigarette in an ashtray. His throat contracted, anticipating a taste that had become a staple in his diet. He stared into the mirrored wall behind Freddy. Darkened images of patrons sat around small round tables. Would he end up like them or old Edgar? With nothing to do but spend pension checks in a bar waiting for their livers to pickle?

Dean lifted the glass to his lips. The aroma made his mouth water. No need to worry about squandered pension checks. Baseball didn't give players pensions. He belted back half the drink. A surge of warmth spread through his limbs. He swirled Jack around until a mini-vortex developed in the middle. Freddy gazed at him while cleaning the bar top with a wet towel. Another tilt of the glass drained all the color.

On cue, Freddy poured a refill. Dean swiped another cigarette from the pack and inserted it between his lips. He patted his pockets for a book of matches.

"You seen this yet, Dream?" Freddy held up an article clipped from the *San Francisco Chronicle* Sporting Green section. "Grady Spencer wrote a column about the Mustangs releasing you. Those dumb sons of bitches probably would've cut Babe Ruth for being too fat."

"Thanks, Freddy." At least Dean had one fan left. He pushed the clipping back to Freddy. These days, bad news traveled faster than a guided missile. "Not interested."

"Hey, Spencer didn't do a hatchet job on you," Freddy said. "The headline reads, *End of the Dream.*" He squinted trying to focus on the small print in the faint light.

Dean shook his head. Freddy cleared his throat, ignoring Dean. Another customer entered the bar prompting the bartender to look up and nod. Then Freddy's eyes shifted back to the newspaper. Dean shook his head again. Freddy was going to read the damn article whether Dean wanted to hear it or not.

For most young professional baseball players the end is predetermined. They live in a jungle of inequities. The conditions are poor and the chances of succeeding are worse. Players are like tickets in the Irish Sweepstakes, waiting for a chance to be chosen. The odds are so incredibly bad, most of them will never see the likes of a major league game unless they pay their way in.

But Dean the Dream Mason wasn't like most young ballplayers. As a teenager, Mason was gifted with more tools than a master carpenter. On the field he could throw, hit, hit for power, run, and field. Scouts predicted nothing less than stardom for The City's best high school baseball player since the great Joe DiMaggio. It was only a matter of time before Dean grabbed the baseball brass ring to go on where Joe left off.

Nine mediocre years later the end has come. Word has it, Mason hung up his spikes at the prime age of 27. The Billings Mustangs, a lowly Class B minor league team waived Dean several days ago. What went wrong? Some people say Mason had been stung by too many B's – booze, broads, and a broken knee. Another source said Mason didn't quit baseball, the game quit him. Whatever the reason, it's the end of an illusion and we're all losers this time.

Wake up, Mr. Disney. This is one dream that didn't come true.

Dean snatched the article from Freddy's hand and crumpled it up into a paper ball. As a sportswriter, Grady Spencer had always treated him square, but the essay was too much like hearing his own obituary. Spencer's words dropped to the floor.

"You've always had a good eye for women, Dream," Freddy said, looking past Dean's shoulder. "But you still haven't learned how to quit pissing 'em off."

"What the hell are you talking about, Freddy?" Dean said, glancing up at the mirror.

Marti Cooper stood behind Dean. She had a derringer pistol pointed at his head. Freddy fumbled underneath the bar and lifted a bat into launching position. Dean grabbed Freddy's arm to stop him. Then he turned around to stare at tiny double-barrels protruding from Marti's hand.

"Didn't your mother teach you that it's impolite to point?" Dean asked.

Marti pulled the trigger.

CHAPTER EIGHT

After a yawn, K.A. closed his eyes for a moment. He had parked his Willy's Jeepster at the far end of the cul-de-sac. The street lights popped on several minutes ago while remaining daylight blended into evening. Scalp itch prompted him to adjust his black wig. This morning's disguise was still in play, with the exception of the white nurse's hat.

The scent of the old woman from the nursing home lingered in his nostrils. He levered the driver's seat back as far as it would go and stretched his legs. He had one more task before leaving San Francisco.

On the opposite sidewalk, a young man combed his greasy hair. His immature mustache resembled dirt more than whiskers. A brown-tipped cigarette lodged behind his ear. He wore the Marlboro flip-top box rolled up in his T-shirt sleeve as an accessory. What were the odds this punk didn't even inhale? His Levi's belt loops fenced a wide black leather belt sporting a huge metal buckle.

K.A.'s eyes zeroed in on the dark leather strap surrounding the young hood's waist. His veins flowed with rage. He steadied his shaky hands by choking the steering wheel. An overpowering desire to kill emerged from its inner hideout. The Urge. Childhood memories of his mustached father whipping him with a similar black leather belt and brass buckle played in his head. He had learned at an early age that the term "bad boy" meant nothing more than being visible around his drunken, short-tempered father. He sensed the odor of the Wildroot Cream-Oil Hair Tonic his father used. The thrashings were often so excruciating, K.A. stopped feeling the pain. His mother never interfered, fearing her own sting of the lash. Instead, she watched in silence.

K.A. reached for a matchbook on the dashboard. The cover advertised opportunities for aspiring artists of any age. He struck a red match head to life to sniff sulfur and eradicate the hair oil smell.

His last memory of his parents had been when he was eleven years old. They were passed out in drunken slumber on their bed. The Urge had overwhelmed him for the first time. He had tossed a lit cigarette onto their bed and waited for the bedding to catch fire. Then he walked out of the burning cracker house and into the night. The cause of the blaze had been determined to be his intoxicated parents smoking in bed. His only regret was that his mother and father hadn't suffered the way they had caused him to suffer.

People had felt sorry for the poor orphan boy with the beautiful face. Many of them lavished attention he didn't crave. They encouraged him to cry, but no tears would come. But he mastered freezing his features into a mournful expression. The doctor had expressed concern that he was hurting himself by keeping his emotions bottled up. They told him over and over that his parent's death was not his fault and not to feel guilty. Freedom, not guilt, was the only thing he felt.

The match's flame bit into his fingers, bringing K.A. back into real time. The young hood had disappeared without realizing how fortunate he was to still be alive.

K.A. flipped the spent match onto the street. Fire wasn't necessary for his next kill.

Without knowing it, the nephew baseball player would be down to his last strike when he returned to his dead aunt's house. A fatal strike he would never walk away from.

CHAPTER NINE

D ean didn't flinch when a flame shot from the gun barrel. Marti moved the derringer lighter close enough to ignite the tip of his cigarette. He'd given the lighter to Aunt Maddy several years ago as a substitute for a real weapon. The way Aunt Maddy drank and irritated people, no one in Visitation Valley would have been safe had the gun been loaded with anything more potent than lighter fluid.

"You left Aunt Madeline's personal effects from the nursing home on Mr. Edwards' desk." Marti dropped the lighter into the oversized envelope. "There's a wristwatch, a few dollars, her social security card, and your copy of the will."

"Thank you." Dean placed the envelope onto the bar top then rotated his body towards the bar. "Now if you'll excuse me—"

"I didn't know you weren't playing baseball anymore," she said, smoothing out the crumpled article. "Nor was I aware you struggled with your career because of an injury."

"No telling how great a ballplayer Dream would have been," Freddy said to Marti. "Every time the man was knocked down he'd get back up, the same way a boxer would."

"More ammo, Freddy." Dean wiggled a finger at his glass and peered at Marti in the mirror. "You obviously didn't come here just to give me my aunt's belongings."

"You're right," she said. "You told Mr. Edwards that you had to meet a friend. Before he or she gets here, we need to talk."

"You're too late." Dean raised a full glass. "Martha Jo Cooper, meet my friend, Jack. Jack Daniel's."

"I don't mean to be rude, Miss Martha," Freddy said. "Are you old enough to be in here?"

"Call me Marti." She removed her driver's license from her purse. "I'm old enough to drive, vote, teach a classroom full of second graders, and have a drink if I so desire."

"Better check to see if her license has expired, Freddy," Dean said.

"A thousand pardons, Miss Marti," Freddy said, squinting at her ID. "You're legal by two years. Fast Freddy at your service, ma'am. What's your poison?"

"My poison?" she repeated.

"I'd like to know your drink preference," Freddy said, showing more gum than teeth.

"Sorry, I don't drink liquor. I'll have a ginger ale."

Dean touched his chin with the glass. Hard to believe the goddaughter wasn't a barfly. Then again, liquor had never appealed to him either until the knee injury.

"You've got no business being in a joint like this," Dean said.

"Hey," Freddy growled, pouring ginger ale from a green bottle into a glass with ice.

"What right do you have to tell me what I can or cannot do?" Marti sat on the stool next to Dean and tugged at her skirt hem. "This should be a perfect place for a . . . what was the name you called me in the parking lot? Oh, yes. A lowlife like me."

Dean saluted her with his glass. Marti had a good memory. And she was right. He had no claim to tell her how to run her life, except she had not picked up on his warning. Freddy's barroom took on a rowdier guise in the evening.

"The lowlife crack was out of line," he said. "I apologize. Again, why did you follow me?"

"I'm not the awful person you seem to think I am. And you're probably not the insensitive ass you want me to think you are. That one is still open for debate."

"You still haven't told me why you're here."

"Whether you like it or not, Dean, your aunt's will and wishes have tied us together." She sipped then crinkled her nose as the bubbles rose from her glass.

"Not as far as I'm concerned," he said. "But maybe you could enlighten me on how you became my aunt's goddaughter? And why she sent you money every year."

"Gratitude. Gratitude to my mother." Marti lifted her glass then put it down. "You probably know that your aunt was married to a Nevada rancher, right?"

"I only knew Aunt Maddy married a man with the last name of Principal."

"Aunt Madeline separated from her husband Calvin Principal," Marti said. "He was wealthy and didn't even know it. After Calvin died, a huge vein of silver was discovered on his property. Your aunt became instantly rich."

Dean studied Marti's face looking for a giveaway tell. If Marti was lying to him, she was damn good. Yet part of the story didn't add up. His aunt had returned to San Francisco rich, but she'd left her sweet personality in Nevada.

"How does my aunt tie in with your mother?" Dean munched on another pretzel then pushed the bowl away.

"Twenty-two years ago, Mother was waiting for a streetcar on Market Street with me in a stroller. She witnessed a young hood-lum snatch a purse from a woman. Then he ran straight towards us. Mother was afraid the thug would crash into the stroller. She stepped forward and tripped the guy with her leg brace. Mother has polio. Then she beat him over the head with an umbrella until the woman came over and knocked the hooligan cold with a suitcase."

"The purse and suitcase woman was obviously Aunt Maddy."

"Yes," Marti said. "Aunt Madeline had just arrived to San Francisco on a bus from Nevada. She insisted Mother should accompany her to the bank. Your aunt wouldn't take no for an answer. That part I know you'll believe."

Dean nodded. Aunt Maddy usually got her way. Someone had hell to pay if she didn't. Dean was often that person.

"Mother and Aunt Madeline met with the bank manager in a private room," Marti continued. "Your aunt opened her purse and dumped out bundles of green bills onto a table. Bills that were blessed with zeros. At first Mother thought the money was coun-terfeit. As it turned out, that was the first and only time my mother would ever see a Grover Cleveland face on a thousand dollar bill."

"You're telling me Aunt Maddy was walking around The City with thousand dollar bills in her purse." Dean squinted at Marti in disbelief. "My aunt wasn't *that* crazy."

"Aunt Madeline was anything but crazy." The timbre in Marti's voice was softer. "Evidently your aunt had more bills in her suitcase. Mother refused to accept the thousand dollar bill as a reward. So Aunt Madeline created a bank account in my name and deposited money every year. Even after we moved to Bakersfield."

Dean stirred the whiskey with a forefinger. Now he understood why his indebted aunt sent Marti money each year. But that still didn't account for the absurd terms in her will.

"Why would my aunt want me to give you a thousand dollars a year, instead of creating a trust account in your name?" He raised his shoulders. "It doesn't make sense."

"You mean provision number eight in the will?" A blush came to Marti's cheeks. "That came as a surprise to me as well. There was a purpose to her folly. Your aunt was a romantic. That provision was Aunt Madeline's way of keeping the two of us tied together."

"Aunt Maddy the matchmaker." Dean roared with laughter. "Like one of those arranged marriages. Lady, you're even crazier than my aunt."

"Still, we are linked whether you approve or not," Marti said. "A small portion of your inheritance is mine."

"So you came here to motivate me to go after my lost money." Dean finished his drink and signaled to Freddy for another.

"The inheritance money isn't the only reason I chased after you. I'm not leaving this bar until you tell me why you think Aunt Madeline's death wasn't an accident or suicide. Mr. Edwards was more than a little skeptical. So am I."

Dean turned to face Marti. The front door opened, spreading daylight into the entryway. A tall, lean man entered the bar.

"Shit," Dean mumbled, shaking his head. "Trouble just walked through the door."

CHAPTER TEN

O n Freddy's jukebox Elvis complained about a hard headed woman being the cause of trouble ever since the world began. The King could have been singing about Marti Cooper, sitting on the barstool next to Dean with both hands posed on her hips. Her brown eyes came alive with annoyance.

The front door creaked to a close. The tall man ambled into the bar. He stopped to allow his eyes to adjust to the darkness. His denim jacket collar stood up like it was starched. His pegged Levi's were tight as skin. He still wore the same dark sideburns and greasy pompadour. Trouble had a name: Boyd Weber, still a hood nine years after high school.

Dean stared past Marti's shoulder at Boyd. Muscles in his chest tensed over a revved heartbeat. If possible, his day was about to go from bad to worse.

"Would you please do me the honor of paying attention when I ask you a question," she said. "What do you think happened to Aunt Madeline?"

"Quiet," Dean whispered. "Whatever you do, don't turn around."

"There you go telling me what to do again," she snapped, turning towards Boyd.

"Get me a Cutty, Freddy," Boyd ordered. "Neat. And don't pour me any of that cheap panther piss you keep under the bar."

"This guy can't be for real," Marti said. "I think he's seen too many Brando movies."

"Damn it to hell, Marti. What didn't you understand when I asked you not to look at him? He's bad news. Especially when it comes to females."

"I can handle myself, thank you," she said.

"His parents, school administrators, and the San Francisco

Police Department couldn't control the son of a bitch." Dean raised a hand yielding to Marti's stubbornness. "At least you can't say that you weren't warned."

"I don't want any trouble tonight, Boyd." Freddy pried a ridged metal cap off a brown Hamm's bottle with a church key. "Last time you were here I had to call the cops."

"Save the sermons for your Sunday crowd and get me my scotch." Boyd wiped his nose on his denim sleeve. "The fight wasn't my fault."

"I'm out of Cutty Sark," Freddy said, checking the bottles behind him. "I'll have to go down to the basement for one." Before leaving he replenished Dean's glass with Jack Daniel's.

"Christ, that figures." Boyd stomped a black boot heel down on the hardwood floor. His elbows leaned into the bar top. He watched Freddy disappear through a side door. Then his eyes settled in on Marti. A cocky smile and a wink soon followed. "Sexpot."

"Oh, shit," Dean grumbled.

Boyd whirled around. He pointed an index finger at the juke-box. Little Richard's "Good Golly Miss Molly" poured through the speakers.

"Who picked this Goddamn jigaboo music?" Boyd's eyebrows stitched together into a scowl as he viewed the room. "I wouldn't admit to it either."

Boyd sauntered towards the back wall. He unplugged the juke-box with an exaggerated tug. The room went silent. Re-plugged, the record player returned to colorful life. He fed a series of dimes into the coin slot and pushed the same button several times. Bobby Darin's "Mack the Knife" filled the room. Boyd's fingers snapped to the beat. His head gyrated from side-to-side. He danced to Marti, mouthing the lyrics.

"Look who's here," Boyd said, after noticing Dean. "The jock who lost his sock."

"Last time I saw you, Boyd, you were running away from a fight. Our fight." Dean pointed to the greaser's hair. "Glad to see our oil reserves are still in place."

"Get bent, Mason. I still owe you for getting me kicked out of high school."

"Correction," Dean said. "You got yourself expelled. I just caught you stealing equipment out of gym lockers, mine being one of them."

"What's a dish like you doing with a wimp like Mason," Boyd said, seizing Marti's hand. "Come on, doll face. Let's see if you can dance as good as you look."

"Thank you for asking." Marti pulled her hand away. "I don't feel like dancing."

Dean exhaled an irritated breath. Marti turned her back to Boyd. Now she was taking his advice. A little late, babe.

"I don't think you heard me right." Boyd swung Marti by the arm, sending her flying off the stool towards him. "I wasn't asking."

"Let go." She yanked her arm again, this time with no success. "Let me go."

Boyd backpedaled towards the jukebox pulling Marti as if she was on skates. Patrons scooted their chairs out of harm's way. Marti screeched out high-pitched protests. Boyd produced an ugly chortle and tugged her close to him. Too close.

Dean ogled his full glass of Jack. He'd come to Freddy's to drink himself into a mind-numbing stupor. Not to tangle with an old nemesis. Or a headstrong woman. He had been in bar fights before. Some of them he even remembered.

"Let her go, Boyd." Dean slid off the stool. "She told you she didn't want to dance."

Boyd responded with a smile. A screw-you smile. A buzz of excitement erupted as if the bell for *Friday Night at the Fights* had sounded.

Marti planted a pointed pump into Boyd's shinbone. His eyes lit up like stadium lights. He gave Marti's cheek an open-handed smack, sending her skidding to the floor.

"Little bitch," Boyd roared, hopping on one boot and rubbing his shin.

Dean charged Boyd in a crouch. His knee rebelled with a jolt of pain. Scenes from their first fight played in his head. Only this time the stakes weren't his baseball gear.

Boyd readied himself. He cocked his right arm, telegraphing his intended move. Just like in high school. He launched his haymaker. Breeze from the punch tickled Dean's hair. Dean buried a shoulder into Boyd's stomach. Boyd landed on his back with Dean draped on top of him.

Dean's fists pummeled Boyd's face. Each blow felt better than the last. Boyd stopped fighting back. Dean hit him one last time then rolled off the prone body. His knuckles were raw.

Marti sat glassy-eyed on the floor holding a hand to her cheek. Dean limped to her. He peeled Marti's fingers away from her face. The cheek was crimson and puffy.

"Are you hurt anywhere else?" he asked.

"I-I don't think so." Her voice was shaky. "Except my ear is ringing."

"Let's get some ice on that cheek," he said. "Can you stand up?"

Dean shifted his weight to his right leg and pulled Marti to her feet. He could feel the shake in her body. She had been lucky. Boyd could have broken her cheekbone had he hit her with a closed fist. Maybe the next time she would listen to him.

Marti's eyes widened. She gasped before coiling away. Dean twisted around. Boyd was on his feet again. His open switchblade shone in the jukebox lights.

"Hope you got pictures of her, Mason." Boyd spit blood from his mouth. "'Cause after I take care of you, her face is only going to be a memory."

"Someone call the police," a voice yelled out.

Boyd inched towards Dean leading with the knife. Dean reached back to make sure Marti was behind him without losing sight of the circling blade. His hand touched nothing but air. Boyd was now close enough to make a strike. Marti became visible on Dean's right. Boyd had stopped moving. So did the knife. Marti's trembling hand was holding Aunt Maddy's derringer.

"Take one more step and I'll fire," she announced. Her left hand united with her quivering gun hand. "I mean it."

"The bullets will shake out of the gun before you pull the trigger," Boyd said in an amused tone. "You won't shoot me."

"The question isn't whether or not I'll shoot you," Marti said, marching at Boyd like a gunfighter. She lowered the barrel at Boyd's groin. "It's *where* I'll shoot you."

"Just so you know, Boyd," Dean said. "The last guy that messed with her is singing soprano."

Boyd stumbled in retreat, righting himself by grabbing onto a table.

"Best watch your back, Mason," Boyd growled, aiming a finger at Dean as he approached the front door. "Or you might wind up doing a Humpty Dumpty nosedive just like your loony aunt."

"What the hell do you know about my aunt?"

Boyd scurried out of the tavern.

Marti choked out a sob. Tears leaked down her face. Dean guided her to the bar and helped her onto a stool. In the morning she would have a nasty bruise and bad memories.

"Nice to see you kids getting along," Freddy said, carrying two bottles of Cutty Sark. He glanced around the barroom. "Where'd Boyd go?"

"To Arthur Murray's for dance lessons," Dean said.

Marti lifted Dean's glass of whiskey with two trembling hands. Her nose wrinkled at Jack's distinct aroma. She took a deep breath then downed most of the drink.

"Careful, Marti," Dean said. "To some people, Jack is more of a fiend than a friend."

CHAPTER ELEVEN

The Ford's right front tire kissed the curb in front of Aunt Maddy's house. The broken streetlight made the area darker than usual. Dean turned around and peered at Marti Cooper's unconscious form lying face down on the backseat. His friend Jack Daniel's had claimed another victim.

A yawn gripped Dean. He had anticipated facing the empty house numbed by Jack—a good plan that didn't reach his desired outcome. He turned off the engine and stared down the cul-de-sac. Most of the neighbors had called it a night. He'd had a long, taxing day that was anything but prosperous.

The car's interior lit up when he opened the door. Mrs. Butera's doberman pinscher, Darko, released a trio of familiar barks from the backyard next door. Dean tested the stability of his knee on the asphalt before shifting his full weight onto the achy joint. Jack often proved to be a temporary pain-cushion, but he'd stopped drinking too early.

An engine's escalating roar prompted Dean to turn towards the dead end. A Jeep sped down the middle of the street without the aid of headlights. He slammed the door shut, keeping his eyes locked on the Jeep.

"Lights," Dean shouted, crisscrossing his raised arms to attract the driver's attention.

The Jeep made a sudden change in direction. The front grill was now aimed at Dean. The engine's whine cranked louder. A one-sided game of chicken? Or was the driver trying to hit him? The Jeep straightened a smidgen to the right. Holy shit, he was the target. Dean dove on top of his car's back end. The Jeep blasted past him after nicking the Crestline's rear side with its front bumper.

The Jeep turned the corner with tires squealing and vanished. Darko's barking intensified. Breathing hard, Dean slid off the trunk, planting his shoes on the pavement. A drunk driver? Sadistic youthful prank? Or had someone tried to run over him on purpose?

"Boyd," he grunted out, recalling the hood's threat before fleeing Freddy's bar earlier in the evening. "The son of a bitch is crazier than I'd thought to pull that kind of stunt."

Dean closed his eyes. He had caught a glimpse of the driver from the working streetlights. Female. Long, jet black hair. Glasses. She wore a white blouse, maybe a dress. Short or she sat low in the seat. Obviously, Boyd wasn't the driver. Nor would Boyd drive an un-cool ride like a green Jeep.

Dean's eyes opened. Hell, most Jeeps were green. The license plate was blue and grey, not California's black and yellow. Could be Nevada, but he wasn't sure. Maybe Boyd had coerced one of his slutty girlfriends to run him over. The Jeep or the plates could have been stolen, all areas of Boyd's expertise. Could the driver also have been involved in Aunt Maddy's death?

Marti groaned. Dean leaned a thigh against the wheel well and peeked into the backseat. Her hand fell limp onto the floorboard. She was still in the land of Never Never. The Jeep would have slaughtered both of them had he been lifting her from the car.

Dean flexed his knee and cringed at the mountain of cement steps leading up to the house. He had every right to make Marti sleep in the car. This neighborhood had always been safe—until tonight. He opened the rear door and shifted Marti's slack form into his arms. She wasn't much heavier than a hundred pounds. His foot kicked the door shut, leaving her soiled blue skirt and jacket inside. Broken glass crunched under his shoes. He looked up at the busted streetlamp. How convenient.

Dean stopped at the bottom of the staircase, inhaled a deep breath, and climbed the stairs making sure of each step. If his knee gave out, they were both in trouble. He would also be the talk of Visitation Valley if a neighbor caught sight of him carrying an unconscious woman clad only in a white slip up his aunt's stairs.

Marti exhaled another soft moan. A familiar scenario, except the only pleasure he derived from having this woman in his arms would be landing safely onto the front porch. If there was any justice, she would have a hellacious hangover in the morning.

The muscles in his arms and legs burned. Marti's head tapped against the front screen door. She moaned again. He opened the screen. After several blind stabs the door key united with the door's lock. Carrying Marti over the threshold was a moment he'd never forget. And she wouldn't remember.

He pushed the light switch up with his elbow. The living room furniture, including Aunt Maddy's prized oriental carved wood lamp and chair were clutter free and dusted. Mrs. Butera must have cleaned and aired out the house.

Marti mumbled. Uh-oh. Was she going to be sick again? He glanced at the darkened bathroom. Her eyelids fluttered halfway open. She lifted her head and threw her arms around his neck. Her face nestled into his chest. She snuggled into him then drooled on his shirt.

Dean hustled her into Aunt Maddy's bedroom. He threw back the bedspread, blanket, and top sheet with one flip. Marti's head bounced on the bed's pillow when he lowered her onto the only available mattress in the house. She rolled over on her side, exposing dark tops to nylon stockings and white garters. Her deep sleep breathing came out in pants. He draped the covers over her shoulders.

Before shutting the door, Dean looked back at Marti. Innocent Miss Martha Jo Cooper spending the night alone with Dean the Dream Mason was more newsworthy than Grady Spencer's column in today's Sporting Green. Especially if Grady reported they slept in different rooms. Hell, the *Chronicle* would have to write a retraction. No reader would believe it, including Dean.

He checked that all the doors and windows were locked. The task didn't take long. Two bedrooms, one bathroom, combined living room-dining room, tiny kitchen, and basement.

The return ascent up the steep basement stairs was slow. He grabbed a blanket, sheets, and pillow from the hall linen closet and tossed them onto the living room couch—the same bed he used in the off seasons when he had lived with Aunt Maddy. The house was in its usual neat condition, with the exception of his old bedroom. His aunt had turned his room into her version of a junk drawer. He hadn't been in there for years.

Darko barked again. Dean crossed the living room rug to the

window and pushed the drapes aside. A neighborhood cat ran from Mrs. Butera's property. Nothing appeared amiss in the cul-de-sac.

On his way to the couch, Dean glanced down the hallway to Aunt Maddy's closed bedroom door. Was Marti somehow involved in his aunt's death? At this point, nothing would surprise him.

CHAPTER TWELVE

The eggs came out sunny side up under cloudy conditions, similar to the sun peeking through the morning overcast. Dean turned off the stove's front burner and scooped fried potatoes from the skillet onto his plate. Two slices of bacon fit snug next to the eggs. A flick of pepper followed a shake of salt. On the way to the table, he reached past folded grocery bags on the counter to notch up the kitchen radio's volume.

"We'll be right back with more of this morning's Don Sherwood show, KSFO, San Fran-cis-co," the radio announcer said over a spirited jingle. Disc jockey Sherwood's trademark infectious giggle never failed to produce a chuckle from Dean. Sherwood, his aunt's favorite radio personality, was as much a part of The City's culture as the Palace of Fine Arts constructed for the 1915 Panama-Pacific Exposition.

"Where am I?" Marti asked in a husky voice.

Dean twisted around holding his plate full of food. Marti's disheveled dark-haired head leaned against the doorjamb, Aunt Maddy's white cotton bedspread draped over her shoulders. One side of the bedspread fell from her hand. Through the milky slip he could see impressions of her bra, panties, and garter belt. She regathered the fabric.

"Aunt Maddy's house," Dean said, extending the plate to her. "Care for some breakfast?"

Pain etched onto her face. She waved off the food. The wrap fell open again.

"Didn't think so," he said, grabbing a knife, fork, and dishtowel napkin.

Her half-open eyes studied his shoes, before rising up to his slacks, button-down shirt, V-neck sweater, and face. The last time he'd had this kind of inspection, the army had classified him 4-F.

"Good Lord." Marti's voice cracked. "Do you have an appointment with Mayor Christopher this morning?"

Dean settled in at the pint-sized Formica kitchen table. He tilted the coffee percolator's spout into a porcelain mug. Then he stabbed a crispy bacon strip into an egg yolk, spreading a sea of yellow across the plate.

"Could you please turn down the sound?" Marti ran her tongue across her teeth. "I think my brain is bruised. And my tongue feels like it's covered with fur."

Dean turned off the radio and returned to his breakfast, smiling. As he expected, last night's dream girl wasn't feeling too bodacious this morning.

"What happened last night at the bar?" she asked.

"It was an experience I'll never forget," Dean said, blowing steam from his coffee.

"Oh, God." Marti stepped onto the linoleum floor like a high-wire acrobat. She put a hand on the table to balance herself. "I don't even remember saying goodbye to Freddy."

"The way you knocked down all those shots of Jack Daniel's, I'm not surprised."

"Jeez, I don't even drink." Marti dropped by stages onto the only other plastic-covered chair. "How many did I have?"

"Too many. It's not like you weren't warned."

Dean scooped a forkful of eggs and potatoes into his mouth. Marti's features scrunched their disapproval. She clutched the bedspread tighter.

"You didn't...Did you slip a Mickey into my drink like in the movies?"

"A Mickey," Dean repeated, wiping his mouth with a towel. "The only Mickey I'm familiar with plays for the Yankees."

"What time is it?" she asked.

"Almost nine o'clock."

"But it's still light out." She squinted at the daylight sneaking through the curtains.

"It usually is this time of the morning."

"Oh, God."

Dean tilted his head to the side to see a better angle of her damaged face. He touched her cheek with a finger. Her head flinched back.

"How bad does it look?"

"Bruised black and blue already," he said. "Probably should put more ice on it."

"If I didn't thank you last night for jumping in," she said. "I want to—"

"Oh, you thanked me last night," he said. "Many times in fact. You also went on a nonstop talking jag, telling Freddy, me, and the whole bar your life's story."

"What do you mean my life's story? And what do you mean by my thanking you?"

The bedspread fell open again. She didn't bother to cover herself. Dean speared another potato. Sometimes a good dose of liquor-shock came in handy. Maybe Aunt Maddy had had the right idea. Marti was better off not remembering.

"Relax," he said. "Nothing happened. I slept on the couch."

"What all did I talk about?"

"Well, there's Brad," Dean said, grinning, "your stockbroker boyfriend who broke off the relationship because he wasn't receiving any dividends. You had the lead role in your high school play. Your rent is two months past due because your roommate swiped $400 and split. You just finished your first year of teaching second grade. But you punched out your principal, Mr. Simmons, for reneging on the summer teaching job he'd promised you—and for copping a feel. Now you don't have your regular school-year job or the summer one. You—"

"It's gratifying that my private life tickles you so much," she said. "And it's Mr. Timmons, not Simmons. I didn't punch him. The heel of my hand accidentally hit his nose when I slapped him. You know more about me than my diary. Where are my clothes? I'm getting out of here."

"There you go." Dean carried his plate to the sink. "Your shoes are in the bathroom. You tossed your cookies before you passed out. This morning I took your jacket and skirt to the cleaners down the street. Mrs. Yee said you can pick up your suit this afternoon."

"My car," she gasped. "My car's still in the parking lot. I don't have enough money to pay the overnight fee. They'll probably tow it away."

"Don't flip out, Marti. I squared things with Mr. Logan, the parking lot attendant." Dean smiled again.

"What do you find so darn amusing?"

"Remember when Mr. Logan thought you looked like Sandra Dee?"

"A lot of people think I resemble Sandra Dee."

"He ought to see you now."

"Very funny." Marti placed her forehead on the Formica table. "God, even my hair hurts. You have no idea how awful I feel."

Dean filled one side of the sink with hot water. He sprinkled in powdered dish soap. The plate, silverware and pan disappeared into the suds.

Marti couldn't be more off base. He awakened most mornings in a groggy, hangover funk. Nothing was more difficult than trying to hit a fastball with crossing eyes and dumbbells banging against a sprained brain. Yes, he knew exactly how she felt. But it had never stopped him from taking another drink.

"If you want to try and make yourself presentable," he said, "I left a clean towel and a new toothbrush and toothpaste in the bathroom, along with an old pair of my sweatpants and a shirt." Dean grinned. "Oh, and there's aspirin in the medicine cabinet. Then I'll drive you back to your car."

"Thank you," she said, struggling to her feet. "Thank you for taking on Boyd. For looking after me, when you could have just left me at the bar. And for not taking advantage. I owe you an apology—"

"You don't owe me a damn thing." Dean scrubbed the plate with a sponge. "Boyd's been a bully all his life. I have a low tolerance for bullies."

He dried the plate with a clean towel. Marti had raised a good point. Why did he take care of Aunt Maddy's goddaughter, especially after she invaded his territory and infringed on his privacy? After all, he wasn't responsible for her. He had every right to walk out of Freddy's and not look back. So why didn't he leave her at the bar?

"Dean, I still don't understand why you turned down Mr. Edwards when he offered to help you get part of your inheritance back."

"You have a thousand reasons a year for not understanding. Edwards wouldn't have offered his services if he didn't believe the charity would be willing to negotiate."

"I admit I can use the money right now," she said. "Honestly, I wasn't expecting anything tangible from the reading of the will— maybe letters or pictures I'd sent." Marti bunched the bedspread with both hands. "I don't recall if you answered my question last night. You told Mr. Edwards that Aunt Madeline's fall wasn't suicide or an accident. You said she was murdered. How could you possibly know someone killed your aunt when you weren't at the nursing home when it happened?"

"I didn't have to be there to know Aunt Maddy was murdered. I'll prove it to you."

CHAPTER THIRTEEN

Dean snuggled the Crestline between two parked cars across the street from Marti's apartment building. He turned to her and stretched his arm across the bench seat. She had persuaded him to drive to her apartment for a quick change of clothes before going to the nursing home. Maybe he was feeling a smidgeon sorry for her. After all, Marti had lost her job, was broke, behind in her rent, ailing from a monster Jack hangover and sported early stages of a black eye, compliments of Boyd.

Marti stepped onto the street on the way to her apartment. Two Marti Coopers could have fit inside the clothes he had loaned her. The long-sleeved, white dress shirt covered the grey sweats like a dress. However, the shoes with two-inch heels lent some dignity to an outfit that resembled upper crust vagrant.

A vehicle appeared in the Ford's side mirror. Small, green, and speeding towards Marti. Was it the same Jeep that tried to run him down last night? Marti didn't seem to notice the danger.

Dean jumped out of his car waving both arms above his head to draw the driver's attention. If he yelled to Marti, she might stop and turn around, making herself an easier target. The Jeep changed course, veering towards Dean, exactly what he wanted the driver to do. He readied himself to jump out of the way at the last second. The Jeep braked to a stop several yards from him.

"Are you in some kind of trouble, sir," a soldier wearing military fatigues asked, leaning out the driver's side window.

"I thought you were someone else." Dean's cheeks warmed. "Sorry, sergeant."

Marti hustled up the building's cement steps. She hesitated at the front door, glancing north and south then behind her like a second-story burglar. She removed keys from her purse. Under the stairs, a potbellied man bolted out a door. He wore a pleated, wife beater T-shirt, black workpants, and a nasty scowl. A slew of obscenities streamed out his mouth as he scurried for the stairs.

Dean watched Marti frantically work the key into the lock. Obviously she was trying to avoid the man rushing towards her. Was this about the unpaid rent? Or was she in some other kind of trouble?

Dean chased after the man. The guy was quick for his size, navigating two stairs at a time. Marti disappeared inside the building with the brute close behind.

Dean's hand caught the door before it closed. His loafer soles slid to a stop on the hardwood floor of an empty, silent lobby. Hallway to his right, the stairway to his left. Which way did they go?

Marti's objections sounded from the right, followed by the man's gruff voice. Dean navigated around the corner and sprinted down the hall where they came into view.

"Take your hands off of me, Jimbo." Marti squirmed to release the man's grip lock on her wrist. "Your mother said I could be a little late with the rent money. Go ask her."

"Two months ain't just a little late." Jimbo pressed his protruding stomach into Marti. "Ma's a pushover for a sappy story. Me, I'm a businessman. Let's go inside your apartment and negotiate the rent with a little poontang barter."

"Need some help there, buddy?" Dean asked.

Dark whiskers peppered Jimbo's cheeks. His upper lip curled up like a vicious dog. He was Dean's height, plus fifty pounds heavier.

"Name's Jimbo." He puffed his chest out. "And I ain't your buddy, but I've seen you somewhere before. Either way, you got no business being here. Get out before I throw you out."

"You're absolutely right, Jumbo," Dean said. "I don't belong here."

"It's Jimbo!"

Marti mouthed the word "no" to Dean while she shook her head, warning him not to provoke Jimbo. Too late, babe.

"I'll leave as soon as you release the young lady's arm," Dean said.

Jimbo squared his shoulders to throw a left-handed punch. Dean's hand encircled Jimbo's neck, cracking the back of his head against the wall. Jimbo pushed at Dean, trying to fight back. Dean pressed a notch more into Jimbo's throat. Jimbo's mouth fell open.

Dean squeezed harder. Jimbo's complexion grew a shade redder. He stopped resisting. Marti's wrist fell free. Dean pulled out a clump of Jimbo's chest hairs for general principal, inducing a gross grunt from the goon.

"The broad owes my ma a bunch of dough," Jimbo choked out.

"Marti, how much money do you owe his mother?" Dean asked, without looking at her. His fingers were numbing.

"A hundred and fourteen dollars."

"Do you have a pen in your purse?" Dean asked.

"Yes, but—"

"Here's my wallet." Dean placed his billfold in her hand. "Take out a hundred and fourteen dollars. On the front of an additional dollar bill, write a receipt acknowledging you paid Jumbo a hundred and fourteen dollars in cash for two month's rent. Jumbo will sign the receipt when you're done, won't you, Jumbo?"

"What 'bout interest?" Jimbo croaked.

"I forgot," Dean said. "You're a businessman. Maybe you're right about interest." Dean's knee connected hard with Jimbo's groin. "Do I have your interest now, Jumbo?"

"Yssss," Jimbo managed followed by gagging.

"I can't take your money, Dean," Marti protested, pushing the wallet back to him.

"Damn it, Marti. Just once, would you do what I ask? My grip's beginning to cramp. This guy could keel over dead any second."

A new level of terror registered from Jimbo's protruding eyes. Marti placed the pen in his hand after inking Dean's instructions. Without hesitation Jimbo signed his name over Washington's face. Dean gradually released the tension on Jimbo's neck. Jimbo scrambled away holding a fistful of bills at his crotch, with the other hand attached to his neck. He'd have a difficult decision where to put an ice bag first.

"I bet we could have him housebroken in no time," Dean said.

"Thank you, once again," Marti said, holding the one-dollar receipt.

"Don't get used to it. Remember, I don't like bullies."

"I'll pay back the money as soon as I can." Marti opened the door. "I won't be long." The door closed.

"A double-dip of female bullshit," Dean muttered, leaning his head against the wall.

CHAPTER FOURTEEN

Dean positioned the Fords' hood to face the Twin Rose Nursing Home. Marti leaned towards the windshield to take in the view. Clusters of rainbow-tinted rose bushes brightened a cement walkway that circled around the building. A luscious green lawn fronted a patio with a statue of St. Francis. Jets of water encircled the statue, providing a tranquil ambiance. From the parking lot, the grounds gave the impression of Twin Rose being a posh resort rather than a private facility for the old and ailing.

Dean cranked up his window until it shut tight. He removed a flathead screwdriver from the glove compartment and placed the tool in Marti's hand.

"What am I supposed to do with this?" she said, waggling the screwdriver.

"Store it in your purse." He opened his door. "There's a chance we may need it."

Dean headed for the entrance at a fast pace. Marti's red flats took two steps to his one. She had changed into tapered black Capris and a yellow blouse with French sleeves. Facial powder masked most of the bruise Boyd had imprinted on her cheek. For a rookie with a shiner coming off her first bender, she looked pretty damn good.

"It's beautiful here," she said, raising her voice to compete with a lawn mower's gas engine. "You picked a nice place for Aunt Madeline, even if she didn't appreciate it."

"Enjoy the scenery while it lasts," he said. "Once we go upstairs, the sights, sounds, and odors can bite real hard."

The front door opened as they approached the entrance. Police Detective Lawrence Lynch's sturdy frame blocked the doorway. He nodded at Dean. The last time Dean had seen Lynch, he wore the same cheap suit and fedora.

"Thought I might run into you here, Mason." The detective

exaggerated the tip of his hat to Marti. "You may have lost your batting eye, Mason, but you still have twenty-twenty when it comes to the ladies. When did you get back in town?"

"Yesterday," Dean said. "About four-thirty p.m."

"Sounds about right," Lynch said, referring to his pocket notebook. "You left the Becker home in Nevada at 7:30 a.m. yesterday. The previous day you were in Montana."

"Should I be offended that you investigated my whereabouts?" Dean said, with a counterfeit smile.

"Just doin' my job." Lynch returned the notebook to his shirt pocket. "Typically, if there's a chance of foul play, a family member is involved. Sorry about Mrs. Principal."

"Any leads on who murdered my aunt?"

"Murdered?" Lynch shifted his view to Marti then frowned at Dean. "Who said she was murdered? Granted, the popular consensus is that Mrs. Principal wasn't the most likable person in The City, but all indicators suggest your aunt took an intentional header. She was old, sick, and from the looks of the scene, on a mission of suicide."

"Is it possible that your negative bias towards my aunt has influenced your judgment in this case?" Dean cocked his head at the detective. "She didn't kill herself, Lynch."

"How would you know?" Lynch asked. "You were away playing bush league baseball when it happened. This is an open and shut case unless you can provide proof otherwise." He removed his notebook again. "What do you know that I don't know?"

Dean locked eyes with the detective. Damn. Lynch had just backed him into a can't-win corner. No one knew Aunt Maddy and her idiosyncrasies better than Dean, but his intuition didn't constitute proof.

"Your silence says volumes." Lynch doffed his hat again to Marti and walked away.

"I got the impression police Detective Lynch isn't very fond of you or Aunt Madeline," Marti said. "How come?"

"My aunt could be any cop's nightmare when she was stinky blotto. Lynch isn't a bad guy. I hit a couple of home runs off of him in a high school championship game. And I also stole his girlfriend, the same woman who spent all my baseball bonus money then divorced me. Instead of holding a grudge, he should be sending me anniversary checks."

"Was there a reason why you didn't tell the detective whatever your theory is about Aunt Madeline being murdered?"

"Lynch wouldn't have believed me."

"What makes you think I will believe you?"

"I figure you're smarter, unbiased, and not job-jaded. We'll soon find out."

Dean opened the door for Marti. Armchairs and couches fronted gold, textured wallpaper and a flower-patterned burgundy carpet. Ostentatious chandeliers hung from the ceiling, but didn't brighten the area. The decor was meant to impress visitors and prospective patients. The lavish lobby would have done justice to the Fairmont Hotel.

"Dean," a familiar feminine voice called out. "I've been expecting you."

Samantha moved with the grace of a dancer to meet them in the middle of the lobby. Her green eyes sparkled. She touched a perfect wave of brunette hair. The long, straight, emerald-colored dress clinging to her body accented a gorgeous hourglass figure.

"I'm Samantha Russell, the General Manager of Twin Rose," she said, offering a hand with lacquered, red fingernails to Marti. "And you are?"

"Martha Cooper." Marti took Samantha's hand. "Mrs. Principal was my godmother."

"Oh," Samantha said, with a smile of surprise.

She towered over Marti by a good seven inches. Marti didn't flinch when they shook hands. But Samantha did. Marti's grip was more than Samantha had expected.

"Honey," Samantha said, zoning in on Marti's cheek, "I hope Mrs. Principal's nephew wasn't responsible for that bruise."

"On the contrary," Marti said, releasing Samantha's hand. "Mr. Mason saved me a visit to a place like this. And I prefer Miss Cooper to honey."

Most people backed down from Samantha's domineering personality. But not Marti. Score a few points for the goddaughter. Dean ran a hand over his mouth to cover a grin.

"I'm assuming this isn't a social call," Samantha said with a razor edge in her voice, turning to Dean.

"We came here to find out what happened to my aunt." Dean noticed a middle-aged couple leaving the elevator. The woman dabbed her eyes with a handkerchief. The man gazed at the floor with a downcast expression. "What is your version, Sam?"

"I'm not going to pull any punches, Dean." Samantha's voice ratcheted higher with each word. "Mrs. Principal was the surliest patient we've ever had at Twin Rose. I lost two maids and a nurse because of her. Carlos, our maintenance man, still has nightmares from seeing your aunt fall from her third floor balcony."

"What a horrible thing for that poor maintenance man to have witnessed," Marti said.

"I'm sorry about Carlos." Dean nodded. "He's a hard worker and a good man."

"You're fortunate I'm not billing you for additional compensation," Samantha said.

"On that note, I paid a year in advance for my aunt to stay here. A refund is in order."

"Refund!" Samantha laughed. "If you recall, the only way we would accept Mrs. Principal into Twin Rose was on the condition of a year's payment up front."

"Which, in good faith, I provided. My aunt's stay at this facility lasted five months. You owe me a seven-month reimbursement."

"You owe me two maids and a nurse," Samantha countered.

"Perhaps my aunt's attorney will change your stance on the subject, Sam, since the Twin Rose staff was negligent by allowing a resident to fall three stories to her death." He moved a step closer to Samantha. "Or could it be that someone here facilitated the fall by pushing my aunt over the railing? That way you could bank the advance money and put a new patient in the same room. Seven months at double the rate."

"That's an interesting theory," Samantha said, "but a swing and a miss just the same. The police report indicated probable suicide. Mrs. Principal had regained much of her strength and was improving – certainly not in temperament – but with her disabilities. Your aunt even put towels down on the floor under the legs of her easy chair to pull it out of her room to the balcony railing."

"Then you believe my godmother could perform a feat of strength like tugging that chair out to the balcony?" Marti said.

"I wouldn't put anything past that woman." Samantha crossed her arms. "If the nurse Mrs. Principal punched out still worked here, she'd concur."

"Did my aunt sign any documents without my knowledge or consent?" Dean asked.

"Not that I know of," Samantha said. "Plus, because of her stroke she didn't have the ability to write."

"But she could move a heavy chair." Dean shook his head. "Doesn't add up. What about visitors, Sam? Did anyone come here to see my aunt while I was away?"

"Still playing Sherlock Holmes, Dean? Yes, as a matter of fact your ex-wife came to visit Mrs. Principal a couple of weeks ago."

"Dede?" His eyebrows rose in surprise. "Dede came to Twin Rose to see my aunt?"

"She told me her name was Claudia. How many ex wives do you have?"

"One," he said. "Which is one too many. Claudia is Dede's formal name. Did Dede give a reason why she wanted to talk to my aunt?"

"Claudia or Dede told me she came here to ask Mrs. Principal a question before it was too late." Samantha lifted her chin as if she had been challenged.

"What question?" Dean asked.

"And too late for what?" Marti added.

"She never said." Samantha shrugged her shoulders. "But the lady claiming to be your ex-wife insisted she be permitted to see your aunt. Since you weren't around. . ."

Dean rubbed the back of his neck. His ex wanted something from Aunt Maddy? Hell, Dede usually wanted something from somebody. What did she covet from his aunt? Money? A place to stay? To be in the will? He peered down at the carpet. For whatever reason, Dede must have been desperate. Those two women had a mutual amount of respect for each other. Zero. Was Dede involved in his aunt's death?

"I'd like to speak to your maintenance man, Carlos," he said.

"I should say no. The police have already talked to him." Samantha eyed a silver wristwatch with diamonds then put a hand on Dean's forearm. "I'm late for an appointment. You may speak to Carlos if you agree to continue this discussion at another time, in a more private place."

"Deal," he said.

"Where are you staying?" Samantha asked.

"At my aunt's house. How do we find Carlos?"

"Almost anywhere inside the building. His supply room is on the third floor. Maybe you can catch him there."

Samantha departed through the entrance door. Marti followed Dean to the front desk. He picked up the phone and dialed an Atwater number. On the sixth ring, the answering service picked up.

"Mr. Spitari's office," the operator announced.

"This is Dean Mason. Message for Harry. Call Detective Lynch at the third precinct for specifics regarding the death of Madeline Principal. That's right, Principal. Harry will know what I'm talking about. Also, I need an update on the whereabouts of a Claudia, AKA Dede, Mason. I'll be at Harry's office later this afternoon. Thanks."

Dean led Marti to the elevator. Nothing had changed since the last time he was here, except Aunt Maddy had been alive.

"It's none of my business," Marti said, "but clearly there's some history between you and Samantha, or Sam as you referred to her. She's very attractive."

"We dated a couple of times. It didn't work out."

"Maybe not for you, but she still has the hots for one Dean the Dream Mason."

"You're reading way too much into it, Marti. Listen, it's not very pretty upstairs. If you want to stay down here, I'll understand."

"No way, buster," she said, jumping into the elevator car. "I go where you go."

He punched the third floor button. The troublesome god-daughter was a distraction. But Marti, like Detective Lynch and Franklyn Edwards, had been disbelievers when he announced his aunt was murdered. If he could convince Marti, maybe the skeptical police and legal system would buy into his theories and help him find his aunt's killer.

CHAPTER FIFTEEN

Dean found Carlos in the maintenance room standing at a workbench. A Miss December centerfold, wearing only a Santa hat and a smile, adorned the wall above the bench. Dean introduced Marti to the handyman. She was honored with the only chair. Dean settled onto an upright, industrial size drum of floor wax. Marti fanned her face with a hand likely to combat the stifling heat and cleaning product fumes.

"Sorry, *Señorita*," Carlos said, swiping a hand over his sweaty forehead. "The heat is on high all the time. The patients, they get colder when they get older." His Adam's apple jutted in and out several times when he peered at Dean. "I know the reason you are here?"

"Dean, perhaps it's too soon to be asking questions," Marti said in an anguished tone. "Poor Carlos is still traumatized."

"Relax, Carlos." Dean leaned forward with both palms facing up. "We're sorry you were a witness to my aunt's death. You didn't do anything wrong. You just happened to be in the wrong place at the wrong time. I was hoping you could shed some light on what happened. What you heard and saw. And what you believe caused her to fall from the balcony."

"Not much to tell, *Señor* Dean." Carlos wiped sweat blisters from his upper lip with a shirt sleeve. "I walk the path every morning to check outside before I go inside. You know, I fix everything here but the patients."

"What time in the morning?" Dean said, pointing to a dusty clock on the workbench.

"Before six." Carlos adjusted a tool belt digging at his expanded waist.

"Isn't it still dark at that time?" Marti said, then squirmed in her seat.

"Half dark, half light." Carlos swallowed hard like he had a sore throat. "The outside security lights on. I hear a noise. I look up. I see her body fall from the sky like a bomb."

"The noise," Dean said. "What kind of noise did you hear?"

"A screech like a scared cat. Is like I tell police. I never forget fear on *Señora* Principal's face. Or sound of her hitting the cement. Never. I jump away into the rose bushes, drop to my knees to pray for her soul. Death is a way of life here, but not like that."

Dean glanced out the third floor window. Carlos' depiction of Aunt Maddy's death didn't jive with Sam's assessment and Lynch's theory. As determined as Aunt Maddy could be, if she jumped deliberately, would she scream or act so scared? On the contrary, a woman who didn't want to die would respond that way.

"Do you recall if my aunt was holding anything in her hands?" Dean asked. "A piece of paper. Pill bottle. A tool . . ."

"Nothing in her hands." Carlos focused on a side wall lined with boxes and canisters. "Her arms were out. The nightgown flap like cape."

"Did you see anyone else? On the sidewalk? On the balcony? In a window?"

"I only see *Señora* Principal."

"Dean, did you read too many Hardy Boys books as a child?" Marti rose to her feet. "You should stop playing private detective and leave this poor man alone."

Marti headed for the door. Dean stretched his achy knee on a gallon paint can ottoman and waited until she left the room to resume questioning Carlos.

"Have you ever seen Marti at Twin Rose before today?" Dean asked.

"No." Carlos grinned and outlined a female figure with both hands. "I no forget *bonita señorita*."

Dean smiled. "You have a good eye, Carlos. That's why I wanted to talk with you. What about your boss Miss Samantha Russell? Did she visit my aunt's room much?"

Carlos shrugged his shoulders. Dean regarded the floor and its different colored paint splotches. Was Carlos reluctant to say anything about Samantha, fearing he'd lose his job?

68

"No secret that my aunt wasn't often the friendliest person to be around," Dean said. "She had a great talent for creating hard feelings, sometimes without saying a word. Do you know of anyone at Twin Rose who would want to harm her?"

"You always nice to me, *Señor* Dean. Give me tickets to Seals Stadium to see Giants play. Put money in my hand to make sure chair in your aunt's room in front of balcony doors and drapes closed." Carlos moved closer to Dean. "I no lie to you. Most people hate *Señora* Principal, including me."

"I appreciate your honesty," Dean said. "Had you ever seen my aunt on her balcony before the day she fell?"

"Never. Not once."

"One last question. Do you think my aunt committed suicide?"

"I no see how she could, *Señor* Dean." Carlos ran a hand through his thick, dark hair.

"Thanks, Carlos. You've been a big help."

* * * * *

Dean found Marti in the hallway gulping in the fresher air. Her arms were crossed against her stomach. She looked up at him with questioning eyes.

"I apologize, Dean. I shouldn't have said what I said. I know you are trying to justify what you believe. It's too bad Carlos couldn't have been more helpful."

"Quite the opposite," he said. "More than ever, I believe Aunt Maddy was murdered."

Marti gasped. She lost her balance and fell into him. The door beside Carlos' room was open. An emaciated old man wearing a white hospital gown sat in a chair with his eyes fixed on the open doorway. Hideous red sores oozed from his arms and legs. Drool leaked down his chin. Dean nudged Marti's elbow, encouraging her to move on.

"I know you warned me about coming up here," she said in a shaky voice. Her eyes stayed riveted to the shiny linoleum floor as they walked. "It's heartbreaking."

"Some of the patients are a lot worse off than that poor guy."

Dean motioned with his head. "Aunt Maddy's room is at the end of the hall. Can you make it?"

Dean stopped in front of room 330. He gazed at the door as if he could see through it. The last time he was in this room, his aunt had been alive, complaining from a half-paralyzed mouth about living at Twin Rose.

He opened a lockless door. A strong, stuffy odor hit him. A finger flip turned on the lights. Marti followed him inside, leaving the door open. The bed, nightstand, radio, lamp, serving table, dresser, and heavy chair in front of the floor-length window curtains remained as he remembered. The linoleum floor needed polishing.

"Aunt Maddy wanted her favorite chair from the house here in her room." Dean patted one heavily cushioned armrest. He pulled each drape open by hand, exposing windows and the French doors to the balcony. "Carlos said my aunt fell from the balcony around six a.m. Doesn't it strike you as odd that a woman would try to kill herself in the early morning?"

"Honestly, Dean, I haven't given much thought about a good time to commit suicide." She raised her eyebrows. "I don't see what difference the hour of the day makes."

"I read a magazine article indicating that the majority of suicides take place in the late morning to late evening. It made sense to me. Most suicides are planned. Notes are frequently left behind. Calls are often made. The point being, I don't believe the first thing a troubled person would do after waking up in the morning is jump off a balcony."

"Maybe Aunt Madeline was awake all night trying to decide if she should end it all."

"If that were the case," he said, "wouldn't it make more sense to jump in the dark of night? There would be less chance of being observed. Or of having someone try to stop her."

"Your theories are subjective—and creepy." Marti rubbed her arms like she'd caught a chill. "So far you haven't offered an ounce of proof your aunt was murdered."

Dean massaged the back of his neck. Marti was right. He needed to up his game.

"Would you please open the balcony doors?" Dean moved the chair a foot away from the curtain.

"Why?"

"Just humor me."

Marti slid behind the chair and twisted the door handle. Nothing happened, like she was attempting to guide a lifeless steering wheel. She tried again with the same result. Then she pulled on the handle, same again.

"The lock must be broken." She peered back at Dean.

"Can you see where the wood near the latch has been notched?"

She ran a finger over the indentation in the wood and paint. "Yes. So what?"

"Take the screwdriver out of your purse and jam the flathead between the latch and door."

Marti exhaled an impatient breath, but followed Dean's direction. When she applied more pressure, the latch moved and the glass-paneled French door opened. She turned to him with dancing eyes. He now had her full attention.

"How did you know about the lock?" she asked.

"Before I left for spring training, Carlos and I took out the lock's carriage so it couldn't retract the latch. The door only opens when levered with a knife or a screwdriver."

"Wouldn't Detective Lynch have noticed the broken door?"

"Lynch probably figured Aunt Maddy was capable of jimmying the door open just like you did."

"Maybe that is exactly what she did."

"That's not likely, Marti. Aunt Maddy was left-handed. The stroke took most of the strength and dexterity from her left side. And she had arthritis real bad in her right hand."

Marti shot a glance out to the balcony. Then she settled into Aunt Maddy's padded chair, apparently lost in thought. Her palms came together at her lips as if she was praying.

"Then you suspected all along that Aunt Madeline might commit suicide."

"No, just the opposite. I never considered my aunt being

suicidal. She was terrified of heights. Traveling over a bridge in a car she would break out in a sweat. She would have milked a rattle-snake blindfolded before getting anywhere near the terrace or railing. I placed her chair from home in front of the door as a first line of defense in case she became disoriented. And she'd still have to figure out how to work the lock."

"Then how was Aunt Madeline able to get out to the balcony?"

"There you go." He smiled. "Aunt Maddy would have had to move the chair away from the drapes, pull the drapes open by hand because I disabled the cords, have the knowledge and ability to pry open the doors, and overcome her acrophobia."

"Jeez, I hate to admit this, Dean, but you're starting to make sense to me."

He took Marti's hands in his and pulled her up from the chair. She stood still while he went into the bathroom and came back with towels that he placed underneath the chair legs.

"Would you please bring the chair out here?" he said, moving out to the balcony.

"So much for chivalry." Marti slid the chair across the linoleum with ease, but struggled when she tried to pull the towels on the terrace's dark gray floorboards.

"I get it now," Marti said, breathing hard. "Aunt Madeline had to be strong enough to push or pull this chair out to the balcony. Wait, Samantha said your aunt had improved physically."

"Come on, Marti. You're much stronger than Aunt Maddy and you struggled to get the chair out here. Now take a look at the floorboards."

"Even with the towels, I made a trail of scratch lines in the paint," she said. "But there are no other marks in the wood."

"Hold that thought." Dean removed the towels and laid them out near the railing. Then he lifted the chair on top of the towels again.

"Someone, obviously not Aunt Madeline," Marti said, "had to be strong enough to carry the chair and place the legs on the towels. It was staged."

"Look who's playing detective now," he said. "You're about the same height as Aunt Maddy. Stand on the chair and look over the railing."

Marti slipped off her flats. She put a hand on a post cap for balance and stepped up. A second hand on top of the railing added stability. She leaned forward and peeked over the side.

"I can see the rose garden and walkway," she said. "But there is no way your aunt could have landed on the cement, unless she fit both feet on the rail top and pushed off like a high diver on a diving board. Either that, or she was thrown over by a very strong person." Her head snapped back. "Dear God. Is that what happened? I need to get down, now."

Marti accepted Dean's hand. Her fingers stayed with him longer than he expected after she stepped down. Then she picked up her shoes and hurried away from the railing to the balcony doorway. He followed with the chair, setting the legs down with a thud.

"Why didn't the police come to the same conclusion as yours based on the evidence you just showed me?" she asked.

"The drapes and doors must have been open when the police got here. A chair was stationed by the railing. Lynch knew nothing about Aunt Maddy's fear of heights and, before you ask, it would be useless for me to bring that to his attention because I could never prove it. So Lynch looks for motive, other than suicide. The logical person who had a motive is me until he discovered I wasn't in the area at the time my aunt was killed. Of course, he didn't know about my aunt's goddaughter Martha Jo Cooper. But you didn't know that you were in my aunt's will. Or did you? Maybe Aunt Maddy told your mother, and your mother told—"

"That's not funny." Marti wasn't smiling. "I didn't know your aunt had a stroke, was in a nursing home, or had a will. Seriously, Dean, what possible reason would anyone have to kill Aunt Madeline?"

"That's the sixty-four thousand dollar question," he said.

"We should go to the police. Tell them what we know."

"I wouldn't say that too loud, missy." A gaunt old man in a wrinkled hospital gown stood barefoot at the doorway. His ashen complexion and wild-gray hair belonged on a mad scientist. "They'll think you're crackers too."

CHAPTER SIXTEEN

The old man in the hospital gown hobbled into Aunt Maddy's nursing home room. He shuffled past Dean, heading straight to Marti. Her eyes widened as he made a slow, careful descent to sit on the bedspread next to her, exposing more of his skinny, hairless legs.

Marti tilted away from the old guy. She looked at Dean, mouthing the word, "help."

"Sir, are you the resident next door?" Dean said, pointing at the wall.

"That would be me." the man said, producing a wicked smile. "Name's George Kopecky. 'Cept around here I'm known as Crackers. Them folks downstairs think I'm nuttier than Mr. Peanut."

"Are you?" Dean leaned a shoulder into the dresser.

"A nutcase?" Crackers rubbed Marti's blouse sleeve with his fingers. "Sometimes."

"Is this one of those times?" Dean asked, ready to spring if necessary.

"I'd say it's a clear day so far. Who the hell are you?"

"I'm Dean Mason. This was my aunt's room. Did you know Mrs. Principal?"

"You mean the woman who bitched 'bout everything, not that I could understand her." He cackled. "No. I didn't know her, but you always knew she was here."

"Mr. Kopecky," Marti said. "Did you see or hear anything the morning of Mrs. Principal's death?"

"Well, Missy, maybe I know somethin', maybe I don't." Crackers' bloodshot, grey eyes focused on her face. "Looks like the nephew's been smackin' you around a little."

Dean raised his palms to the ceiling in disgust. Marti answered the old coot with a headshake and a smile.

Why did everyone think Dean would rough her up? He had never physically hurt a female in his life. Conversely, irate women had slapped and punched him countless numbers of times for not being committed to a relationship.

"What did you mean by maybe you know something?" Dean asked.

"If you got a sawbuck, maybe I do know somethin'."

Dean plucked a ten dollar bill from his wallet. He tore Hamilton's face in half and placed one half into Crackers bony hand, in case the old bird was hustling him. Or worse. Could this frail man have been capable of killing his aunt?

"Maybe," Dean said, snapping the half bill with both hands, "I'll fork over this if you convince me your recollection of what happened to my aunt is genuine."

"Gonna play that way, huh, Sonny?" Crackers' scratched his hip. "Okay, I'll tell you what I told them two cops. 'Course, they didn't believe a word I said. There was a nurse in the old bat's room—"

"Whoa," Dean said. "Timeout. How'd you know a nurse was in my aunt's room?"

"Ya gonna let me tell my story or not, Sonny?" Crackers glared at Dean. "You're kind of like your aunt."

"Mr. Kopecky," Marti gave his skinny forearm a reassuring pat, "you'll have to excuse Dean. He's obviously still upset about the death of his aunt. Please continue."

"Thanks, Missy. Like I was saying, I heard a heavy thump like somethin' dropped on her balcony. Then I hear a banshee cry. So I pound on the wall. I pound some more. It got quiet, 'cept for wailing outside. Then I heard someone running. I opened my door to give a few whys and wherefores and see a nurse hurrying out of the room."

"Did you know the nurse?" Marti asked.

"Nope." Crackers eyeballed the bill in Dean's hand.

"Can you describe the nurse to me," Dean said in a softer tone.

"Good lookin'," Crackers gummed a grin at Marti, "but not as attractive as you, Missy. Long hair the color of a crow. White dress, shoes, and rounded hat. Nylons."

"How tall was the nurse?" Dean asked.

"You about six feet, Sonny?"

"Five ten and some change," Dean said.

"The nurse was two to three inches shorter than you." Crackers wiggled an index finger at Dean. "But I never said the nurse was a she."

"What the hell are you talking about, Mr. Kopecky?" Dean moved towards the man.

"The nurse was a guy wearing a black wig and dressed as a gal. Them feet was too big and wide to be female. Plus I never seen no gal with an Adam's apple like that."

Dean ran a hand across the back of his neck. He flashed on the Jeep that had almost flattened him. The driver hadn't worn a hat, but had black hair, sat low in the seat, and...

"How about eyeglasses," Dean asked. "Was the nurse wearing dark-framed glasses?"

Crackers rubbed his grey chin stubble. "Come to think of it, yeah. Glasses."

"How did you know about the glasses, Dean?" Marti questioned.

"Lucky guess." Dean stared out at the balcony. His speculation was based on fact, not luck, or coincidence. Crackers had just bolstered his theory that Aunt Maddy had been murdered. And the same person had tried to kill him. But why?

"Which way did the nurse go when she left the room?" Dean glanced at the doorway.

"To the stairway," Crackers answered.

Dean nodded. A real nurse is on her feet all day and would probably take the elevator. A killer, posing as a nurse, would take the stairs to avoid being seen.

"Mr. Kopecky," Dean said. "What happens on your bad days?"

"I hallucinate. Well, they tell me I see people and things that aren't really there."

"Was the person rushing out of my aunt's room real?"

"As real as the two of you," Crackers said. "Now gimme the rest of the ten, Sonny."

"Are you saying the nurse pushed Dean's aunt over the balcony?" Marti asked raising her voice.

"Negative, Missy." Crackers wiggled a finger in his ear like a drill. "I'm sayin' the nurse was in the room when his aunt took her plunge. Maybe she was pushed, maybe she wasn't. Don't know. Don't care, 'cept its been a lot quieter around here since then."

Crackers snatched the half bill from Dean's hand with surprising deftness. He scooted for the door, his ass smiling at them through the gown's opening in back. His cackle echoed from the hallway.

"Do you believe him?" Marti asked, peering up at Dean

"I believe Crackers saw a real person leave Aunt Maddy's room. I'm still not sure he saw a man posing as a female nurse."

"We need to go to the police, Dean."

"Obviously, the police didn't buy Crackers' story," he said, heading to the door. "And they won't buy mine, which means they won't help. But I know someone who will, for the right price."

"And who would that be," she asked, rushing after him.

"A man named Scary Harry Spitari."

CHAPTER SEVENTEEN

The office door to Scary Harry Spitari's private detective agency was locked. Dean glanced down at the gap between the hallway and door bottom for a telltale shadow of light. None. Harry was either on a case, at the track, or hiding inside from bill collectors. Dean reached above the door for the skeleton key resting on the molding.

"Are you breaking into this scary guy's office?" Marti took a step back.

"How could it be a break-in if I've got a key?"

Dean entered with Marti close behind. He switched on the light. The reception room was a hodgepodge of office furniture. A 1959 Tanforan Racetrack calendar was the only wall decoration. Harry's place of business was the antithesis of attorney Franklyn Edward's upscale building in a respectable part of town.

Harry's voice filtered from the second room. Dean cracked open the door. The back of Harry's bald head glistened at Dean. Harry had a phone receiver pinned to his ear and in his other hand waved a rolled up sports page like a conductor's baton. His desk chair was tilted back—almost horizontal. Scuffed brown oxfords were propped up on the windowsill.

"Put a C-note on the nose for Freaky No Peeky in the third tomorrow," Harry said in his deep nasal voice. "You know I'm good for it. I've got a good feeling about this one."

Harry slammed the black receiver down, causing its bell to sound a note. Next he flipped the newspaper towards a second phone on his cluttered desk. Then he swiveled around.

"I knew you were there the whole time, Dream. Who's the good-lookin' broad?"

"Scary Harry Spitari, meet Marti Cooper." Dean pulled one of the wooden chairs out for Marti, then sat next to her. "Marti is Aunt Maddy's goddaughter."

"Madeline Principal's goddaughter?" Harry flashed Marti a crooked-tooth smile.

"Somehow, I had you pictured differently. Wonder why?"

"Yes, I wonder why." Marti scowled at Dean as she sat down next to him.

"Harry has a PhD in shit-disturbing," Dean said, grinning at the little detective. "But his investigative intellect is close to genius. And, as you can see, he's been blessed with a mug few mothers could love but a natural disguise for his line of work."

"I was wrong." Harry adjusted wire rimmed glasses on his lengthy nose without shifting his eyes away from Marti. "Shiner or no shiner, you're not a broad. In fact, you kind of look like that new Hollywood cutie-pie in the flicks."

"So I've been told," she said. "You don't appear very scary to me. Why the name?"

"Coined the moniker myself," Harry said. "Placing the word scary in front of Harry Spitari has made me a San Francisco icon."

"Careful, Marti," Dean warned. "Harry has black belts in jujitsu and exaggeration. Last time I saw you, Harry, you were trying to grow a mustache. What happened?"

"My dog licked it off, wiseass," Harry said, sneering at Dean.

"What's the haps from your police department connections?" Dean asked.

"According to Detective Lynch, the case is closed." Harry scanned notes scribbled on a racing form. "Word from the nursing home staff was your aunt had been despondent. A psychotic neighbor saw a nurse leaving her room, but that didn't hold much validity. No nurse on the staff fit his description. The coroner didn't find anything unusual, except balcony rail splinters under her fingernails. No suicide note. As far as Johnny Law is concerned, Madeline Principal offed herself."

Dean flexed his knee. A woman fighting for her life would most likely have splinters. Not a woman trying to kill herself. Was Harry testing him?

"Mr. Spitari," Marti said. "Dean doesn't believe Aunt Madeline committed suicide. He pointed out a number of discrepancies the police may have missed—or don't care about. I have to admit the inconsistencies seem plausible."

"Call me Harry, sweetheart. If it's Mr. Spitari, I won't be able to have lewd and indecent thoughts about you. I'm sure you know Dean assists me with my caseload during his baseball off-seasons. The man could be a crackerjack investigator. However, in this particular case, his objectivity might be more than slightly impaired."

"So that's what Samantha meant about you playing Sherlock," Marti said, squinting one eye at Dean. "Why didn't you tell me?"

"It was none of your business. And I'm not a detective in spite of what Harry says."

"Let's talk nitty-gritty here, shall we?" Harry removed his glasses and cleaned the lenses with his tie. "I read about you in the paper, Dream. Tough break. Then again, your aunt should have left you a bundle. Welcome to easy street. Why, then, are you still sniffing around for inside cop stuff."

How did Harry know Aunt Maddy had been wealthy? Dean himself never knew. Plus Harry had been too damn quick to dismiss foul play as the cause of his aunt's death. He knew more than he was letting on.

Dean snatched a baseball with his autograph from the desk. He placed two fingers across the red seams. If the ball had any value besides sentiment, Harry would have sold it years ago for track money. Dean underhanded the ball to Harry and narrated the reading of the will in Franklyn Edwards' office, then this morning's nursing home visit. He didn't say anything about last night's near-death Jeep experience. Harry would have told him he was being paranoid.

"Madeline left all of your inheritance money to a charity?" Harry cranked out a sharp sarcastic laugh. "Why doesn't that surprise me? But you believe she was murdered. There are no reliable witnesses. No viable motives. No police support. No suspects, except the infinite number of people who despised the wicked witch of Visitation Valley, including myself. That list is longer than the line at the Mission Street soup kitchen. On the other hand, pissing people off isn't usually a cause for murder."

"What did Aunt Madeline ever do to you, Harry?" Marti leaned forward in her seat.

"Harry once did a job for my aunt," Dean said. "Then she stiffed him on the bill. Harry's rule number one: Never work for free. At least now you can tell me the reason why she hired you. And what you discovered."

"Believe me, some things are better left buried, Dream. Especially now."

"Would that be for your benefit or mine?" Dean asked.

Harry reached into the bottom drawer of his desk. He twisted the cap off a bottle encased in a wrinkled paper bag and took a swig. The back of Harry's hand wiped a white smear of Milk of Magnesia from his lips.

"That ulcer of yours would cease to exist if you quit playing the ponies," Dean said.

"I'm in a slump, that's all." Harry turned to Marti. "Madeline didn't pay me because she couldn't handle cold hard facts. Her nephew seems to suffer from the same affliction."

"Cut the crap, Harry. We both know Aunt Maddy was murdered. But everyone keeps trying to guide me in a different direction, even you. I'll find the killer. And in the process, maybe I'll get some or all of my money back."

"I told you he was good." Harry winked at Marti.

"You're going to steal money from a charity?" Marti said.

"Why would it be stealing if the money is rightfully mine?" Dean countered.

"Waste of time and energy, Dream." Harry said. "Unless you come up with real proof or the killer, the cops will continue to treat you like Typhoid Mary with the Asian flu."

"Have any better ideas?" Dean queried.

"Nothing is going to stop you from trying to shakedown the charity." Harry scratched his scalp. "But the odds of you getting your inheritance back from the orphan people on your own are worse than a three legged horse winning the Kentucky Derby. Unless..."

"Unless what?" Dean and Marti said at the same time.

"With my assistance, you've got a chance." Harry removed a cigar from his coat pocket. "While you're doing a face-to-face in Nevada trying to intimidate the charity people, I could work my network of contacts from here. As a team, we might find the person who killed Madeline and get your money back – like winning the daily double."

"Then you're going to help us?" Marti said.

"Us?" Dean threw Marti a hard stare.

"A definite maybe." Harry sparked a wood match to life across the desktop, holding the flame to a cigar tip until it glowed red. "Under the right circumstances, I could make myself available."

"Real charitable of you, Harry." Dean waved away a smoke cloud. "Available at what price? In other words, what do you want in return?"

"I need someone to work a case for me," Harry puffed. "It's right up your alley. Should only take you one night. Two at the most."

"Deal," Dean fired back before Harry could up the stakes.

"And," Harry continued, "if we're able to retrieve any or all of your inheritance, I want you to cover what your aunt owed me, plus a bonus. A lot cheaper than what Madeline's legal mouthpiece would've charged."

"That seems fair," Marti said.

"Fair is paying off Aunt Maddy's debt, which I will do," Dean said, with a nod to Harry.

"Before you blast off to Nevada to learn as much as you can about the charity, get more information." Harry blew another cloud of smoke at Dean. "Don't go in blind."

"Right, Harry." Dean placed the business phone receiver to his ear and dialed 0.

"Who the hell are you calling?" Harry bellowed, stretching to retrieve the phone.

"Operator, I'd like to place a person-to-person call to a Beals Becker in the state of Nevada. The number is Elko 6-5539. My name is Dean Mason."

"Do you have any idea what a person-to-person long distance call costs these days?"

"Less than what you're going to lose on Freaky No Peeky

tomorrow," Dean answered.

"Is that really you, Dream," Beals said on the other end of the telephone line.

"How many other Dean Masons do you know?"

Beals laughed. The flick of a metal Zippo lighter lid came across the line. Dean had given Beals the rectangular lighter as payback for all the Camels he'd bummed while under Jack's influence. The scratch of the tiny lighter's wheel against the flint sounded. Dean pictured his young ex-teammate with a cigarette dangling between his lips while playing with a pimple on his face. Beals exhaled into the receiver.

"Have you ever heard of a town in Nevada named Charity?" Dean asked Beals.

"Sure. But it ain't much of a town. 'Bout sixty miles from my daddy's ranch."

"You once told me you'd like to be a private eye," Dean said. "How would you like to play detective for me?"

"You razzin' my berries? I'm your man."

"There's a charity in Charity," Dean said. "It's called The Billy Orphan Foundation. When I call them, all I get is their answering service. Find out as much as you can about their operation. I need the name or names of whoever runs the show and how to contact them. See if you can get a license plate number, home address, or a phone number I could use to track them down. Don't let on that you're snooping. That's really important, Beals. Otherwise, you could be in some serious danger."

"I'm hip, Dream. Nobody's better at playing dumb than me. I'll borrow Daddy's truck and go this afternoon. Hey, thanks again for talkin' Mr. Finley into keepin' me on the team as long as he did. I had a blast, man."

"That's the way it should be. Most people forget that it's a game. I appreciate your help, Beals. Maybe you can save me another trip to Nevada. Call me back at the number I gave you before I left your parent's ranch."

Dean placed the receiver in Harry's anxious hand. Harry hung up as quickly as he could. Then he shuffled through the mess on his desk and passed a case file to Dean.

"Everything you need to know is in that file," Harry said, pointing his cigar at Marti. "Ever consider partnering up with the goddaughter? She's different than the fillies you usually run with."

"How ironic," Marti said. "Aunt Madeline had the same idea about us teaming up."

"Yeah, and look what happened to her." Dean rose from the chair and opened the door for Marti. "It's time for you to pick up your car and disappear from my life."

CHAPTER EIGHTEEN

The door to Dean's old bedroom would only open halfway, as if someone or something was pushing back. Dean patted the wall until his fingers found the light switch. He squeezed into the room and couldn't believe his eyes. No wonder Aunt Maddy had made him vow to never set foot in this room while she was alive.

Only small patches of grey carpet were visible. The bed he had slept in as a teenager sagged beneath cardboard boxes, newspapers, clothes, furniture, and stuff he couldn't put a name to. Some of the paraphernalia he recognized from the basement garage, things his aunt no longer found useful for the house. Why would she go to the trouble of shifting unwanted objects into his room?

He kicked a broken fan out of his way. Aunt Maddy was the queen of eccentric, but she had also been a neat freak. The other rooms in the house were in order.

"I don't get it," he muttered. "This room is a like an alter ego."

The bat he had used in high school came into view. Dean resisted the urge to choke the wood handle with both hands and take a swing. Did Aunt Maddy create an illusion of clutter on purpose? Was there something of great value or importance hidden in this room for him to find after she passed?

"Or is this mess your revenge?" he said, peering up at the ceiling. "Payback for my not being here when you needed me the most?"

He plucked a dusty *Look Magazine* from the top of a two-foot pile. The cover pictured undefeated heavyweight boxing champion Rocky Marciano. He threw the magazine back onto the stack, raising a cloud of dust. The task of sifting through all this junk was mind-boggling. Then again, if he ignored his instincts, would Aunt Maddy's secrets remain buried forever?

"Damn that woman. At the very least she could have left me a hint or a clue."

He moved further into the room. Maybe she did leave him a

sign and he hadn't recognized it yet. How long would it take to solve the mystery of this mess—if there really was one? He only had nine days to take up the old carpeting and refurbish the hardwood floors per his aunt's will, or the house would be sold with the proceeds going to an orphan charity. Restoring the floors, however, would be a task of futility if he didn't obtain legal title by paying the delinquent taxes, interest, and penalties. Money he didn't have. Yet.

Dean removed a watch from his jeans pocket. Almost 8:30 p.m. He was anxious to leave for Nevada instead of working Harry's case. But a deal was a deal. Plus, Harry had made a salient point. Dean's chances of finding the person who murdered his aunt would be hindered if he were to do a solo on this venture. He needed Harry's expertise and connections. Case in point, Harry had called earlier after an initial inquiry into The Billy Orphan Foundation. All information leading to the foundation stopped and evaporated in the town of Charity, an odd occurrence for a legitimate philanthropic organization as large as The Billy Orphan Foundation seemed. Dean would have to pick up the trail from there and feed it to Harry piecemeal.

The phone rang. Dean wiped his hands on his hole-infested Levi's. Was Harry calling a second time to see if Dean was working his case? Dean was tempted not to answer the phone. But it could be Beals Becker with a report on The Billy Orphan Foundation. He backed out of his room and rushed to the kitchen.

"Hello, Dream," the familiar sexy voice purred on the other end of the line.

"Samantha," he said, his shoulders slumping in disappointment. "I was just on my way out the door."

"We kind of got off on some wrong footing this morning. Why don't you come over to my place for a peace offering drink?" She snickered. "Perhaps we can agree on a deal that will satisfy both of our needs."

Sam's giggle and sexual innuendos were obvious tells she was several fingers into the sauce. Or did her invitation involve an ulterior motive? Either way, her timing couldn't be worse.

"Thanks for the invite, Sam, but I'm working a case for Harry tonight. How about if I call you—"

The doorbell chimed. Jesus. Aunt Maddy's place was jumping like downtown Broadway on a Saturday night when the fleet was on shore leave.

"Someone's at my door. And I'm late for work. After that, I'll be traveling for a few days. When I get back, we still need to discuss the overpayment issue."

"That's not all we need to talk about, Dean. You had asked me if your ex, Dede, told me why she came to Twin Rose to visit your aunt. I didn't lie. She didn't tell me. But that doesn't mean I don't know the reason. Don't take too long to call me."

"Sam, wait—"

The dial tone seemed louder than normal. Did Sam just throw him a red herring as a ploy to attract him to her house? He stared at the receiver then dialed the first number to get Samantha back on the line. The door bell rang again. His body tensed. He hung up the phone. Who could be on his doorstep at this hour? It was too late for the neighbor, Mrs. Butera, to be calling on him. Or for a Fuller Brush man hawking his wares. But it was never too late for a killer, like the Jeep driver, to make another attempt. Or could it be Boyd Weber itching to finish their fight?

The bell rang twice more. Dean went back to the bedroom and grabbed the bat with one hand. On the way through the living room adrenaline jacked his senses up to red alert. He raised the bat into smashing position and opened the front door.

"Oh, shit," he grumbled, lowering the bat. Through the screen he saw a distorted form in dark clothing standing on the unlit landing. "What are you doing here?"

"Before you go ape," Marti said, "please hear me out."

Dean flicked on the outside light. A black coat covered most of the outfit Marti had on when he had left her earlier this afternoon. The lamppost across the street shone down on her Studebaker loaded similarly to his old bedroom. She tugged the screen door open. There was nothing between them except an invisible wall of tension.

"I realize that seeing the horrible goddaughter on your doorstep just hours after you thought you'd rid yourself of her is a terrible shock."

"So far you're making sense." He leaned the bat against the entryway wall.

"Do you always answer the door with a club in your hand?" she asked.

"I thought you were the Fuller Brush man." He reached for the door handle. "Look, I don't mean to be rude, but I'm on my way out."

"You're going out looking like that?" Marti grimaced at his clothes.

He touched the coat he'd purchased from Goodwill after dropping Marti off at the parking lot – the most grotty-looking jacket they had, but perfect for Harry's case.

"Is that why you're here, to critique my clothes?"

"I wish it was," Marti said. "Jimbo talked his mother into evicting me from my apartment. I need somewhere to stay until I can find another job and a new place to live." She pushed her palms out. "Before you say no, you should consider that Aunt Madeline would have approved. I'll help you with the floors, cleaning, organizing—

"Whoa." Magic words. Dean glanced back at his old bedroom. The light was still on. Unlike Samantha, Marti's timing couldn't have been better. He sneaked a peek at his watch. "Okay, you can live here."

"I'll cook for you" Marti continued. "Run errands . . . Did you just say yes?"

"You can stay here," he said. "For a short time. Under certain conditions."

Marti's back stiffened. Her eyes narrowed as if he'd become a predator. She let go of the screen door and backed away. He caught the door before it hit him in the face.

"W-what kind of conditions?" she asked.

"There's a little project inside the house. Uncharacteristically, my aunt piled almost everything unattached into my old bedroom. I've got a feeling she hid something in there, something that would lead me to better understand many of her idiosyncrasies. I need someone to clear out the room and sort through what's in there." He smiled. "A perfect project for a patient, former second grade teacher who's good at organizing things, don't you think? You can start tonight."

"What am I supposed to be looking for?"

"I'm not sure," he said. "Maybe you can unveil some of the secrets of my aunt's past. As a young boy, I remember how sweet she used to be to everyone. Her drinking habits and personality changed when she came back to The City after living in Nevada. Is there a connection to The Billy Orphan Foundation? Or the man she married, Mr. Principal?"

"Is that all you want me to do?" she asked.

"Well, since you offered, you could help with the cleaning. And cook, if you know how, before I go to Nevada." He extended a hand. "Do we have a deal?"

"I also have conditions," she said, ignoring his hand.

"You have conditions!" Mrs. Butera's doberman barked back at his raised voice. "Did you wake up this morning and say to yourself: Today I'm going to mess with a man's life? I'm going to drive Aunt Madeline's nephew crazy in less than twenty-four hours?" He zipped up his jacket. "A few seconds ago, you were pleading for a place to stay. You can't make stipulations without leverage. Now, do we have a deal or not?"

"What are the sleeping arrangements?" she asked in a firm voice.

"Same as before. You sleep in my aunt's room. I'll take the couch."

"Actually, that was my second condition," Marti said. "As long as I stay here, there will be no liquor in the house. No drinking." She offered her hand. "Deal?"

"Are you out of your mind, lady?" He pushed past Marti heading for the stairs. "And I thought Aunt Maddy was tough to live with. Whether you decide to stay or not, lock the door."

CHAPTER NINETEEN

From the creek bed, K.A. gazed up the dirt embankment. Last night he had failed to eliminate the ballplayer, a first for the Kill Artist. This morning, he would make up for his lack of success by killing two people–one scheduled, the other impromptu.

K.A. took short, careful steps climbing back to the road. If he stumbled or fell, he would soil his pristine white uniform which would raise suspicion. After all, who would want dairy products from a filthy-looking milkman on his early morning delivery route?

He dusted his pants at the cuff when he reached the top. From this vantage point, the body lying on the creek bank face down in the water was hardly visible in the light of dawn. The small boulder K.A. had used to bash in the man's forehead was now positioned near the water, blood side up. K.A. had then pushed the milkman down the embankment and unzipped the trousers. To the police, it would appear the milk jockey had stopped to take a leak, lost his balance in the darkness, slid down the hill, and hit his head on a large rock before landing in the water headfirst. Not foul play. Just an unfortunate mishap. And another K.A. masterpiece.

The oversized white hat, stuffed with wadded newspaper, had Perry's Wholesome Dairy printed on both sides in bold red letters. The clean uniform he'd pilfered from the milk truck hung baggy on him. The white belt around his waist was hitched into the last hole otherwise the pants would be around his ankles. "Johnny" was stitched in red thread on the jacket and shirt pockets. It looked and felt like he was wearing another man's uniform. Not a problem. He would only need the outfit for a short time.

He boarded the truck and grabbed the clipboard. His forefinger ran down the milk route schedule, stopping at the name Harold Meade. The order was for two bottles of cream. The list didn't say how many people were in the Meade family. But K.A. knew old Harold lived alone. What did Meade use the cream for? Coffee?

Cold or hot cereal? Or was it just a fattening substitute for milk?

K.A. went to the back of the enclosed truck. He snatched two bottles of cream from a crate and inserted them into the open squares in the metal bottle carrier. He placed the carrier onto the floorboard next to the driver's seat. This would be a very special delivery, with no extra charge. He removed a box from a paper bag and poured a portion of the contents into both bottles. Then he replaced the thin cardboard stoppers over the openings.

The truck's brakes squealed to a stop in front of Harold Meade's house. Faint light emitted from inside. Meade must be awake. The house had been completely dark when K.A. had cased the property last night. With a flashlight in hand, he had discovered empty cream bottles on the back porch. Those bottles had been his inspiration.

The box fit easily under the jacket which he zipped closed. Before leaving the truck, he checked the street in both directions to make sure no one was watching him. His blond hair hid underneath the oversized hat pulled low on his forehead, making it difficult for anyone to identify his face.

Hard-soled black shoes scrunched his presence in the gravel driveway. The cream bottles jiggled in the carrier. Inside the house a volley of sharp barks sounded like a small dog. Shit. There had been no indication of a dog last night. Animals could screw up any plan, even a good one. He picked up the empty bottles from the creaky porch and placed them in the carrier. The dog's bark rose to a more frantic pitch when K.A. knocked on the window of the back door. A light came on in the kitchen, but the door curtains obstructed his view.

A heavy man with deep wrinkles and thinning brown hair opened the door. His bifocals were thick enough to be bullet proof. He wore black Ben Davis workpants held up by suspenders that draped over long sleeved thermal underwear. The man's slipper held back the yapping little terrier.

"Glad you came here early," the man said, watching the bratty dog. "I'm out of cream." He looked up at K.A. for the first time and double blinked. "Where's Johnny?"

"Johnny took the day off." K.A. pointed to the stitched "Johnny" on the jacket. "I'm new. They gave me one of his old uniforms. I'm really sorry to bother you, Mr. Meade, but there aren't many public johns on this route. Mind if I use your bathroom?"

"Of course not." Meade opened the door wider. "Come on in. Johnny makes an occasional pit stop here too."

A box of Wheaties with a smiling Stan "The Man" Musial on the front stood tall on the kitchen table. A spoon, coffee mug, and sugar container was next to the bowl filled with cereal. Meade had been patiently waiting for Johnny to arrive with the cream to have his breakfast. The dog growled at K.A. as if it knew something was wrong. Smart dog.

"Goddamn it, Parky, shut up. The little shit hates men in uniforms. Especially the meter man." Meade pointed to a hallway. "Bathroom's second door on the right."

"I'm a breakfast of champions man too," K.A. said, handing him the bottles of cream and putting the carrier with the empties on the counter. Then he moved from the kitchen to the darker hallway. At the first door on the right, he looked over his shoulder to observe the old man.

Meade put one bottle of cream in the refrigerator. Then he eagerly popped off the other bottle's top and poured a generous amount of cream into the coffee mug and over the cereal. He slurped several sips of coffee, before shoveling spoonfuls of sugar into the bowl of Wheaties. The spoon pinged against the porcelain bowl in a steady rhythm.

K.A. left the bathroom door ajar. He sat down on the toilet lid and began a slow count to one thousand. The cereal bowl crashed to the linoleum floor, followed by the loud thump of Meade's body.

When K.A. re-entered the room, Meade's limbs were spastically jerking. Blood from a gash on Meade's forehead commingled with the white puddle and soggy Wheaties. Meade must have smacked the side of the table with his forehead before hitting the floor. Parky lapped up tainted, spilled cream like there was no tomorrow.

K.A. was careful not to make footprints in the cream. He dislodged eye glasses from Meade's nose and positioned them on the counter. Then he poured the unused, tainted cream from the bottles on the table and in the refrigerator down the sink drain and rinsed out the bottles. He returned one empty bottle to the table, and put the other in the carrier. He tipped the sugar container over the drain until all the sugar was gone. Then he removed the box of rat poison from under his jacket. He refilled the porcelain sugar bowl with the powdered poison, making sure to spill a little on the counter. He placed the box next to the glasses. Finally, he put the deadly sugar bowl beside the empty cream bottle on the table. Police would most likely survey the scene, assume Meade confused the sugar box with the rat poison box and not investigate the old man's death any further.

K.A. opened the freezer and rifled through the frozen food. He was about to give up when his hand latched onto a bundle wrapped in layers of wax paper. He removed the package of green bills – cold hard cash. Freezers were a common place to hide valuables. He stuffed the money into his pocket.

K.A. headed for the porch door then turned and surveyed the scene one last time. The only chore that remained was to return the milk truck to the road overlooking the creek. He left the kitchen lights on and opened the door. For Harold Meade and his snarky dog Parky, the Wheaties people would have to change their slogan to "Breakfast of Death."

CHAPTER TWENTY

D ean poured the pale remains of a Thunderbird Wine bottle onto the cement in the back alley. A puddle spread to his worn tennis shoes. He tossed the empty bottle into a dumpster and hurried away from the rear of the grocery store.

"A case right up my alley," Dean muttered. "Real funny, Harry."

Dean arched his nose towards an ebony sky sprinkled with vivid white dots. He rubbed three days worth of unshaved whiskers. He had solved Harry's case. No more stakeouts or impersonating a wino, but the stench from cheap wine, unwashed bodies, and the other foul smells from being without shelter would stay with him for a while.

A man covered in a newspaper blanket snored from inside his cardboard house. Hard times for those impoverished souls dwelling in The City's back street squalor. Marti had also been homeless when she rang Aunt Maddy's doorbell three nights ago. What would have happened to her if he had turned down her offer to barter for their temporary living arrangement? A moot point. He would have let her stay in any case. But she didn't know that. Nor was Marti aware how much he enjoyed their time together in the house. She was a good roomie, giving him space when needed, yet filling a void that he had forgotten needed satisfying. He looked forward to her company, plus she was a hell of good cook.

Dean raised the collar of his fifty-cent Goodwill jacket. He patted the inside pocket which held an envelope. The result of a good faith gesture for a task he performed earlier this evening. Marti would be one surprised former homeless lady when he returned to the house tonight.

He flapped his arms across his chest to keep warm. Marti was upholding her end of their agreement by diligently analyzing items stored in his old bedroom – now the only room in the house with a rug. After he removed the carpeting from the other rooms this morning, Dean was surprised to find the hardwood floors in great shape. He expected his bedroom floor should be in the same condition. A quick wax and buff would make all the floors inspection-ready, satisfying provision number seven of Aunt Maddy's will.

His chilled lips cracked into a smile. Just how good a deal-maker had he been with Aunt Maddy's naïve goddaughter? He had neglected to give her a time limit. The slower Marti worked, the longer she had a nice place to live rent free. Was Marti the kind of woman who would take advantage of a convenient situation? The cold had nothing to do with a shiver that gripped him. If his ex wife Dede had discovered something of value in the house, she would have kept it and not said a word. What if Marti was cut from the same mold?

Dean turned the corner onto Third Street and fished the watch from his pocket. It showed 10:15. He stopped at a phone booth and pushed open the accordion door. One of his street comrades had curled up asleep on the metal floor with a bottle of wine wedged in his armpit. The man reeked worse than an outhouse at a chili con carne cook-off. Dean straddled the vagrant and inserted a dime into the coin slot.

Harry answered on the second ring. His voice had a razor edge, an obvious sign that Freaky No Peeky, along with his other hairy mates, hadn't come into the money.

"Perk up, Harry," Dean said. "You were right about City Market. The product theft is an inside job, with the help of a city cop on the take. I witnessed their operation from the alley. Have to admit, though, the bad guys came up with a great little hustle."

"Hit me with the details, Dream." Harry's voice and probably his mood rose. "Starting with the name of the dirty cop."

"Hold on a sec," Dean said. The vagrant snorted then rolled over knocking Dean off balance. Dean shifted his feet. "At least three of the market employees are dirty. They stash the stolen items in the alley dumpster as trash. An accomplice in a pickup truck picks up the goods. And get this, Harry. I know the driver. He used to run with Boyd Weber's Royal Rogues gang back in high school."

"Good job," Harry said. "Give me names, descriptions, make, model, license number of the truck, and the cops—"

"You know it's really cold out here, Harry." Dean sniffed several times into the receiver. "And I kind of barged into someone's stinking home to make this call. Tell you what. Meet me at Fast Freddy's. After you ply me with a couple of drinks, I bet the info you've requested will teeter off my tongue."

"Horseshit," Harry roared. "Give me the Goddamn information."

"Hey, Harry. I'd hurry if I were you. You know how my memory fades after I get together with my friend Jack. See you at Freddy's."

* * * * *

A second cup of Freddy's stale coffee made Dean's inside embers glow searing hot. Ten minutes ago he was freezing cold. Now he was sweating enough to unzip his jacket. Dean reached inside his coat and touched the envelope intended for Marti. He wanted present the gift without being under the influence of his friend Jack.

Freddy rolled him another Pall Mall across the bar top. Dean scooped up the cigarette like a quick-handed shortstop and parked it behind his ear.

"Why do you keep this place so damn hot," Dean asked, touching his wet forehead.

"You're hot," Freddy said, wiping a glass with a towel. "Rudy at the end of the bar is always cold. Speaking of hot stuff, did Miss Marti survive the morning after?"

"Like a champ," Dean answered. "She may be the only person I've ever met to honor the vow of never drinking again."

"If you ask me, Dream, you'd be wise keepin' that lady."

"Nobody asked you, Freddy."

"Mack the Knife" crooned from the jukebox. Dean jumped off the stool looking for Boyd. Rudy was soft shoeing by himself in front of the music maker. Dean blew out a relieved breath and reclaimed his barstool.

An illuminated Hamm's beer clock behind the bar pointed a couple ticks before eleven. Where the hell was Harry? Recalling the license plate number of the getaway pickup truck wasn't a problem. Numbers and statistics stuck to Dean's brain like pine tar. But names often drifted off to parts unknown.

"In case Harry calls, I'll be outside," Dean said, snatching a book of matches.

A slight mist fell. Dean sniffed in a breath of San Francisco's sea air that wafted across town from the Pacific. This section of downtown was quiet for a Saturday night. He looked in both directions up and down the street. No sign of a green Jeep. Or Harry. He eyed his watch again. Harry should have been here by now.

Dean reached for the cigarette behind his ear and struck a match. A gust of wind blew out the flame. A second match died from the same fate. Maybe he should invest in a Zippo lighter like the one he'd given to Beals Becker. Another person he was waiting to hear from. Beals hadn't called him back since their phone conversation in Harry's office. Perhaps Beals had left a message with Marti this evening while Dean played street bum.

Dean struck another match, cupping it in his palm this time. Same results. He moved several doors down to a dark, sheltered doorstep and sparked a match to life.

A fist full of brass flew in his direction. Dean flinched. The cigarette dropped from his lips. The blow glanced off his forehead above his eye.

Dean fell back, spreading his arms to maintain balance. Vagrants were notorious for verbally attacking anyone who invaded their territory. Since when did they start using brass knuckles?

"Remember me, Mason?" Boyd growled. "Said I'd be back."

Dean sidestepped Boyd's next punch. He shook his head to clear a spastic brain and regroup from Boyd's sneak attack. Warm, sticky fluid invaded his left eye, bringing on a stinging sensation. The clear eye blinked to stay focused. He threw a wild hook and missed both of Boyd's faces.

Boyd's next punch landed hard on the side of Dean's head, knocking him to the cold cement. The night lit up with white and red flashes. Boyd's leather boot eluded Dean's forearm defense before connecting with his chest.

"Is that little bitch of yours in the bar?" Boyd spit out. His leg reared back as if he was placekicking a football. "I feel like dancing again."

Dean caught Boyd's boot with both hands. Boyd hopped on one foot. Dean twisted the boot then let go. Boyd fell backwards hitting his head with a loud thump against a lamppost's rusty, sculptured base. Garbled words escaped Boyd's throat. Dean slithered across the rough sidewalk and sent a momentum-packed, bent elbow into Boyd's groin. Boyd bayed up to the sky like a castrated hound.

With great effort Dean rose to a knee and struggled to his feet. His brain spun. He moved to a building with waist-level brick siding, holding on to stay upright.

"Don't pass out," he whispered. "Stay awake." His breath came out in pants. A familiar click sounded. He rocked back. "Oh, shit."

Boyd, hunched over, inched towards Dean. He covered his groin with one hand, the other held an erect switchblade. This time the bastard wouldn't stop at just hurting him. This time he'd go all the way.

Dean's finger's slipped from the brick. His floating brain urged his legs to move, with no results. The only part in his body that didn't hurt was his damaged knee.

Boyd grunted with each choppy step. Dean's hands closed into fists. In spite of the dark, the blurred background behind Boyd looked like a colorful LeRoy Neiman painting. Dean had one punch left – a home run or nothing. Boyd raised the knife high with the blade aimed down at Dean's chest. Dean closed his eyes and fired an uppercut with everything he had.

CHAPTER TWENTY-ONE

The sound of flesh striking flesh was followed by a metallic clank. How could that be? Dean's punch had hit nothing but air. His functioning eyelid lifted open. Boyd was clutching his wrist, ogling the switchblade lying harmlessly on the cement.

Scary Harry Spitari stood beside Boyd poised in a martial arts stance. His next jujitsu blow landed at the nape of Boyd's neck, sending him down to the pavement in a collapsed heap. Harry blew on his rigid hand as if it was a smoking gun.

"What the hell took you so long?" Dean stared down at Boyd's prone body.

"I thought my timing was near perfect," Harry said.

"Perfect? You sadistic son of bitch. I bet you enjoyed watching Boyd coldcock me."

"It was rather entertaining." Harry adjusted his brown fedora. "For an athlete who has the strongest hands of any man I've ever seen, you're pitiful as a fighter. Why won't you let me teach you some basic jujitsu moves?"

"Because I'd use the moves on you," Dean said, touching his sore ribs.

"Poor sport." Harry kneeled down and placed two fingers on Boyd's neck. "He'll be out for a while. First telephone booth we see, I'll make an anonymous phone call to the police and report a mugging. It's best we both keep a low profile."

Harry riffled through Boyd's pockets. He took the hood's wallet and knife, leaving only a greasy comb and the brass knuckles decorating Boyd's fingers. The cops would have a hard time determining if Boyd was the mugger or the muggee.

Dean's equilibrium reacted as if the 1906 San Francisco earthquake was happening again. He held Harry's shoulder before he lost his balance and joined Boyd on the cement. Harry whipped out a small notebook and touched an equally small lead pencil to his tongue.

"Better educate me on the grocery store scam before you pass out," Harry said.

"Your compassion overwhelms me, Harry." Dean hitched up the collar of his jacket. "Ply me with a couple of dogs from Doggie Diner, and I'll give you all the names and numbers of the bad guys."

"You're in luck." Harry patted his coat where Boyd's wallet was stored and steered Dean towards Freddy's. "I happen to have come into a few bucks."

* * * * *

Thirty minutes after Harry had come to Dean's rescue, Dean entered Aunt Maddy's house. Water pipes were humming with activity. Marti must be in the shower. Damn. He placed a hand at the back of his hurting skull. The dizziness he'd experienced from Boyd's sneak attack had transitioned into a pounding headache. He needed aspirin in the worst way, but the bottle of Bayer was in the bathroom medicine cabinet.

He placed his Polaroid camera on the coffee table, along with an envelope with Marti's name scribbled on the front. The contents would most likely alter their living arrangement. A good night, except for the beating he took from Boyd.

Dean peeked inside his old bedroom. Aunt Maddy's jumbled heap of clutter had been transformed into organized piles. Marti had accomplished a great deal in a short period of time. If his gut feeling from a few nights ago had been correct, maybe Marti was close to discovering what his Aunt had wanted him to find.

The water pipes turned silent. Marti's singing resonated from the bathroom. She obviously didn't know he was home. It sounded like the song "Someone To Watch Over Me" by the Platters. How could a woman that attractive have such god awful pipes?

Dean switched off the bedroom light. The tip of his tennis shoe bumped the bottom of the door before he closed it. Marti stopped singing. He moved to the bathroom door. What would be the best way of warning Marti he was home without frightening her? A soft knuckle-knock with an ensuing hello. Or a hello and then...

The bathroom door flew open. Lavender-scented steam floated from the room. A baseball bat appeared out of the fog launched towards his head, followed by a wild cry.

Dean caught the meaty portion of the bat with his palm. Dark circle smudges tattooed the wood from contact with a horsehide baseball. He yanked the handle out of her hand, indignant for almost being belted by his own bat.

"You scared the bejabbers out me," Marti said, panting. "Guess I'm still spooked from the other night. I thought you were Boyd."

"Good thing I wasn't Boyd. You've got one hell of a good swing. You could've killed the sleazy hood. Or me."

Marti threw him a meek, apologetic smile. Her shiny, wet, black hair was combed straight back. She wore a long white T-shirt that stopped at mid-thigh. So did Dean's eyes. She reached behind the door and produced her fuzzy bathrobe that must have been hanging on the hook.

"Good heavens, what happened to your face?" Marti tied the robe's belt in a bow and inched closer to him, staring at the cut above his eye. "You probably need stitches."

"It just needs to be cleaned up," he said. "Hazards of working a case for Harry."

"Speaking of cases, Mr. Edwards called. He wants you to reconsider his proposal. And also to remind you there are only six days left to refurbish the floors."

"I'm not surprised. Edwards wants to make sure I have enough money to pay his fee by getting a portion of my inheritance."

Dean opened the medicine cabinet, jiggled two aspirin from the bottle into his mouth, and chewed.

"Yuk," Marti uttered, making a sour face. She removed iodine from the cabinet and began painting Dean's cut. "I'm glad you're home. We need to talk about—"

"That can wait," he said, dodging another dab of iodine. "There's something in the living room I want you to see."

Dean pulled on Marti's sleeve, guiding her to the coffee table. He handed her the envelope. Marti's features brightened as if she was receiving an unexpected present. In a sense she was. She lifted the envelope flap and removed several Polaroid photographs. Her mouth opened but no words came out. Then she slapped his cheek.

Dean rubbed his face. Not exactly the reaction he had been expecting. The photos fell to the floor. She poked a finger on his chest where Boyd had kicked him.

"Is this your idea of a joke?" she exclaimed. "Showing me dirty pictures. I can't believe you'd do something like this."

"Whoa." Dean bent down to pick up the black and white Polaroids. "Slow down, Marti. Try looking at the faces."

Marti snatched the snapshots from his hand. Her mouth opened again. She glanced up at Dean then back to the pictures.

"That's my principal Mr. Timmons with . . . Cynthia Bolin."

"Yep. You're looking at extracurricular activities by your former principal and the teacher who took your summer school teaching assignment. I caught them at a drive-in movie playing backseat bingo. They couldn't even wait until it got dark."

"That cad." Marti's hand formed a fist. "He's married. And Cynthia. I thought she was my friend. How did you ever find him?"

"Harry has connections everywhere. One of his cop friends provided Timmons' address and license plate number. Before going on Harry's case tonight, I followed Timmons around. Got lucky." Dean flipped over the envelope. "It seems your sleazo principal has had a change of heart. He even wrote you a note of apology to that effect and signed it. You've got your teaching job back in the fall."

"I can't thank you enough, Dean." Marti beamed as she stuffed the pictures back into the envelope's seclusion. "Did you intimidate Mr. Timmons similarly to what you did to Jimbo in front of my apartment?"

"Intimidate is such an ugly word."

"How about blackmail then?"

"I prefer persuasion," he said, painfully removing his jacket.

"Why did you do such a sweet thing for me?" she said, not hiding her emotion.

"Had nothing to do with being sweet," Dean said in a firm tone. "Timmons is a bully. He tried to use his position of authority to get what he wanted from you. But you stood up to him. Even if it meant losing a job you needed and deserved. I admire you for that."

Dean avoided her searching, watery eyes. Not a total lie. He just hadn't told her the full truth. Someone had tried to kill him. If Marti continued to live with him in Aunt Maddy's house, she was in as much danger as he was. Now, with her teaching position reinstated, she could afford to find a place of her own.

"Is that the only reason you persuaded Mr. Timmons?" she said. "Because he was a bully. No other motive?"

"Just leave it at that."

Dean touched sticky iodine and blood mixed on his forehead. There was another reason. She was getting to him in a disturbing way. The same way he had felt about his ex wife Dede when he'd first met her. But he still didn't know if he could trust Marti.

Marti inched towards Dean. She got up on tiptoes and wrapped her arms around his neck. The move caught him off guard. He squeezed back, a reflex reaction. Or was it? Her hair smelled delicious, like a combination of soap and flowers. He loved the feel of Marti's softness pressing against him. Too much. Their eyes locked. This wasn't the message he wanted to convey. Or was it?

The phone rang. Their embrace separated as if they'd been caught doing something wrong. He rushed into the kitchen with Marti trailing him.

"Yes, this is Dean Mason," he said, pressing the phone harder to his ear. "I can hardly hear you. We must have a bad connection. Please speak up."

Marti sat down on one of the kitchen chairs. She seemed to be reading his expression, trying to figure out who was on the other line. He turned his back to her.

"Dean, this is...this is Amos Becker, Beals' father. Can you hear me better now?"

"Yes, Mr. Becker," Dean said. "Much better. I've been waiting to hear from Beals."

"The wife said I shouldn't call you this late," Mr. Becker said, after a long pause. "Beals talked all the time like you was Mickey, Willie, and the Duke all in one uniform. He said you were responsible for that Montana team keeping him on the roster." Mr. Becker broke into sobs. "That meant so much to my son, Dean."

Pressure mounted in Dean's chest, making it difficult for him to breathe. He shifted his gaze to the kitchen ceiling.

"What happened to Beals, Mr. Becker?" Dean choked out.

CHAPTER TWENTY-TWO

The phone receiver dropped from Dean's hand after Mr. Becker clicked off. Dean stared up at the ceiling. His young buddy Beals had one hell of a good reason for not calling him back. A myriad of emotions tugged Dean in different directions – sorrow soon turned to guilt before settling into anger.

"Please tell me what's going on," Marti said, kneading her fingers into his forearm.

"Beals Becker is dead." Dean's voice came out low, raspy. A stranger's voice.

"Oh my God. How...what happened?"

"Beals drove his father's truck over a cliff. A deputy sheriff told Mr. Becker his son had been drinking."

Dean went to a cabinet and kneeled to the floor on both knees as if he was praying. He couldn't remember the last time he'd said a prayer. Not that it mattered. No Godly words would bring Beals back to life. He opened the door and reached blindly inside. His hand returned choking the neck of an unopened bottle of Jack Daniel's.

"Please don't," Marti said, grabbing the bottle's body with both hands. "Look what happened to Beals."

"You picked the wrong time to climb onto your Carrie Nation soapbox, Marti. There are things you don't understand."

"Here's what I do know, Dean. My father was a heavy drinker. He was a good man, but he just couldn't give up his dependence on alcohol. It cost him his job then his dignity. I watched him literally drink himself into protracted suicide. It's wasn't pretty. Liquor never solved his troubles. Nor will it eliminate your problems."

"I'm not your father," Dean said, breaking the seal with a thumbnail.

"Physically, Daddy was a strong man. Just like you. It will kill you too. Just a matter of when." She removed her hands from the bottle. "That's my last pitch, slugger. But you'll be losing more than an inheritance or your aunt if you drop the ball on this one."

"What the hell is that supposed to mean?" he said, holding the bottle in one hand.

Marti straightened her back and answered with a defiant stare. Dean's tongue skimmed across dry lips. The cork top popped off in his hand. He considered himself unwilling to stop drinking, as opposed to unable. Was he incapable of facing his demons without Jack? Marti's luminous eyes continued to bore into him. Was her pep talk meant to encourage him for his own good because she cared? Or was she attempting to inspire him into sobriety as motivation to seek her lost $1000 a year inheritance?

Jack's familiar scent made him swallow hard. His body and mind thirsted for the liquid fire to work its magic of a painless temporary escape. But Marti had been right about one thing. When Jack's influence wore off, the problems were always still there accompanied by a hangover.

"Sure as shit, I killed that poor boy," he said. "I'm responsible for Beals' death."

"That's crazy talk." Marti shook her head. "You're not to blame."

"I sent Beals to the charity. He'd still be alive if I hadn't called him."

"I know you feel bad," she said. "But you're not thinking straight. You had nothing to do with the accident. Beals was in the wrong place at the wrong time doing the wrong thing. You didn't get him drunk. Beals did that all on his own volition."

"Beals didn't drink, Marti. He was allergic to alcohol. Liquor made him violently ill. It was impossible for Beals to get drunk."

"Then none of this makes sense. Why would Beals imbibe if he knew he'd get sick?"

Dean swirled Jack around until several drops spewed from the top. One sip and he wouldn't stop until the bottle was half empty. One tiny taste. That's all it would take.

"Are you telling me someone made it look like Beals had been drinking?" Marti pressed a hand over her heart. "That Beals was murdered."

"Two people in my life have died in less than a week under suspicious circumstances. Two is more than a coincidence." He ogled the bottle's small opening. If that Jeep had come at him thirty seconds later, two more people would be dead. "The only connection between my aunt and Beals is The Billy Orphan Foundation and me. You do the math."

"Please, listen to me." Marti tugged on his shirt. "Before you do something foolish, let's go to the police with everything you know. They have to believe you. Believe us."

"And tell the police what? A charity in Nevada is offering a rather unique program. They kill people in my life who ask questions or invest money in their organization. No, officer, we don't have any real proof to back up what we've just stated." His head tilted back. "Come on, Marti. It's time to move out of Fantasyland and into Realsville."

"What choice do you have other than the police?"

A good question. Two choices came to mind. He could drink himself into a comfy state of oblivion. Or he could find the people responsible for the deaths of Aunt Maddy and Beals. But he couldn't do both. One direction was alluring and easy. The other course was complicated and damn near impossible.

"Don't go to Nevada," Marti said. "At least not now. There are only six days left to refurbish the floors or you'll lose your house."

"What difference does it make? I can't pay the back taxes and penalties anyway."

"Aunt Madeline wanted you to have this house." Marti clutched his bum shirt. "Can't you get a loan from the bank?"

"No bank will lend me money without collateral. The house isn't really mine. Nor do I have a job. The only asset I had was my ability to play baseball. Now I don't even have that."

"You know a lot of people . . . like that owner of the baseball club you were telling me about, Mr. Finley. Maybe he would lend you the money."

"Mr. Finley is in poor health. I can't bother him or anyone else with my troubles."

Dean dislodged Marti's fingers from his shirt. His mouth watered, desiring Jack's effect. He lifted the bottle to his lips then hurled it against Aunt Maddy's squat refrigerator. Marti cried out in surprise. The bottle didn't break, but Jack spilled his brown guts into a puddle on the linoleum.

"I'm heading to Nevada tonight," he said.

"I'm going with you."

"The hell you are. But it's not safe for you to stay in this house alone, Marti. I'll put you up in a hotel until I get back."

"The hell I'm not going with you. I have a stake in this too."

"Oh, I get it," he said. "You want to be my bodyguard to protect your $1,000 a year asset just in case I negotiate to get part of my inheritance back." His fingers made a snapping sound. "Or maybe you're afraid I'll get the money back and won't tell you?"

"The money is secondary," she said, pounding a forefinger into his sore chest again. "I'm going with you because I owe it to Aunt Madeline. And I owe it to you, too."

"Like I said before, you don't owe me a damn thing." Dean pushed past her. "I'm going to Charity alone. And I'm not returning until I have proof The Billy Orphan Foundation is involved in the deaths of Aunt Maddy and Beals Becker. You're not coming with me. That's final."

* * * * *

After a quick shower and shave, Dean rushed towards the living room with his suitcase. He couldn't drive nonstop to Charity without sleep. He would travel as far as he could on Highway 80 then pull over for a few hours. Maybe he could make it to Reno.

"Oh, shit." His bag dropped to the floor. Marti stood next to her suitcase barricading the front door. "What part did you not understand when I said you couldn't go to Nevada with me?" Dean demanded.

"I have a feeling you're about to change your mind," she said, smiling.

Dean threw Marti an angry stare. He didn't have time for her games. She wore jean pedal pushers with a red belt, a white sweat-shirt, pigtails, and a smug expression. Marti looked more like a pretty college coed than a second grade school teacher, come wanna-be adventurer. She would be much safer in the classroom.

"If I have to, I'll physically move you out of the way," he said in threatening voice.

"You won't have to." She hitched her thumbs into her waist-band like a gunslinger and stepped aside. "I think you will want me to tag along with you."

"In college, did you major in pissing people off?" He picked up his suitcase and marched towards the door. "Get out of my way, lady."

"Before you leave," she said, "you should ask me why my presence would be of great benefit to you."

"I'll ask that question when I get back." Dean's hand encircled the doorknob.

"Earlier tonight in your old bedroom I found and read Aunt Madeline's diaries." Marti's expressive eyes brightened. "Your aunt's most private thoughts and secrets. A literal bank of information. In essence, answers to most of your questions are in there. But if you're not interested. . ."

Dean's fingers released the knob. Was she jiving him? There was only one way to find out.

"You could have mentioned this little tidbit to me earlier."

"If you recall, Mr. Mason, I started to tell you. But you wanted to show me the pictures of Mr. Timmons and my ex-friend Cynthia. By the way, that meant more to me than you'll ever know. Then the phone rang." She put an unlaced white tennis shoe covered foot on the suitcase. "Here's the deal. I'll share everything I learned about Aunt Madeline if you take me with you."

"That's freakin' blackmail," he barked.

"I think you mean extortion," Marti said. "Either way, I figure the lowdown on your aunt is worth a ticket to Nevada. And I'll tell you this much, Aunt Madeline wasn't as batty as she led people to believe. She had reasons for most of her bizarre behavior."

"Those diaries happen to be my property. You have no right to keep them from me."

"Yes, I'm aware of that," Marti said. "But if I left the diaries exactly where they were hidden then I've committed no crime." She smiled again. "My guess is, by the time you search for and find the diaries, the state of Nevada will have seceded to California."

Damn it. He looked down at his desert boots then at Marti. She had him by the gonads and they both knew it.

"Okay, you can go," he said. "Now tell me what you found. And it had better be good."

"Not so fast, slick," she said, pointing to her mouth. "No information passes through these lips until we get to Nevada. If I share what I know with you now then I lose every bit of my leverage. You taught me about leverage the night I rang your doorbell."

"I said you could go, damn it. Do you think I'm going to just dump you off on the side of the road once I get the goods? That's not very trusting of you, Marti."

"I trust you more than any man I've ever known, Dean." Her features hardened. "What's more, you're a nice guy. I know you wouldn't just park me on some isolated road. Especially in the dead of night."

"Then we don't have a problem, do we?"

"But you might be tempted to turn around and bring me back here," she said.

Shit. He hadn't thought of that. Marti wasn't only smart, she was devious too – a fact that bothered him. And he was wasting valuable time arguing with her.

"Get in the car," Dean groused, picking up her suitcase. "But let me warn you, Martha Jo Cooper. If you're bullshitting me about the Aunt Maddy information, you'll quickly find out I'm not such a nice guy. Two people are dead already. I don't want you to be number three."

CHAPTER TWENTY-THREE

The lights of Sacramento grew smaller in Dean's rear view mirror. 1:50 a.m. on the dashboard clock. He stifled a yawn, fighting fatigue. His foot pushed down harder on the accelerator. The Nevada state line seemed light years away rather than two hours.

On the radio Frank Sinatra crooned "Blues in the Night", masking Marti's silence. Dean had been driving with a passenger who should have stayed home for her own good. Marti wasn't aware someone had tried to ram him into oblivion in front of Aunt Maddy's house. Most likely the driver was the same person who murdered his aunt. Dean would be just as vulnerable to another attack until he could piece together a picture of who and why someone wanted him dead. Being on the road, especially in the dead of night, provided a temporary cover, but how was he supposed to protect Marti when he couldn't defend himself from an invisible assassin?

Dean held the steering wheel with his left hand and rubbed tired eyes with the fingertips of his throwing hand. Then he stretched his arm across the seat back until his hand landed near Marti's left shoulder. She didn't seem to notice. He had hoped for a reaction from her. His hand rejoined the steering wheel.

He yawned. His eyes shifted to the rearview mirror. A pair of headlights appeared as two decimal points in the darkness. Could the killer be following him? He eased his foot off the gas, slowing well below the speed limit. The headlights gradually became larger. Dean drifted towards the road's shoulder when the car signaled to pass him. Being overly suspicious, if not paranoid, could be a lifesaver.

Marti turned her head away from the passenger window. Dashboard lights illuminated her stare aimed at Dean. He should have driven her straight to a San Francisco hotel. But he needed the information about Aunt Maddy that was locked in Marti's pretty head. Once she revealed his aunt's secrets, however, their

111

agreement would be voided. To renege on a promise was unethical and cold hearted, yet necessary for Marti's own welfare whether she realized it or not.

Dean's eyes watered after another yawn. He pinched his cheek hard then cracked open the window. The cold air was just as effective, and didn't hurt as much.

"Would you like me to drive for a while?" Marti asked, rubbing her arms.

"What I would like is for you to share what you found in my aunt's diary."

"Do you promise not to turn around and drive me back to San Francisco?"

"You have my word." Dean held up two fingers. "Scout's honor." His pledge didn't cover depositing Marti at the nearest safe haven in Reno.

"You probably got your scouting merit badge from a sorority." Marti folded her dungaree-clad legs underneath her. "Did you know you have a cousin, Dean?"

"A cousin?" His head recoiled like he'd been hit in the face. "What the hell are you talking about? I don't have a cousin."

"Oh, but you do," Marti said. "Aunt Madeline had a baby boy out of wedlock. I won't go into detail, but your aunt was quite promiscuous in her younger years. Some of her early diary reads like one of those pocketbook midnight readers that I'm told you men are so keen on. After she separated from her husband Calvin Principal, Aunt Madeline met a soldier in a Reno bar one night, got drunk, and woke up alone in a motel room the next day. The creep took her purse and clothes. She didn't remember what the guy looked like or having sex with him. Months later, she learned she was pregnant."

Dean touched the cut above his eye. Now it all made sense. No wonder Aunt Maddy had been so private about her past. She didn't want anyone to know about the baby.

"When did this happen?" he asked. "And what did she do with my cousin?"

"Your cousin was born in 1934, twenty-five years ago. That would make him two years younger than you. Aunt Madeline left the baby in a satchel at the Reno bus station bathroom. But the shame of abandoning her son haunted her. She wrote page after page about guilt being her companion for the rest of her life."

Marti had just unveiled the reason why his aunt gave so much money to orphan organizations. And why she had taken on the responsibility of caring for him after his parents were killed in the train wreck. Aunt Maddy must have been trying to atone for her sins and the guilt that possessed her.

"I'm assuming Aunt Maddy never knew what happened to her son," he said.

"There were newspaper clippings about a baby found in the restroom at the Reno bus station. He had blue birthmarks on his forehead and stomach. The articles referred to him as the 'The Blue Birthmark Baby.' The authorities took him to a hospital."

Dean blew out a troubled breath. The shocking information Marti just shared meant he may not be the last surviving member of the family. Did the house he had almost inherited now legally belong to Aunt Maddy's son, along with the inheritance money invested with The Billy Orphan Foundation? A question for attorney Franklyn Edwards.

"Is that where the baby's trail ended?" he asked.

"No, there's more. When Aunt Madeline considered making out a will, she hired Harry Spitari to find her son."

"I'll be damned." Dean spanked his thigh with an open hand. "So that's the mystery assignment my aunt gave to Harry. How far did Harry get?"

"Her son's trail stopped at a boy's orphanage in Nevada. He was in his teens by then."

"Then my cousin is still alive."

"There was a fire at the orphanage. Harry told Aunt Madeline no one survived. Even the man who ran the orphanage died. I'm sorry, Dean."

Heavy pounding invaded Dean's chest. How strange to feel pangs of grief for a total stranger. If he had accidentally bumped into his cousin, neither one of them would have known they were related.

Dean's eyes squinted at an oncoming car's bright lights. He tapped the high beam button on the floorboard several times with his foot until the driver responded with low beams.

What was Harry's reason for not sharing the outcome of the investigation? Dean yawned again. Was Harry trying to shield him from the truth and potential hurt? That wasn't Harry's usual modus operandi. Or did Harry have an ulterior motive influenced by Aunt Maddy's unwillingness to pay Harry's fee?

"Did my aunt convey why she didn't pay Harry?"

"It took Harry several months to track her son to the doomed orphanage. When he gave Aunt Madeline a final report and bill, she didn't believe him. She thought he either invented the fire story or used it for his own convenience to end the case and get paid."

"That doesn't make sense," Dean replied. "Aunt Maddy was frugal about many things, but she was also honest."

"In her heart, she believed her son was still alive. Maybe she was right."

Dean shrugged his shoulders. He had read about mothers being spiritually connected to their children. Similar to the type of bond twins have with each other. Conversely, Harry dealt with fact. If he had, in good faith, taken his investigation as far as it could go, Aunt Maddy should have paid Harry for his services. Then again, maybe she thought Harry knew more about the investigation than he was telling her.

"I lived with my aunt all those years with no knowledge of what was tormenting her. No wonder she drank so much. Her story would have made a good novel."

"I agree," Marti said. "Even if we weren't involved, Aunt Madeline's diary was intriguing. She also wrote some spicy pages about your ex-wife Dede. In fact, that stuff Dede pulled on you, including spending all of your baseball bonus money, your aunt predicted in her diary." Marti cleared her throat. "I'm curious, not that it's any of my business, but what happened to Dede after she depleted your bank account and filed for divorce?"

"It wasn't long before she left San Francisco with a well-heeled older man. My last off season, someone told me she was no longer with her sugar daddy."

Dean turned on the heater. Aunt Maddy had warned him not to marry Dede. Nothing new there, a young man disregarding an elder's advice. If he had listened to his aunt, he would still have enough money in the bank to pay off the taxes and penalties on the house, hire someone to refurbish the hardwood floors, and have cash left over to. . .

Holy shit. He almost swallowed his Adam's apple. Calvin Principal never filed for divorce, allowing Aunt Maddy to become wealthy by inheriting her deceased husband's silver-enriched property. What if Dean was still legally married to Dede? She probably knew his net worth wouldn't fill a newspaper coin box, but maybe she discovered that Aunt Maddy was wealthy. Was that the reason Dede contacted Samantha at Twin Rose Nursing Home to see his aunt? Would that prompt Dede to kill Aunt Maddy? And him? Dean smacked his temple with his palm. Jesus, what the hell was he thinking? He had signed the final divorce papers. More paranoia. Lack of sleep must be catching up with him.

"I also found correspondence from The Billy Orphan Foundation and other orphan charities explaining how an annuity trust account would benefit Aunt Madeline." Marti rubbed her hands together. "Their strategies were quite similar in pursuing money. The more money your aunt gave them, the more the charities urged her to send greater amounts. She always complied."

"I don't know about the other charities, but someone from The Billy Orphan Foundation maliciously misled my aunt. Maybe that's why she was murdered."

Dean shifted his foot to the brake. He sent the car to the road's dirt shoulder and stopped. His eyelids felt heavier than a rain-soaked tarp covering an infield.

"Do you think you could drive for a while without killing us?" he asked.

"I'm a very good driver, thank you," she shot back. "Just because I accidentally bumped into you in the parking lot doesn't mean—"

"Wake me up when we get to Reno."

Dean pushed the door open and walked around to the passenger side. Marti had provided invaluable pieces to Aunt Maddy's jigsaw juggernaut. But he needed to shut his eyes. Clear his brain. Catch a few hours of sleep. Maybe he'd wake up and find he was still a professional baseball player. Aunt Maddy and Beals Becker were still alive. And that he didn't like the goddaughter.

CHAPTER TWENTY-FOUR

Sweat trickled down K.A.'s cheeks. His body was sprawled across a threadbare mattress that covered a portion of the bedroom floor. He rested his hands behind his head as a pillow and stared at a pitch-back ceiling. The windows in the stuffy cabin had been boarded shut to keep unwanted visitors out of his rural seclusion. An oscillating fan would have helped. Then again, electricity would have been nice too. Safety always outranked luxury.

An obnoxious owl's screeching penetrated the thin walls. He could identify most noises from lurking night critters, human or otherwise. The abandoned cabin, located a mile away from The Billy Orphan Foundation, was his favorite haven in spite of the lack of amenities. Unruly weeds, underbrush, and trees provided a natural camouflage for this cabin which hid his costume disguises, vast stash of cash, and the Jeep parked in back.

The static from the Zenith transistor radio annoyed him. He was half listening to a program out of Idaho, the only station that came in this late at night. Crunching sounds competed with the commentator. K.A.'s smoky-grey roommate was having a late night snack. The cat and K.A. tolerated each other at best, but they had two things in common. The moody feline had a strong dislike for humans. And Cheetah was an expert exterminator.

A series of yawns gripped him, yet sleep wouldn't come. The radio host spoke passionately about pork bellies and other commodities. K.A. pictured him as bald, skinny, and for some reason, wearing suspenders. But voices could be deceiving. So could faces. Strangers trusted K.A.'s comely features and disarming smile without question. Like that old fool Harold Meade who allowed an unfamiliar milkman into his house without a second thought.

K.A. angled the radio's position on the floor for better reception; why he wasn't sure. Farming held no interest to him. Nor did he know what a commodity was, except it obviously had to be something of value. Cold hard cash was his commodity. It would take him dozens of lifetimes to spend all the money he hoarded just in this cabin. Money was the secret ingredient to his existence or nonexistence. Money gave him power. Power represented the autonomy to roam as a phantom assassin.

From his back pocket he removed a wallet filled with stolen Social Security cards and driver's licenses and placed it next to the radio. Hell, his victims didn't need the ID cards anymore. As far as the United States government was concerned, he didn't exist either. The last official record that used his birth name, Tyler Wilkes, was a death certificate.

K.A. closed his stinging eyes. His troubled mind had shifted into overdrive. Someone had sent Beals Becker to nose around The Billy Orphan Foundation and ask questions he had no business asking. The zitty-faced kid was too young to be a private dick or a G-man investigating the foundation. Plus, Becker had the subtlety of a slug, but slugs leave trails.

K.A. had befriended the Becker kid with a lure of information about the charity. A handkerchief full of chloroform left Becker unconscious. K.A. poured whiskey into the boy's mouth, on his clothes, and in the cab. Then he sent Becker and his truck with Nevada license plates over a cliff. A regrettable accident. The dumbshit never learned that drinking, driving, and sticking his nose where he shouldn't don't mix.

The rhythmic sound of Cheetah's chomping stopped, followed by water being lapped up from a metal bowl. K.A. smashed a fist into the mattress. Who sent Becker? Soon, others would be coming. If K.A. wanted to remain invisible, everyone connected to the charity would have to be eliminated, including the ballplayer in San Francisco who left all of those messages with the answering service.

His eyes popped open. Maybe the voice on the radio was keeping him awake. He reached for the transistor. His hand stopped in midair at the sound which preceded a serious bulletin. He positioned the transistor on his chest and fine-tuned the dial.

"We interrupt our regularly scheduled program, *Today's Commodities*, for a special news report on the Black Belt Killer," the voice announced. "Murder is running rampant in Idaho, Nevada,

Utah, Oregon, and California. To date, a killer referred to as The Black Belt Killer is believed to be responsible for the strangulation of nineteen men, baffling the highway patrol, police, and the FBI. The Black Belt Killer is currently ranked number seven on the FBI's Ten Most Wanted Fugitives list."

K.A. smiled. He had finally made the FBI's Ten Most Wanted list. Like a hot rock 'n' roll singer with a hit song, he was moving up the charts. They called him the Black Belt Killer. He liked the name, but it was a misnomer. The Urge inside of him had killed those nineteen men. Setting fire to his parent's bed had opened a door The Urge had been hiding behind. He could better control The Urge when he was younger. As an adult, The Urge was controlling him, growing stronger and more intense each day, making it difficult to separate business from need. Even seeing a man on a movie screen or a billboard who wore a black belt and smoked a cigarette prompted The Urge to emerge. How many more kills would it take to become public enemy number one?

"When and where will the Black Belt Killer strike next is anyone's guess," the radio voice said. "Men are staying home or carrying weapons to protect themselves. Local law enforcement is concerned that innocent people will be hurt or killed by nervous male citizens with itchy trigger fingers."

"If they're frightened now," K.A. said, "how would John Q. Public react if they knew I'd killed over seventy people?"

"The killer's MO has not changed," the announcer continued. "He strangles his victims with their own black leather belts. We still have not been offered an explanation of what sets off this psychopathic killer. The only connection is the black belt. Authorities caution all male citizenry not to wear black leather belts in public until this homicidal maniac is captured."

"Psychopathic killer! Homicidal maniac!" K.A. threw the radio against the wall. Parts splattered in different directions, but the radio continued to play. The cat scurried out of the room. "They think I'm crazy."

A match strike off the wood floor soon illuminated the lantern by his side. The radio's white plastic cover had broken into a number of pieces. He seemed to lose control more frequently now, something that never used to happen. Willpower over matter. They would never capture him as long as he maintained his discipline. He was too intelligent. Too strong. Too motivated. He killed his victims without one iota of doubt or pity, taking pleasure in reviewing the memory over and over again. The Black Belt Killer was invincible as long as he stayed invisible.

With both knees on the floorboards, he picked up the radio pieces. Noteworthy men, geniuses like Einstein, Hitler, Van Gogh, and Jack the Ripper were thought to be off-kilter. They were crazy in their own special way.

"If I'm so friggin' crazy, how come they don't have one sniff of who The Black Belt Killer is? Or why multitudes of rich, old people are expiring from accidents or suspected suicides."

K.A. grunted out a throaty laugh.

"My old man, in his drunken gibberish, often told me I would never amount to anything. Well, Daddy, I'm number seven on the FBI's Most Wanted List and climbing. Before I'm done, I'll be more famous than all of them. And I will do it sober. How crazy is that?"

CHAPTER TWENTY-FIVE

Marti's shriek jolted Dean awake. She struggled with the steering wheel while pounding her foot on the brake pedal. The front end of the Ford was skidding sideways across the center line of Interstate 80.

Dean latched a hand onto the wheel, wrestling Marti for control. From the opposite direction, a semi truck's long horn blast was followed by the sound of locked brakes and squealing tires. Dean's foot extended to the gas pedal, sending his car into a spin across the pavement until all four wheels left the highway. The truck rocketed past them with its horn still blaring.

Dean dislodged his foot from the accelerator. A tornado of loose dirt funneled around them. The speedometer needle receded to the left, belying the sense of velocity. He released relieved breath. An obliterating collision with the truck had somehow been averted. And they call baseball a game of inches.

A boulder the size of a building grew larger in the car's path through the fog of dust. Dean jerked the steering wheel in the opposite direction, sending them into another dizzying spin. Marti shielded her face with crossed forearms. The driver's side smashed into the stone, launching Marti across the bench seat. All sound and movement stopped.

Dean's eyelid's crept open. Marti was sitting on his lap with his protective arms around her. They stared at each other in silence.

"Are you hurt?" he asked, aware of Marti's trembling limbs.

"Just a little shook up."

The driver's side door of his once classy ride was scrunched against the boulder. They had just experienced a real life amusement park ride and lived through it.

"What happened?" he said, still holding Marti. "Did you fall asleep?"

"I swerved to avoid a bunny running across the road."

"A rabbit," he barked. "You almost got us killed over a—"

"He deserved to live too."

"You have my permission to slap the bejabbers out of me if I ever ask you to drive again. I'll take the wheel."

Marti didn't attempt to move. She adjusted her shoulders to lean into him. Her body nestled perfectly into his lap. Their eyes fixed and stayed. Her lips parted.

Hard knocks on the window caused them to jump in unison.

"You kids all right?" A squinting man straightened up and took a step back.

The interior temperature rose several degrees. Dean rolled down the window, welcoming the cold air and the truck driver.

"We're fine." Dean lifted Marti and scooted to the center of the seat. "How about you, mister?"

"Man, in my twenty odd years of drivin' that is the closest I ever come to buyin' the farm." The driver tilted the bill of his cap back exposing a lined forehead. "You young lovers should wait to do your lip-lockin' when the wheels ain't rolling."

Dean settled in behind the steering wheel. Marti hugged the passenger door watching the truck driver's boots create a trail away in the sandy dirt. Her cheeks had turned crimson. Did the lover insinuation embarrass her? Or was she uncomfortable about what would have happened had the trucker not knocked on the window? Perhaps her thoughts now were similar to his. This was not a good time to involve himself in anything except his mission to find The Billy Orphan Foundation in Charity.

Dean's swallow did little to lubricate a dry throat. A reservoir of water would not quench his craving. His lightheaded brain ached. Marti's presence and driving had nothing to do with his condition. His body throbbed for a shot of Jack. Dean entwined his fingers to stop the shakes. He had encountered these symptoms more times than he could remember, always giving in to his need for a drink.

He squeezed his eyelids shut for several seconds then concentrated on the task at hand. Scraping metal against rock, he finessed his car away from the boulder. Much to his surprise, the door creaked open when he pushed the handle. His shoes sank into the loose earth. The entire driver's side was maimed with dents and scratches. A loose piece of metal stripping came off in his hand. He wasn't sure how Marti felt about him, but the lady had one hell of a vendetta against his car.

Dean guided the Ford back onto a road that he assumed was Highway 80 heading east. The visor shielded his eyes from the first light of a red dawn. Marti had rolled up her window, but cold air shot through new cracks in the driver's side window frame. He turned on the heat full blast. Desert surrounded the highway lanes. There were no landmarks. He could be driving into the bowels of Idaho and not even know it.

"Do you know where we are?" he asked, wiping sleep from his eyes.

"I drove past Reno over an hour ago." Marti yawned and curled her legs underneath her. "We're in Nevada, somewhere."

"You were supposed to wake me up when we hit Reno."

"You were sleeping so soundly, I didn't have the heart to disturb you."

Dean shot Marti a searing glance. Was she telling him the truth? Or was she trying to cover her shapely wazoo? Maybe Marti suspected that he intended to park her at the Reno bus depot with a one-way ticket back to San Francisco.

His shoe punched down on the gas pedal. He knew their approximate vicinity now, a good four hours away from The Billy Orphan Foundation in Charity. What the hell was he going to do with this perplexing woman?

Marti's eyelids closed, rose slowly then closed again. She had been up all night without sleep. Her nap would serve both of them well.

"Did I tell you that I found your divorce papers?" she said in a tired voice.

"Did you notice if both signatures were on the document?"

"You both signed it. Dede used her given name Claudia. She has nice handwriting."

"Perhaps you and Dede can become pen pals." Dean cheered

in silence about the confirmation.

"While you were sleeping I recalled something else from your aunt's diary," she said. "If I remember correctly, your friend Valerie from Mr. Edwards' office contacted Aunt Madeline about writing a will *pro bono*."

"Mr. Edwards told us he assisted folks getting up in their years." Dean said. "Then again, how would Valerie know to call an old lady with big bucks named Madeline Principal?"

"Good question. Maybe I got it mixed up. Maybe Aunt Madeline heard about the free wills and called Mr. Edwards. I'm so tired. Can't think straight anymore. . ." Marti's head scrunched into the seatback. Her breathing was audible, deep. The heat and lack of sleep had overcome her.

Dean notched down the temperature. He struggled out of his jacket one arm at a time and draped it over Marti's shoulders. She snuggled into the warm blanket with sleeves. He switched on the radio, changing stations until the end of a twangy country and western song filtered through the dashboard speakers.

"A nice little ditty from Conway Twitty," the deejay announced in a southern drawl. "Real name Harold Lloyd Jenkins. Speaking of names, it has just been brought to our attention that The Black Belt Killer has murdered another Nevada man. Please be alert and careful until this psycho killer is apprehended. In other words, partners, if you want to hold up your trousers and keep your life, use suspenders."

The deejay's suggestion sounded like a country and western song title. Dean glanced down at the ebony leather belt encircling his waist. This was the first time he had heard about a Nevada mass murderer called The Black Belt Killer. The deejay had warned men not to wear a black belt in public. Every baseball player in the country wore a black leather belt as part of his uniform.

Marti mumbled something in her sleep. Her nap would give him time to sort questions jumbling around in his head. Questions that had no answers. The person who murdered Aunt Maddy was clever enough to make it appear like an accident or a suicide. If Crackers' story at the nursing home was lucid enough to be true, why would a man dressed as a woman throw his aunt over her balcony? And then try to run Dean down. Obviously, someone out there was hell-bent on terminating all branches of the family tree.

Dean's stomach fluttered like a knuckleball. What if his aunt had been the secondary target? Was she killed as a way to pull him back to San Francisco? An angle he hadn't considered before. Who hated Dean enough to kill him? Boyd. The hood had held a grudge against him since high school. And Boyd knew about his aunt's fall from the balcony. Yet Boyd had not been the person driving the green Jeep. And Boyd wouldn't hire an assassin to do the dirty deed, illustrated by the chickenshit brass knuckle attack outside Freddy's Bar.

Dede, his ex-wife, was another story. Engaging the services of a killer would be Dede's style. She had hired a thug to assault Dean when he objected to giving her the Ford Crestline Victoria, the only asset he retained after she spent all his baseball Bonus Baby money. Dean had decked the hooligan with one punch and retained ownership of his car. What if Dede had sent an assassin to kill Aunt Maddy and then Dean? But what good would it do Dede to eliminate both of them if she was not legally married to Dean anymore? Was there a divorce law he wasn't aware of, where the money would go to the closest living person? Did his ex-wife force his aunt to sign a document leaving all of her assets to Dede without Samantha's knowledge? What a legal nightmare that would be. Another question for attorney Franklyn Edwards.

Dean shook his head. Crazy thoughts. Or were they?

He was wide awake now. His heartbeat revved in sync with the car's engine. Samantha had the temperament to take no prisoners. But what would Sam gain from murdering his aunt? A few extra months of double fees and Twin Rose would be minus one difficult patient. Was that enough incentive to kill a person, even an ornery old lady like Aunt Maddy?

A road sign appeared indicating 142 miles to Winnemucca. Charity was somewhere north between Winnemucca and Elko.

What about Scary Harry Spitari? How did Harry know Aunt Maddy was rich? For good reason, Harry had an intense dislike of Aunt Maddy. His gambling habit usually kept him cash-deficient. Who would be more capable than Harry to work a scam? But his private eye buddy would never try to kill Dean. On the contrary, Harry saved Dean's life after Boyd's sneak attack. Then again, was Harry so broke that he had no choice but to go after Aunt Maddy's money? More insane thinking. Or was it?

Dean passed a slow-moving station wagon. None of his far-fetched theories tied in with The Billy Orphan Foundation. But they were somehow involved. Beals Becker's death was more than a coincidence. With Harry's help, he would find out if The Billy Orphan Foundation was a legitimate charity. And he would also research the background dope on this Billy Orphan cat, if that was his real name. In the 1920s, General Mills created the fictional Betty Crocker to be a spokesman for their products. Odds were Billy Orphan was a contrived name to play on the public's sympathies.

Dean veered back into the correct lane. He tucked his coat higher on Marti's shoulders. Where had Marti been when Aunt Maddy was killed? He had never thought to ask her. He could be riding with the enemy. What if. . .

"Damn it." Bright red glowed in Dean's rearview mirror like a live ember. The speedometer needle flirted with eighty-five. As if it had a mind of its own Dean's foot jumped to the brake. The motor-cycle highway patrolman motioned with a gloved hand for Dean to pull over. Dean angled his car towards the shoulder. Why the hell was this law enforcer wasting time citing Dean for speeding when there were killers on the loose?

CHAPTER TWENTY-SIX

The four-hour old speeding ticket on the dashboard slid closer to Dean when he turned onto Lonesome Pass Road from Highway 80. He stuffed the ticket into his shirt pocket. The town of Charity was somewhere on this curvy road. Each turn seemed like the last turn of sandy dirt, low-lying brush, occasional trees, and distant, dark mountains. A pack of cars and trucks whizzed by from the opposite direction. The road wasn't as solitary as advertised.

Marti had been awake since Dean stopped for gas twenty minutes ago. The lady was a freak of female nature. Three hairbrush strokes and two swipes of lipstick rendered her camera-ready. She stared out the side window taking in the sights in silence. Was Marti having second thoughts about finagling a ride to The Billy Orphan Foundation? Or was she planning her next coup? She had successfully countered his plans by holding back information about Aunt Maddy. She allowed him to sleep until they were well past Reno. If the charity people were involved in the deaths of his aunt and Beals Becker, Dean was doing exactly what he had not intended to do—put Marti in jeopardy. Now it was too late to abandon her like an unwanted orphan in some Podunk Nevada town.

"Oh, look," Marti gushed, pointing to a parcel of vacant land by the side of the road. "A Burma Shave sign." She read, "These signs are not..." then waited for the next little sign to appear. "For laughs alone... The face they save... May be your own. Burma Shave. I just love their little rhyming roadside ads."

Dean's fingers kneaded the soft tissue around his achy knee. The Burma Shave punch-line was apropos, but the large road sign that followed stole his interest. WELCOME TO CHARITY – HOME OF THE BILLY ORPHAN FOUNDATION. PLEASE HELP BILLY'S ORPHANS WITH A DONATION. The billboard's bold black letters on a bright yellow background stood out from a distance. Underneath the copy was a color pictorial of a striking fair-haired boy about five years old. The child's sad face intrigued Dean, forcing him to focus on it. His foot lifted from the gas pedal as the boy's features became larger and more striking.

"The Billy Orphan Foundation uses that boy's face on their brochure," Marti said. "It breaks my heart every time I see him. Makes me want to help every poor, abandoned child out there. Aunt Madeline must have felt the same way."

The Ford coasted past the billboard. Moments later, Dean braked to a stop. On Marti's side of the road stood a one-story wood structure the size of an A & W Root Beer stand. The building was fronted by a potholed dirt parking lot and one car. A shake roof supported a smaller Billy Orphan Foundation sign with the same boy's face. A small grocery store with two gas pumps neighbored the charity ten yards to the right.

Dean stared through the windshield at an empty paved road and the back frame of another billboard for traffic approaching from the opposite direction. The other side of the road was touched by nature only. The town of Charity consisted of two buildings and a pair of billboards.

"Am I missing something?" Marti asked, throwing her hands up in confusion.

"No wonder we couldn't find Charity on a map. It doesn't even warrant a dot."

"That's why the service station attendant on Highway 80 told us to take Lonesome Pass Road and don't blink." Marti kept turning her head, as if looking for something to materialize. "I assumed The Billy Orphan Foundation was a large orphanage in a city."

"Exactly what they wanted people to think."

"But the brochure I found in your old bedroom had pictures of a sprawling estate with a school, playground, and hordes of happy children." Marti pointed at the small building. "They are deceiving the public. Isn't false advertising against the law?"

"What if The Billy Orphan Foundation acts as a conduit to funnel a percentage of their donations to the orphanage you just described, as well as to other orphanages around the country? That would, arguably, make them affiliated. In essence, the donations are sent here and then distributed to the orphanages. Although their brochure presents a false impression, it is probably legal. No different than putting the word NEW on a box of soap, but the only thing different about the product is the word on the box."

Dean shoved the gearshift into park and removed his foot from the brake pedal. His fingers choked the steering wheel. But there was nothing legal or ethical about murdering people for their money. All he had to do was back that up with proof.

"Then you are saying the foundation is operating within the law?" Marti placed both hands on the dashboard and turned to Dean.

"Maybe."

"What is that supposed to mean?"

"What if," he said, "The Billy Orphan Foundation receives a million dollars a year in donations then splits a hundred thousand dollars with all the orphanages? The foundation pockets nine hundred thousand dollars and who is the wiser?"

"That's fraud, for orphans' sake. They would be stealing money from homeless children."

"There you go," he said. "The government must have some sort of check and balance system to oversee the integrity of non-profit institutions. But think about it, Marti. It would be next to impossible to monitor a charity's receivables, especially with cash gifts and checks in small denominations."

A fast moving car appeared in the rearview mirror. Dean goosed the Ford towards Ida's Grocery Store. His tires skidded to a stop on compacted dirt between two gas pumps. He beeped his horn for service.

"Why are we stopping here?" Marti stretched her arms. "You just filled up."

"Homework." He honked again and rolled down his window.

A man wearing a straw cowboy hat moseyed into the afternoon heat from the darkness of a mechanic's garage attached to the building. The stained hat and pointed black boots pushed his frame over the six-foot six-inch mark. A faded red rag hung from the back pocket of his jeans. He gnawed at a forefinger then spit a piece of nail onto the dirt. "Elbie" was stitched in white thread above the front pocket of his blue uniform shirt. His weathered features scrunched together like he was facing the sun, except the bright yellow ball in the sky was behind him. An ugly scar shaped like a frown marked his left cheek. Definitely a face best suited for under the hood.

"What's it gonna be?" Elbie said to Dean in an impatient tone. Sweat lined his leather-skinned face. "Regular or Ethyl?"

"Filler up, Ethyl," Dean said.

Elbie removed the pump nozzle and wedged it into the gas tank. He contorted his body to swipe a peek at the yellow on black license plate above the back bumper. Some people play the license plate game. Others are nosy. Which one was Elbie?

"Is the little boy on the billboard really an orphan?" Marti asked, after sticking her head out the passenger window.

"Beats me," Elbie said.

"Where are the orphans housed? Marti continued. "It certainly can't be in that small building."

"Beats. . ." Elbie's eyes widened when he noticed Marti's face for the first time. He hitched his head at an older couple standing on The Billy Orphan Foundation porch. "That youngin's face on them signs gits 'em every time, ma'am. Most everyone stops to give 'em money, especially pretty women."

"The wife and I were thinking about donating a few bucks to the orphan foundation," Dean said. Marti batted her eyes at him in surprise before he creaked open the driver's side door. "Right, dear?"

"But sweetheart, we don't have much cash on us," Marti said in a soft voice. "And we left our checkbook at home." She smiled at Elbie again. "Do you have the foundation's mailing address? We could send them a check when we get back to California."

"Don't know the address. All the mail in these parts goes to the Gumption Gap Post Office."

"Gumption Gap?" Dean said.

"Yep. Gumption Gap is the next town down the road about nine miles."

Elbie reached for a bottle of windshield wiper spray and a

long-handled squeegee. The numbers on the pump stopped flipping. He rolled his eyes at the nozzle, reinserted it and pulled the trigger again. Gas spilled over the car's paint until he stopped the flow.

"Didn't need much gas, did ya?" Elbie spit out.

The question sounded more like an accusation. Was Elbie irritated that Dean requested service with a near full tank of gasoline? Or could he be suspicious that Dean was up to something?

"We're on our way to Oregon," Dean said. "I wasn't sure we'd find another gas station on a road that starts with the word Lonesome."

"Makes sense." Elbie's questioning expression eased away. "After Gumption Gap, it's 'bout ninety miles before you find the next gas."

Dean nodded then walked towards the charity's building. The older couple was still on the porch, arguing. At the sound of a sharp whistle Dean turned his head back to the pumps.

"Put your money through the slot in the door," Elbie said. "Nobody's ever in there."

"What if I have a question?"

Elbie shrugged his massive shoulders and turned his attention to the windshield.

The couple exited down three wood steps as Dean approached the porch. The woman jabbed an incriminating finger at her bald mate. Ma and Pa Kettle they weren't.

"When I suggested we stop and make a small donation," the woman said, "I was talking about a couple of dollars. How much money did you put in that envelope?"

"Never you mind," the man said. "It's for them poor orphan kids. My daddy was an orphan child. I'll never forget the stories he told us about being hungry and unwanted."

"You gave away our food money for the week," she said.

"What if I did?" He rubbed a hand over his bare scalp. "At least some of them kids, like the boy on the sign, will have some food on their table."

"You old fool. If you keep this up, we're going to need charity ourselves."

Dean moved past the bickering couple. What had he learned so far? Not a hell of a lot. The town of Charity in the state of Nevada was a pair of buildings sandwiched in between two billboards. Their phone number went directly to an answering service that took messages only and did not provide information. The Billy Orphan Foundation building was for show only. Was the answering service inside? Mailed donations went to a post office box in a town called Gumption Gap. But the charity also received donations from drive-by traffic. Who collected the money from the post office and from this store-front address? A man named Billy Orphan? If there really was such a person. Where did the donations go after being picked up?

Dean glanced back at his car. Marti was doing what came natural, being a distraction. Elbie sprayed window wash on the windshield for the third time—the cleaner the glass, the better the view. Was Elbie and whoever worked inside the store affiliated with the charity? If so, in what capacity? Someone from The Billy Orphan Foundation had talked Aunt Maddy into investing a fortune in their charity? Who was that person and where could Dean find him?

He studied the structure. Iron bar impressions showed through the darkened windows like a jail. These bars were meant to keep people out, not in. He knocked on a sturdy front door. Then he knocked again. Still no answer. The door handle didn't budge when his thumb pressed down on the lever. He lowered his head next to the slot in the door hoping to hear the female voice of the answering service. Nothing.

He straightened to full height. Next to the door frame, two wooden racks filled with donation envelopes were nailed into the building, along with a yellow pencil attached to a string. On the envelope Dean wrote "Casey Stengel", the New York Yankees' manager who was nicknamed "The Old Professor." The address of Yankee Stadium would do. He pantomimed placing a bill inside the envelope, before inserting it through the slot. Paper plopping onto paper sounded back. How large was the pile?

While Marti distracted Elbie, Dean walked around the structure. The entire trip took less than a minute, enough time for another car to park in front of the grocery store. The only way to enter or leave The Billy Orphan Foundation was through the building's front door. A phone line fed into the roof from the back. Was that the answering service line? Elbie had told them no one was ever inside the foundation. How did someone collect the donations dropped through the slot? Did Elbie mean there was never a person inside to interact with the public? If the phone line wasn't dedicated to the answering service, then who used the phone?

Dean hurried back to the pumps. He had come here to find answers to his questions. The answers were here, if he could just find someone willing to talk with him.

"Are there any cold Nehi sodas in the store?" Dean asked Elbie.

"Refrigeration's against the back wall." Elbie pointed a finger at the store entrance.

"What are you drinking, Elbie? You look like a man who could use a cold one."

"Much obliged." Elbie's face puckered in surprise. "Ida don't like me drinkin' up the profits. Make mine a grape."

"Me too, honey," Marti called out, with a pixie grin.

Dean entered the store. The man who had parked his car in front conversed with the lady behind the counter. Ida no doubt. Dean found a public phone attached to the side wall. He inserted a dime into the slot and dialed a familiar number. On the fourth ring, his party picked up. One of his questions had just been answered.

CHAPTER TWENTY-SEVEN

The public phone attached to Ida's General Store wall was fifteen feet away from a partially open door labeled PRIVATE. The door, sandwiched between racks of canned and boxed food, was several inches ajar. With the phone receiver pinned to his ear, Dean could hear the same female voice echo from that back room and on the telephone line. He pushed the phone hook down with a finger. From the room the operator repeated "hello" three times then disconnected the call.

Dean replaced the pay phone receiver. The location of the answering service for The Billy Orphan Foundation was no longer a secret. Why would the service be inside this store instead of the charity building?

Dean moved several feet towards the door marked PRIVATE. From an angle, he caught a glimpse of the operator sitting in front of a miniature switchboard. She was younger than he thought, maybe late teens or early twenties. Puffed-out red hair was squished down and divided by a headset. She held a movie star magazine in her left hand, licked two fingers on her right hand, and turned a page.

The hanging bells on the front door jingled when the man who had been at the counter left the store. Dean headed to the back wall. He selected one Nehi orange and two grape bottles from a glass-enclosed refrigerator unit and approached the cashier. The middle-aged woman wore a frilly apron over a checkered red and white dress that could have doubled as a tablecloth. Her face was an older version of the girl behind the door.

"You've got a nice little business here." Dean placed the bottles onto the counter. "Are you the manager?"

"I'm Ida, the owner." She bagged the three sodas and chucked in a miniature bottle cap opener. "You'll thank me later. They always do."

"I got the impression that the gentleman pumping gas was the owner."

"Don't doubt that a bit," she said in a snippy tone. "My brother helps out when he can't find other work." Her finger pushed the cash register key numbers until the money drawer slid open with a ring tone. "That'll be a grand total of 48 cents."

"The wife and I are looking for a business to get into," Dean said, sliding a fifty cent piece to Ida. "You know, something that would provide a decent living in a nice quiet place. You interested in selling?"

"You've got yourself a pretty good eye, mister." She placed two shiny new 1959 Lincoln pennies into his hand. "But I doubt you could afford to buy me out."

"If it's that good, you're probably right. Maybe we could open a little diner across the road. Do you know who owns the land around here?"

"Don't know," she said, jutting out a defiant chin. "Wouldn't tell you if I did. We don't need no competition."

"Can't blame a fella for trying." Dean said, with a smile. "Hope I wasn't too pushy."

"On the contrary, you're the type of young fella who'll go far in this world 'cause you're ambitious and know when to stop asking questions." Ida notched her head towards the entryway. "Which way are you and your wife heading?"

"State of Oregon." Dean lifted the bag.

"Then you might want to stock up on some eats." She pointed to sandwiches wrapped in wax paper on the counter. "Not a lot of food vendors between here and Oregon. And the sandwiches are freshly made."

"No wonder you do so well, Ida. You're a great salesman. I'll check with my wife to find out what kind of sandwich she prefers."

Dean hurried outside armed with a tad bit more knowledge. Ida ran the show here under an iron apron. More than likely, her daughter was the operator in the side room. And brother Elbie worked the pumps when he was broke. She had a country personality in a hold-you-at-a-distance way, and was wary of answering nosy questions about the store. Was Ida affiliated with The Billy Orphan Foundation? Quizzing her about the charity would most likely prove counterproductive. He had a better idea of how to open Ida's bag of secrets.

The heavy air around Dean's car was inundated with ammonia essence from window washing solution. Dean knocked the metal cap off a grape Nehi and handed the bottle and a dollar bill to Ida's brother Elbie. The cold glass first went to the gas-jockey's forehead then he drained the purple liquid from the bottle in five gulps, followed by a belch. He unlocked a metal change drawer next to the pump with a key on a chain attached to his belt loop. Elbie calculated the change out loud. He lost his place and recounted. The change was a nickel short. Elbie ogled Marti through the clean windshield one last time then returned to the garage shadows.

A red Pontiac with long tail fins pulled into The Billy Orphan Foundation parking lot. A pregnant lady carefully removed herself from the driver's seat and waddled up to the front door with her purse. She stuffed several green bills into a charity envelope and slid it through the mail slot just like Dean had done several minutes earlier. She returned to her car and drove away.

Dean stared at The Billy Orphan Foundation door. One way in, one way out. If this was the charity's headquarters, why wasn't it open to the public? How often would someone go inside to collect the money? Once a day? Twice a week? How many donated dollars passed through the mail slot per year?

An older model Oldsmobile towing a small trailer parked in front of the grocery store. A family filed out of the car heading for the entrance, the mother holding her daughter's hand. Dean needed to slip inside the store as soon as possible, but it would be pointless without Marti's cooperation.

Dean removed the cap from the other grape bottle. He leaned into Marti's open window and handed her a soda. Before she could take a sip, he whispered what was on his mind.

"You want me to do what?" she said, handcuffing his wrist with her fingers.

"Impersonate Sandra Dee," He said. "Everyone thinks you look just like her. I don't have time to explain, but the masquerade could help lead us to the person we're after."

"You are certifiably off your onion." Marti released his arm.

"Just because I resemble Sandra Dee a little doesn't mean I can impersonate her. Sandra is beautiful. Blonde. Has a different voice. Different nose. I think she is taller than me. And she is a talented actress. You might have better luck asking Sandra Dee to play Marti Cooper."

"Do you have a scarf and sunglasses?" he asked.

"In my purse. Why?"

"Movie stars sometimes try to hide their identity. I'll bet you would look just like Sandra Dee traveling incognito by wearing a black wig."

"You are not scoring many points by saying my hair looks like a wig." Marti opened her purse. She draped the scarf over her head, tying the ends into a knot under her chin. A portion of her black bangs showed on her forehead. She adjusted the rearview mirror after donning sunglasses. "This is insane. I look like someone who's trying to impersonate Gidget. Sorry Dean, I don't even own a bikini. I'm not doing it."

"You can pull this off, Marti. You're just as pretty as Sandra Dee. You told Freddy and the whole bar that you had the lead in your high school play, which means you can act. Just ask Boyd Weber. He fled the bar because you convinced him you were going to fire a real gun at him. I also haven't forgotten how you finagled your way to Charity on the premise of helping me. Here is your chance to prove it."

"You want me to walk into that grocery store as Sandra Dee."

"No," he said, leaning back into the bright sunlight. "I want you to remain seated in my car and act just like Sandra Dee would if she was on the road traveling."

"No offense, Dean," Marti said, wrinkling her nose. "But Sandra Dee wouldn't be caught dead traveling in this car."

Ouch. He had not considered the crumpled condition of his car. The Crestline Victoria was well past being a showpiece ride. Then again, maybe that was a good thing.

"Can you think of a better car for Sandra to be traveling in anonymously?"

Marti shook her head. She disengaged eye contact with Dean

and gazed into the mirror again. How heavy was the debate going on in her pretty head?

"You're not going to take no for an answer, are you?" Marti adjusted the sunglasses. "Okay, I'll do it. Why? I'm not sure. Either your family's craziness has rubbed off on me, or that little guilt dart you threw at me about helping you penetrated. Next time you get to play the star."

"I've been there." Dean knocked off the cap of his orange Nehi and took a long swig. Pulsating cold rushed to his forehead. "It's not all that it's cracked up to be."

CHAPTER TWENTY-EIGHT

Dean re-entered the grocery store unnoticed. At the counter, the Oldsmobile man asked about the charity and requested change for a twenty-dollar bill, while his wife roamed the aisles with their children. Ida readily traded the man seven green bills for his twenty, but was stingy about providing information regarding The Billy Orphan Foundation. Nice to know she treated all her inquiring customers the same way.

Dean veered past the pay phone and, without knocking, entered the windowless room marked PRIVATE. A blast of air from an oscillating fan cooled his afternoon sweat. The young operator's mouth formed a circle, halting her discourse into the receiver centered above ample breasts.

"You scared the country out of me." She squirmed in her seat pointing the magazine in her hand at Dean then shifted her view back to the PBX switchboard and said, "No ma'am, I wasn't talking to you. Like I was saying, I'm just the answering service operator. But I do know you can write a check to The Billy Orphan Foundation. Yes, Ma'am, I'm sure they will also accept cash. No trouble at all. You're welcome."

"Sorry if I frightened you." Dean eased down onto a folding chair two feet away from the young operator.

"Keep your voice down and shut the damn door." She jerked a metal-tipped plug from the board and snatched off her headset. Ten fingertips patted a red bouffant hairdo likely stiffened by hairspray. "Ma will go apeshit if she sees a strange man in here. Or any man for that matter."

"It wasn't my intention to get you in trouble." Dean said, closing the door.

"You're the kind of trouble I like," she said, with a hint of southern. Her bosom beneath a frilly, tan cowgirl blouse seemed to expand. She crossed her denim-clad legs. "Sit down and tell me your name, cowboy."

"My friends call me Dream." He sat down again.

"Bet I can guess why." Her pudgy cheeks reddened "I'm Peggy."

"Can you keep a secret, Peggy?"

"You can tell me anything, Dream." Peggy painted an invisible cross over her heart.

Dean peered down at his callused hand. Seated before him was a younger version of Ballpark Beddy—a bored and impressionable small-town, young woman seeking excitement, even if it meant inevitable trouble. Most of the ballplayers he knew took advantage of a sure outcome that would ultimately give both genders bragging rights.

"I couldn't help but notice that you were reading about Hollywood movie stars," he said, touching the magazine in her hand. "You may find this difficult to believe, but there is a movie star traveling in disguise outside in a car. She's wearing a black wig and sunglasses so no one will recognize her."

"Are you pullin' on my petticoats, Mister Dream? Bet my Uncle Elbie sent you in here. He likes to mess with my brain 'cause it ticks my ma off. I swear that man is dumber than a crankshaft."

"Have you seen the new Gidget movie, Peggy?"

"Are you kidding? Four times so far." She thumbed through the pages of her magazine. "There's a swell article and picture in here about Sandra Dee."

"Sandra Dee is sitting in a car, waiting for me. I'm that beautiful young lady's agent."

"You lie," Peggy exclaimed in a husky voice. She jumped to her feet, forgetting that the receiver around her neck was still attached to the board. "No one is a bigger Sandra Dee fan than I am. I even know her birth name is Alexandra Zuck."

"You are a big fan." Dean just learned Sandra Dee's real name. "We are on our way to do a benefit. Miss Dee likes to travel incognito, as witnessed by the wig and the state of the car I'm driving. You'd be amazed by what some of her fans will do to get near her. Talk to her. Or get her autograph. So when Miss Dee is in transit, she likes to go unnoticed. But she asked me to stop after we saw the billboard."

"There aren't many drivers who can resist stopping at the charity after seeing that little boy's face."

"Any idea who that boy is?" Dean asked.

"Nope, not a clue. Maybe he's Billy Orphan."

"Does that mean you haven't seen Billy Orphan in person?"

"Maybe I have and didn't know that it was Billy Orphan." Peggy squinted at Dean. "Are you shittin' me about Sandra Dee being in a car in the parking lot?"

"Peggy, there's a reason why I offered to disclose Miss Dee's identity to you. As you probably know, Miss Dee is an extremely generous person. She's contemplating giving The Billy Orphan Foundation a rather large donation. However, Miss Dee has given money to several philanthropic organizations that have turned out to be less than honorable. We went to the foundation first, but no one was inside to answer our questions. And your mother and uncle were less than willing to tell me anything about the charity. Before Miss Dee authorizes her accountant to cut a check, I need to garner some information. We're on a tight time schedule. In other words, it's up to you whether The Billy Orphan Foundation gets that big donation."

"You really know how to pressure a gal." Peggy grinned. "I bet that comes natural to you. We're not supposed to say nothing to nobody about the charity. I don't know much anyway, 'cept I don't want to get into no trouble."

Dean studied Peggy's features. Her blinking pale blue eyes revealed trepidation. Was she afraid of being reprimanded by her mother? Or was something else scaring her?

"Then again," she said, leaning forward and placing a hand on Dean's knee, "I'd do just about anything to see Sandra Dee in person. If I answer your questions, will you let me talk to Sandra?"

"I'm under strict orders to keep the public away from Miss Dee when she travels," he said, reading the disappointment taking over her face. "However, how can I say no to Sandra Dee's biggest fan? If you confide in me, Peggy, I'll let you talk to Sandra. Actually, it's not a bad deal. After all, you might be helping the orphan kids too."

Peggy gaped at the closed door first then at a clock on the wall.

Dean wiped sweat from the back of his neck. The room became stuffier by the second. She nodded her consent.

"Is The Billy Orphan Foundation legitimate?" he asked. "In other words, have you heard any complaints from donors?"

"Not as far as I know. Folks seem right content to keep giving them money."

"Good to hear," he said. "Why aren't you supposed to talk about the charity?"

"That's the way Ma wants it." Peggy blew out a troubled breath. "In this store, there's no other way but Ma's way."

Ida never mentioned a husband. Where was Peggy's father? The old man probably discovered the way out of Charity and never came back.

"Does your mother work for The Billy Orphan Foundation?" he asked.

"Nope."

"Who owns this building?" he asked. "And the land?"

"Don't know," she said, exposing her palms.

"I think you do," he said. Peggy revealed a real tell, like a pitcher sticking his tongue out every time his catcher called for a curve ball. "Let me reiterate something. There's a lot at stake here, including your meeting with Miss Dee."

"If Ma knew I was talking to you—"

"The only way your mother will find out we've been talking is if you tell her," he said. "I don't mind admitting that I'm confused by all the secrecy. Nor can I figure out why the switchboard is in the grocery store and not at The Billy Orphan Foundation?"

"'Cause no one's supposed to go inside the charity."

The switchboard buzzed. Peggy hastily put her headset on again, turned her attention to the board and spoke into the receiver hanging from her neck. After a brief conversation, she penned the caller's name and phone number on a pad of lined paper then removed the headset. This time she didn't fluff her hair.

"The charity people own the buildings, billboards, and the land. Ma don't have to pay them rent." Peggy's eyes squinted at the doorknob again. "They even give her money to watch over the charity and for me and my sisters to work their switchboard to give them messages. I think they gave her such a good deal 'cause people who stop here at the store wind up donating to the foundation."

"Then, in a sense, you're working for the charity," he said.

"If you put it that way, I guess. Sometimes people even give us money to take to the charity. Rumor has it, the couple who ran the store before ma kept some of the donations. Then one day they were up and gone. No one knows where they went. Or why they left."

Dean nodded. No wonder she was so nervous and Ida was so secretive.

"How do you relay the telephone messages to the orphan people?" he asked.

"I write them down on this pad and put the pages through the charity mail slot."

"Obviously someone goes inside to collect the donation money and messages. Would that person be Billy Orphan?"

"Don't know," she said, rubbing the side of her nose.

Dean cleared his throat. Peggy was lying again. He'd been trying to avoid applying pressure. Now he had no choice.

"You know who that person is, don't you, Peggy?"

Peggy scratched her nose again. Either she was having an allergy attack or she was lying.

"You're not going to get into any trouble," he said. "I promise."

"Oh yeah." Her face flushed. "The last guy who promised something stood me up and got his skinny ass killed."

Air hissed from Dean's mouth as if Peggy had punched him in the stomach. He couldn't breathe. Was the guy who made the promise named Beals Becker?

CHAPTER TWENTY-NINE

The temperature in the operator room surged in a matter of seconds. Dean dabbed a sleeve against his sweaty forehead. He looked away, struggling to conceal the turmoil churning inside of him. His throat craved a shot of Jack Daniel's and a cold glass of water chaser. How much did Peggy know about Beals Becker's death?

"Is something wrong?" Peggy's fingertips caressed the tissue above his bum knee. "Are you okay?"

Dean managed a weak smile. Peggy leaned towards him, studying his clammy face. If she got much closer, he would drip on her.

"A good friend of mine died recently," he said. "Your no-show date reminded me of the loss. Sorry. Were you close to this guy?"

"Never got the chance." She squeezed his knee one last time before taking her hand away. "He was just a guy passing through the area asking a bunch of questions. He wasn't much of a looker. And he had a bad complexion. But he was nice, respectful. Not like most of the dickheads around here. So when he asked me out, I said yes." Tears formed in her eyes. "Instead of picking me up after work, he got drunk and drove over a cliff. I've been stood up before, but nothing like that. Guess I'm fortunate, though. I could've been in that truck drinking with him. He never got to find out that I'm a liquor-works-quicker kind of gal."

Dean swallowed hard. She had just described Beals. People allergic to alcohol become extremely ill before they get drunk. But Peggy didn't know about Beals' condition. Did Beals ask her out on a date to pump her for information? Or to get lucky? Probably both.

"I'm curious about the fella who was killed," Dean said. "Did you detect an odor of liquor on him when he asked you out?"

"Nah." She touched her hair again. "And I've got a good smeller. I was outside bringing the phone messages to the charity when I saw him. I could smell tobacco on him, so I bummed a cig. Happened that he smoked Camels, my brand. We started yackin'. Beals was his name, but I'm not sure if that was his first or last name. He said he used to be a professional baseball player. Then he asked me out for dinner after work." Her eyes widened. "No guy around here asks you out for dinner on a first date."

"How did you find out this Beals guy was drunk when he drove over a cliff?"

"The Deputy Sheriff told Ma that the inside of Beals' truck smelled like a distillery. He had to be bombed out of his skull to do something like that. Plus they found an empty scotch bottle in the cab."

Dean turned his head to enjoy a full blast from the oscillating fan. Maybe in this part of the country they use assumption rather than autopsy to determine cause of death.

"Peggy, didn't it seem rather odd that a guy would go out and get smashed before his date with a hot chick like you?"

"Sure did," she said, smiling. "But that wasn't the only peculiar thing. He had stuck around for awhile. Ma got real suspicious when she saw him snooping near the charity after he had asked her a bunch of questions."

"Maybe your mother chewed out Beals' butt so bad he went and got drunk?"

"Nah. Ma mentioned it to K.A. when he was getting gas...Oh shit!" Peggy's face flushed red. "Forget I just said that."

"K.A. Who is K.A.?"

"Please." Peggy's eyes blinked like a Broadway Street sign. She bit down on her lower lip and turned away. "I've already said too much."

"Are you afraid of this K.A. person?"

"You aren't from these parts, Dream. Ma's scared of K.A. Even Uncle Elbie won't mess with him."

"I presume K.A. works for The Billy Orphan Foundation," he said.

Dean waited for Peggy to respond. Could K.A. and Billy Orphan be the same person?

"No one goes inside the charity 'cept K.A. The man's scary mean. You would be wise to stay away from him."

"I appreciate the warning. But I wouldn't be doing my job for Miss Dee unless I contacted K.A. How can I get a hold of—"

"Peggy!" Ida's voice boomed from inside the store. "You got someone in there with you?"

"Oh, crap." Peggy's hand covered her lips.

She peered at Dean in a panic, her eyes asking him what she should do. The poor girl's body shook. If Ida opened the door, Peggy was in some serious trouble, plus his information stream would dry up. He glanced around the room then pointed to a radio butted against the floorboard. His fingers pantomimed a twist movement. Peggy nodded, leaned down and fiddled with a knob. A weather report filled the room. The male deejay warned of a summer storm coming in a matter of hours.

"No, Ma. Just getting a weather update. It's gonna rain soon. Is it too loud?"

"You always have that blasted radio on too loud. Thought I heard a man's voice. Turn it off."

"Sure, Ma." Peggy switched off the radio. "Sorry."

Peggy wrapped her trembling arms around herself. They stared at each other in silence. Dean couldn't help but feel a twinge of guilt. He was taking advantage of this naïve girl under false pretenses. Yet, he still needed to ask a few more questions.

"You have to get out of here, Dream."

"I know," he whispered back, taking her hand. "I need to talk to this K.A. guy."

"Haven't seen K.A. since the day Beals was killed. He travels a lot of the time. A couple of day ago, he told Ma he'd be gone for at least a week."

"Where does K.A. live?"

"Nobody knows where K.A. lives," Peggy said, looking at the doorknob again.

Damn. Dean peered down at the floor in disappointment. If K.A. was traveling, how long would he have to wait for this guy?

"Nobody knows where K.A. lives," Peggy repeated in a low voice, leaving her hand in his. "'Cept me. That bit of knowledge alone should get me a visit with Sandra Dee, don't you think?"

"Maybe even a part in her next movie," he said. "Can you give me directions?"

"Maybe I'm just a sucker for them blue eyes, but I trust you're a straight-shooter."

Peggy drew in a deep breath. She turned his hand over palm up and snatched the ballpoint pen from his shirt pocket. Her forefinger ran over his life-line like a fortune teller. An omen? At the touch of the pen's point his skin tingled. Peggy sketched lines on his hand that formed a map. She stopped after marking an X.

"One day my ex-boyfriend and I were looking for an isolated spot to, you know, fool around. We saw this abandoned cabin and stopped to check it out. The windows were all boarded up. But I saw K.A.'s green Jeep hiding in some tall weeds in back." She poked tiny dots circling the X and finished with a set of numbers at the bottom. "K.A.'s place is about a mile from here. None of the roads are marked and the cabin is easy to miss if you're not looking for it. If you pass a giant oak tree on the left, you've gone too far. Just in case you get lost, or even if you don't, that's my phone number at the bottom."

Peggy had said K.A. drove a green Jeep. Was that a coincidence? Or was K.A. the driver who had tried to run him down in front of Aunt Maddy's house?

"Describe K.A. to me, Peggy."

"K.A. doesn't look nothing like his surly disposition, that's for sure." She produced a weak smile. "No offense, Dream, but he's the best looking fellow I've ever seen. Brunette hair and a beard that doesn't hide his handsomeness. He's an inch or two shorter than you. Kind of lean, but strong. I mean really strong. My sister and I have seen him carry heavy boxes and bags like they don't weigh nothing at all."

Dean shook his head. Her description of K.A. wasn't like the person he saw driving the Jeep. Too bad.

"How old is K.A.?" Dean asked.

"Hard to tell 'cause of the beard. He's about your age, maybe a little younger."

"One last question, Peggy. What do the initials K.A. stand for?"

"Beats the shit out of me," she said, "exactly what K.A. will do to me if he finds out I was talking to you."

Peggy hitched her purse over her shoulder and planted a quick smooch on Dean's cheek. She opened the door far enough to scope out the store. Then she was gone, leaving the door ajar.

"Taking messages to the charity, Ma."

"Don't take too long," Ida responded. "You might miss a call."

Dean waited until he heard the front door bells ring. He opened the table's only drawer and found loose paper clips, magazines, pencils, pens, pads of paper, a pair of scissors, lipstick, and a printed directory of the businesses in the town of Gumption Gap, including the post office. The real phone number of The Billy Orphan Foundation was nowhere to be found. The post office was open Monday through Saturday, eight a.m. to six p.m. Good to know. If K.A. was the only person allowed into The Billy Orphan Foundation, he would also be the only person to pick up the mail. The Gumption Gap postmaster could fill in some missing pieces about K.A. and the charity.

Dean returned the paper to the drawer and slipped out of the room. At the counter Ida was ringing up purchases. Dean went to the center aisle and grabbed a bag of Granny Goose potato chips and a can of Planters Peanuts.

"Took your wife a good long time to decide," Ida said. "Men will eat anything when they're hungry. Women are picky." She pointed to the sandwiches wrapped in wax paper. "We've got three different kinds: peanut butter and jelly, baloney, and ham and cheese."

"I'll take two of each," he said. "How late do you stay open, just in case we get hungry on the way back from Oregon?"

"We close at seven in the summer. I'll look forward to seeing you on your return trip."

Dean carried the bagged food outside. He'd be back a lot sooner than Ida anticipated. Marti had creatively re-parked his car with the driver's side facing the sun.

"This is such a thrill for me, Sandra," Peggy said, squinting. "To actually get to talk to you in person. Sorry about your laryngitis. You can't imagine how excited I am."

"Remember your promise, Peggy," Marti said in a hoarse voice. "You can't tell anyone I was here for a few days. The gossip spreads like crazy. People chase after me." Marti pointed to Dean. "Several reporters even have me romantically linked to my handsome agent."

"Who could blame them?" Peggy said, leaning her shoulder into Dean. "Can I please get an autograph?"

Peggy gave Dean's pen to Marti along with a notebook from her purse. Marti looked up at the Ford's ceiling in thought then began writing. She handed the pen and notebook back to Peggy when she finished.

"Thank you for being my biggest fan," Peggy read. "I'll never forget our visit to Charity. May all of your dreams come true. Fond regards, Sandra Dee."

Peggy rushed back to the store holding her Sandra Dee autograph and Dean's pen. On the porch she turned and waved to Marti before disappearing through the front door.

"I feel horrible about misleading that girl," Marti said, removing her sunglasses.

"It's possible," Dean said, "that meeting Sandra Dee will be the highlight of Peggy's life." He handed her the bag of food. "In fact, your Hollywood movie star performance was so convincing, you may want to start with the ham sandwich first."

Dean studied the ink map on his hand. If Marti felt guilty about deceiving someone, how would she feel about breaking and entering?

CHAPTER THIRTY

Sarah Henderson had been asleep on her couch when K.A. entered through the front door. Most people, especially folks in rural areas like this, left their doors unlocked or wide open. How simple it had been for K.A. to don his gas mask, close a few windows, and turn on the gas stove full blast to make sure she didn't wake up. She wore a ragged housecoat over a nondescript dress. Her open-mouth breathing had become labored. Not a pretty picture for a woman worth more than a half million dollars.

A series of framed Henderson family photographs placed prominently on the fireplace mantel intrigued K.A. Most were of children and young adults, except for three pictures of a man in a military uniform, in a suit, and in a sports shirt. More than likely he was Mr. Henderson, the dead husband. Where were the children and grandchildren now? Clearly, they lived somewhere else, expecting their yearly Christmas and birthday checks. In a sense, Sarah had been abandoned like an orphan. No wonder she invested the bulk of her money in The Billy Orphan Foundation.

K.A. moved away from the living room. The gas mask made his breathing audible. He found the woman's purse hanging on her bedroom doorknob. She had twenty-six dollars in her wallet. Money wasn't his quest. Nor would he need her driver's license. He removed Sarah's Social Security card and placed it in his pocket. A lost Social Security card would not arouse suspicions of foul play in the same way missing cash or valuable personal items would. The card was insignificant, but the numbers were as much a part of his disguises as wigs or makeup. His bank's saving accounts had a variety of Social Security numbers, compliments of the people he murdered. He was careful to close each account several times a year and open new ones with different Social Security numbers. By the time bank authorities discovered something was amiss, he was long gone. Nor could they provide an accurate description of a person with more than thirty disguises. Nor could they trace that person to an individual who no longer existed.

He re-hung the purse on the doorknob and headed for the kitchen. The burners on the stove hissed out the deadly, odorless gas that had sent Sarah into a stage close to death. K.A. switched the dials off, halting the gas, and returned to the living room. His gut told him Sarah didn't seem the type to commit suicide.

K.A. lifted Sarah's limp body from the couch and placed her face down on the shiny kitchen linoleum next to a metal bucket. He grabbed her hair, lifted her head then let go. Her face smashed into the floor. He poured a bottle of ammonia into a bucket of bleach. The toxic vapors from the mixture would quickly overwhelm what was left of her life. He dipped a sponge in the deadly solution and crammed it into Sarah's hand. What a perfect way to die. For a growing number of old people, he had become as lethal as a major heart attack. In a sense, he had done many of them a favor by ending their lives prematurely—like the old woman, Madeline Principal, at the nursing home. What kind of quality existence would she have had if he had not thrown her over the balcony?

He sat down in an end chair at the kitchen table and leaned back. Sarah's stomach barely moved. Watching her die brought him back to boyhood memories. What kind of life would he have had as Tyler Wilkes if he had allowed his parents to live? His father had been like a master puppeteer, pulling and controlling the invisible strings of their lives. When his mother cooked his father's meal the wrong way, or didn't clean their cracker house to his father's specifications, or disagreed with her husband about anything, his father would take his aggressions out on mother and son.

On one occasion, Tyler had tried to protect his mother, but his father beat him so badly with the black leather belt and big buckle that Tyler could not move for days. His mother only nursed his injuries when that evil man was gone. Tyler soon developed a hatred for his mother that almost rivaled his loathing for his father. He tried his best to stay out of trouble, but his father found fault with whatever he did. Hell, sometimes that brute would slap him across the face just for kicks then laugh. His father never once apologized for beating him. Instead, Tyler was told he deserved it.

At an early age, Tyler began torturing neighborhood animals, making them suffer the way he wanted his father to suffer. The more he mauled them, the greater the thrill. A neighbor once caught him in the act and confronted his parents at their house. After the disgruntled neighbor left, his father tortured Tyler as he had tortured the animal.

Tyler first tried to run away at age nine. He made another attempt when he was eleven. His father found him each time. The punishments were more violent and lasted longer each time. Fleeing the house was not the answer for survival. The only way Tyler could escape would be to eliminate his father before his father killed him.

Tyler could still feel the last severe beating dished out by his inebriated father, with his mother a silent spectator. That night Tyler set their bed on fire. Hot tears streamed down his cheeks— tears of jubilance. He had finally liberated himself from his father's striking, black belt. Free to unleash a gift he had been blessed with. He graduated from hurting animals to killing humans, an act he found even more stimulating. That night, Tyler had become K.A.

Chimes from an old grandfather clock returned K.A. to 1959. Sarah's body was still. He removed his gas mask and slipped through the front door as fast as he could to keep the toxic fumes from escaping. The nearest neighbor lived a good fifty yards away. The odds of him being seen were slim, but someone might think Martians had invaded the tiny Oregon border community if he had been spotted wearing a gas mask.

A waft of warm afternoon air greeted him. K.A. turned and stared at the door. He was always cautious, yet lately he felt as if he had been making mistakes – like how he missed running over the ballplayer with his jeep. Or not checking Sarah's pulse before he left? Should he go back inside? Indecision had never been a problem for him. He shook his head. If Sarah wasn't gone, she would be soon. The windows and doors were still shut. Chloramines were lethal in an enclosed area. Why, all of a sudden, would he doubt himself? Was he losing his edge—his will to kill? Or was it fear? Fear of being caught?

A growl emerged from his throat. His mind was playing games on him like never before. He was the Kill Artist, the Black Belt Killer.

Number seven on the FBI's most wanted list. They would never catch him as long as he didn't make mistakes.

K.A. hustled down Sarah's creaky wood steps. How long would it take for her to be discovered? Often it took days, sometimes weeks. The Henderson family would experience even more losses. They had seen the last of their Christmas and birthday checks. The bulk of Sarah's fortune would stay with The Billy Orphan Foundation.

He hiked to his Jeep. It was 2:30 p.m. by his watch. He had a three hour drive back to his Nevada cabin hideout. Sarah Henderson was his last kill for The Billy Orphan Foundation. The charity's pay-days were coming to an end. He could sense it. The same sense that had kept him from being apprehended all these years.

In a normal world, he would give his employer two week's notice and a termination letter. But he had never existed in a normal world. The only termination would come from executing the principals involved in The Billy Orphan Foundation. What other choice did he have? He had always known the day would come when they would have to be eliminated for him to remain a shadow in the dark.

He kicked a rock to the side of the road. His kill list was growing at a rapid pace. Anything or anybody that connected him to the charity had to be eliminated. He still had time to make the town of Gumption Gap before the post office closed at 6:00 p.m. On Saturday postmaster Fuzzy often locked the doors a few minutes early to get a head start on happy hour at a local saloon. The unsuspecting postmaster knew just enough about K.A.'s operation to be expendable. A creative fatal accident would make Fuzzy's last hour anything but happy.

He tossed the gas mask into the back of the Jeep and climbed in behind the wheel. After adjusting the rearview mirror his real face stared back at him. He opened the makeup kit on the passenger seat. His brows darkened after several eyebrow pencil strokes. A short-cropped brunette wig covered his blond hair. Gluing the brown beard onto his face came next. He threw a menacing stare at the mirror to practice the character. Acting came as natural to him as killing. People around Charity and Gumption Gap had grown accustomed to his permanent scowl and surly disposition. Many of them thought his initials stood for kick ass. Even bulk-brain Elbie at the gas station, built like a Sherman tank, wouldn't challenge him.

The engine rumbled to a start. By the time he shifted into third gear, the Jeep had passed Sarah's house. He would call in his latest kill from the telephone at The Billy Orphan Foundation like it was business as usual. Then he would wipe out all traces of the charity in Charity.

CHAPTER THIRTY-ONE

The sweet scent of country on a slow moving afternoon challenged Dean's sense of urgency. Dark clouds had come from nowhere to dominate the sky, notching down the temperature. Wind propelled the air like it was driven by a jet engine. A summer downpour loomed minutes away.

Dean had parked past a large oak tree on the left side of the road per Peggy's directions. Marti leaned against a dented fender and re-examined the ink map on Dean's palm while he scoped out the area. No cabin was in sight. He could have made a wrong turn. None of the roads had identifying signs. The trees, rocks, sandy dirt, and weed fields they had passed had no distinguishing features. Marti pointed to a hodgepodge of overgrown nature and hitched her shoulders into her neck as if to say that was her best guess.

Dean agreed with a nod and hurried through tall weeds. Marti followed from close behind with fingers clutching to the back of his shirt. With K.A. away traveling, finding the cabin would be the next best thing.

"Mind telling me whose house we are looking for?" Marti asked. "And why?"

"A man named K.A. who works for the charity. He'll lead us to whoever is running The Billy Orphan Foundation."

A portion of the cabin appeared. Dean stopped. The front windows were boarded up. The exterior had not seen fresh paint in years. The blemished roof had lost some shakes, and several bricks had departed the smokeless chimney. Why would K.A. live in such a ramshackle place? Or did Peggy dupe him, just like he had deceived her?

Dean knocked on the warped front door. He knocked again, this time harder. A crow cawed its disapproval from a nearby tree. The doorknob wouldn't budge. He leaned into the decayed wood. The door was sturdier than it looked. Maybe it was nailed shut from the inside. Ramming it down with a shoulder might prove futile and painful.

"I doubt anyone lives here," Marti said. "It looks abandoned and ready to collapse."

"Maybe that's the occupant's objective," Dean said. "To keep people like us away."

"Well, if this K.A. gentleman lives here then we're trespassing on his property."

"All in the way you look at it," he said. "By Peggy's description, K.A. is anything but a gentleman. I don't see any warning trespassing signs or fences. Besides, we're just two innocent hikers looking for shelter to get out of the rain."

"But we're still trespassing—"

A skinny, greenish-gray lizard scurried past them, prompting Marti to jump towards the door. She gripped Dean's arm standing on her toes.

"That little guy is more afraid of you than you are of him," Dean said, with a grin.

"You don't know that for sure. What if he was having a really bad day and wanted to bite the first person or thing that got in his way?"

"The only bad day a lizard has is when a predator decides to have him for dinner."

Dean took Marti's hand and headed for the side of the cabin. He pushed through invasive plant life using his legs and arm as bushwhackers. Tiny prickers stuck to his pants, socks, and shirt, poking at him from all angles. He eyed each step. There had to be a herd of other little creatures lurking in the weeds ready to jump them for disrupting their environment. Or worse, a snooper trap set by a larger varmint named K.A.

Dean nodded when they reached the rear of the cabin. Peggy hadn't been jiving him. A dilapidated outhouse stood on the left about thirty feet into the weeds, flanked by a well on the right. A matted weed trail in the center led to a clearing near the back porch. This was K.A.'s private driveway and parking space. Not exactly the Ritz, but more than likely K.A.'s accommodations.

Porch planks shifted under Dean's weight. The back door was also locked, but not as rigid as the front door. He cupped his eyes with a hand and peered through a gap between the boards nailed over a window. It was too dark to see inside.

"Guess we are out of luck," Marti said, sounding relieved. "Where do we go next?"

"Inside the cabin to stay dry."

Dean caught renegade raindrops in his hand. Three hard tugs on the boards freed the window cover. He took one of the boards and rammed it through the glass. Most of the broken pieces fell inside the cabin. He knocked the remaining glass from the frame and threw the board into the dirt.

"Are you out of your mind?" Marti charged him like a raging bull at a red commies convention. "Trespassing is bad enough. But breaking into a man's house is a major crime. If they don't lynch you first, you will spend the rest of your days in some hick prison, pounding rocks with a sledgehammer."

"You've been watching too many westerns like *Gunsmoke* on television. But you do raise an interesting point, Marti. You're already an accomplice, aiding and abetting me in said crime." He threw a leg over the window sill, landing a shoe inside the cabin, and standing half in and half out. "As my co-conspirator, would you rather be an outside lookout, or tag along with me?"

"I go where you go." She glanced over her shoulder at the weeds.

Dean climbed through the window and helped Marti into the cabin. Their shoes ground glass shards into the wood floor. He waited for his eyes to adjust to the darkness. She held his arm again, her hip adjoined to his leg like they were in a potato sack race. Images appeared. A lantern sat on the kitchen's lopsided table with one chair. He scratched a wood match on the table and illuminated the lamp. Canned goods lined an open shelf. A pot, pan, bucket, and a Coleman stove sat on the counter, along with eating utensils and one plate. Obviously, entertaining others wasn't K.A.'s strong suit.

"Dean, what are you going to do if K.A. comes back and finds that you—excuse me—that we broke into his place?"

"Odds are that won't happen." Dean went to the shelf and read the labels on the cans. Marti moved with him. K.A. had a hankering for beans, fruit, and soup. "K.A. travels a lot. Peggy told me he'll be gone for a week."

"What in particular are you looking for?"

"I'm waiting for something to jump out at me," he said. She pinched his bicep. "Not literally. I'll know it when I see it."

She followed him into a front room that consisted of a fireplace and a chair with stuffing oozing from filthy fabric. A steady melody of raindrops beat on the roof. Water dripped from the ceiling. Logs were stacked neatly next to the fireplace stones. Slivers of light penetrated the boarded windows. The cabin was hot in spite of the change in weather.

A two-by-four braced against the front door. Dean twisted the lock and lifted the board from its frame. He opened the door far enough to provide ventilation and light then moved to the fireplace. The hearth held an abundance of cold charred wood and ashes, which shouldn't have come as a surprise. Nevada was enjoying a warmer than usual summer this year, taking the bite out of desert nights.

"This place reminds me of pictures I've seen in history books of life back in the 1800s," Marti said. "There is no electricity. No plumbing. No phone. No modern conveniences. What kind of person would want to live like this?"

"A man who cares more about his privacy and being alone than he does about comforts. A man who will safeguard his secrets as if they are as valuable as gold."

"Dean, how can you be so sure this K.A. guy lives here?"

"This is K.A.'s place all right," he said, holding the lantern high and walking the room. "I can feel it."

"Putting your sleuth instincts aside, we have not seen anything that identifies the occupier. What if this place belongs to a grouchy hermit with an itchy trigger finger?"

"One look at you would take the grouch out of any geezer, armed or not," he said.

"Nice try." She tugged on his shirt sleeve. "I will remind you of what you just said when you are lying on this dirty floor in a pool of blood after being peppered with bullet holes."

He stared at a door concealing the only room they had not seen yet. The door didn't have a lock. Then why was it closed?

"Maybe you should go back to the car, Marti," he said, extending his hand to the doorknob.

"I told you, I go where you...Wait..." She leaned her head towards the door. "What was that? I heard something."

"Your nerves are playing tricks on you." He raised the lantern higher.

"I'm telling you I heard something," she said, moving back.

Dean released a nervous breath. He twisted the knob until the door groaned open a few inches. He had heard the same noise.

CHAPTER THIRTY-TWO

A wicked stench hit Dean the moment he opened the room's door. Holding the lantern and his breath, he stepped inside. An angry hiss sounded from the dark corner to his right. Instinctively, he turned towards the noise. An obscure image flew at him. He jumped back, but too late. Sharp claws tore into his upper body. The hiss elevated into a high-pitched screech. Dean fell to his knees.

Marti rushed into the room. She snatched the lantern. Dean fought off the animal's vicious attack, grabbing handfuls of cat fur with both hands. Finally, he dislodged the claws and heaved the dark grey beast into the front room. The cat slid across the floorboards then scampered through the open front door. Had the door to this room been closed to keep the cat caged? Or was the cat's presence meant to deter anyone from going further inside the room?

"I've never heard of a guard cat before," he said, peering up at Marti. "Maybe I should have knocked first."

"Dean, you're bleeding."

Marti kneeled in front of Dean and tore at his shirt decorated with splotches of blood. He pulled Marti's hand away from his chest. She was hurting him more than helping. He stood and reclaimed the lantern from her.

"I packed Aunt Madeline's bag of first aid supplies in my suitcase," she said. "I'll go out the front door and be right back."

Dean waited until Marti left the cabin. He gritted his teeth and removed the tattered shirt. Hot stings from the cuts and scratches made him feel like a slow heifer at branding time. He held up the lantern and scoped out the rest of the room. Nestled into a corner at the far end was a mattress, no box springs, and a rumpled green army blanket. On the floor next to the bed were a second lantern and a transistor radio missing most of its white cover. Against the opposite wall was a bucket of cat food, water bowl, and a cardboard box filled with cat litter.

The back of Dean's hand wiped a sweaty forehead. The disabled radio represented the only personal luxury item inside the cabin. What kind of music tickled K.A.'s tastes? Peggy had told him K.A. was about Dean's age, maybe a bit younger. Did Fats Domino's "Blueberry Hill" give K.A. a rock 'n roll thrill? Or was he a Hank Williams country and western kind of guy? Dean twisted the knob, clicking the radio to life: An agriculture program aired.

Dean went to the wall where the cat had been waiting to ambush him and picked up the stinky box. He rushed from the bedroom into the kitchen and chucked the box through the broken window.

Glass crunched beneath his shoes. A few minutes ago, he had been relieved when K.A.'s green Jeep hadn't been parked in back. Now, after finding the cabin unoccupied, Dean was looking at a full plate of disappointment with a side of frustration. Marti had been right. So far, not a damn thing confirmed this place was used by K.A., the man Peggy described from The Billy Orphan Foundation. Someone, presumably a Jeep driver with a vicious cat, ate, slept, and listened to farming programs on the radio here. Dean touched his sore chest and winced. The scratches had stopped bleeding. If this wasn't K.A.'s place, he was back to a square one where all sides weren't equal.

Marti waited for him in the mattress room holding a paper bag and a clean shirt. Rain water dripped from her clothes and hair. She dabbed iodine on him, which ratcheted up the throbbing. Dean's cuts and scratches changed from crimson to bright orange. She wrapped several layers of gauze around his chest and back, finishing her nursing with strips of white adhesive tape. Then she kissed his cheek. His eyebrows arched in shock. This room offered many kinds of unanticipated surprises.

"What was that for?" he asked.

"For being such a good patient." She touched the kissed area with soft fingertips. "I didn't have any lollipops."

"Lollipops are highly overrated."

Disappointment registered on Marti's face when he reached for his new shirt and carefully buttoned the front. She was sending him more hints than a catcher using both hands to signal the next pitch. And he was more than tempted to reciprocate. Whether Marti knew it or not, she kindled a passion buried inside that he had not felt in a long time. What the hell stopped him? History. The last lady he gave his carte blanche trust to bailed out on him when he needed her the most. He hadn't allowed himself a second chance, building an invisible barrier instead. He wanted to believe in Marti. Yet Marti could be another Dede in different wrapping. How would he know, really know, which team she played on unless he removed his wall of doubt?

Pounding rain sounded like nails hitting the roof. They looked up at the same time. The intact ceiling allowed no visible leaks in this room. Amazing.

Dean lifted the thin, clumsy mattress and threw it against the front wall. It crumpled into an awkward heap. Another dead end. An organized neatnik lived in this old and cruddy cabin.

Marti nudged his hip with her elbow. She looked at all four walls with an exaggerated head shake, silently telling him they were wasting their time in the cabin. He couldn't blame Marti for being uncomfortable. Nor would he debate the issue with her. Hell, she wouldn't listen to him anyway. Instead, he turned in a slow circle, eyeballing the walls, ceiling, and floor. Something about this room was out of proportion.

He went to the wall with the boarded window and knuckle-knocked from one end to the other. His foot stomped on the floor at the same time. He performed the same routine on the far wall. Marti's frowning features advertised more disapproval. He beat on the cat's wall. The sound changed from solid to hollow. He walked the entire wall rapping on each board. They all sounded alike.

Dean stepped backwards and examined the wall from across the room. Marti's scowl had transformed into a nodding grin. Foot-wide boards stretched from the floor to the ceiling. Everything conformed except in the middle by the cat's food bucket. Three boards had an inch gap from the floor, something he'd missed before. He went to the cat's wall and ran a hand underneath. Nothing but air. Air meant space.

"Better stand back," Dean said. "After dealing with that devil cat, there's no telling what kind of booby trap K.A. has rigged."

She moved out of his sight. Dean tugged at the boards until they shifted. He tensed, waiting for another sneak attack. Nothing jumped out at him, nor could he hear intimidating sounds. He inched the boards away a bit more then looked over his shoulder at Marti. Her head bobbed up and down urging him to continue. He yanked harder. The hidden door gave way with ease. He lifted the lantern to examine a narrow closet that ran the length of the room.

"Harry was right about your investigative skills," Marti gushed. "Every time I doubt you, Dean, you prove me wrong. You're like an all day pass to the funhouse at San Francisco's Playland at the Beach."

"Never been compared to a funhouse before," he said. "Does that mean you have finally changed your mind about being my accomplice?"

"Just call me Marti-the-Moll. I can't wait to see what we will find inside."

CHAPTER THIRTY-THREE

The Jeep's windshield wipers struggled to keep up with a relentless storm. K.A's head ached from squinting at the blurry windshield. The speedometer stuck at forty to avoid an accident and confrontation with the law. At this rate, he would make Gumption Gap with little time to spare before Fuzzy closed the post office at 6:00 p.m.

A drenched young man appeared further up the road with his thumb out. K.A. ignored the hitchhiker, concentrating instead on keeping the Jeep's tires connected to the slick pavement. Some drivers pick up hitchhikers to be Good Samaritans. Or they are lonely and in need of conversation. K.A. preferred his own company, regardless of how troubled or stranded a ride-seeker might be. Hell, one could not be too careful. Some nutcase out there could be planning to rob or harm him.

The Jeep passed the hitchhiker without slowing. K.A.'s glance in the rearview mirror revealed the young man's thumb gesture had transformed into a middle-finger, accompanied by an expression of contempt. The same look on his father's face before beatings. He could smell the memory of Wildroot Cream Oil hair tonic.

K.A. managed to brake to a stop without skidding off the road. He crammed the gearshift into reverse, traveling backwards at reckless speed. The smiling hitchhiker ran towards the Jeep, his battered suitcase swinging like a clock pendulum.

K.A. squeezed the gearshift knob. The Urge had trounced every ounce of his self-discipline and was now in complete control. The hitchhiker's last ride would take him to a dead end.

* * * * *

Dean turned up the volume on the transistor radio to counter the rain pelting K.A.'s cabin. A weatherman warned of a fast-approaching summer storm. Dean exchanged a smile with Marti. He ignited the second lantern and handed it to her.

Marti followed him to K.A.'s hidden closet. The radio voice turned somber with a new update about the Black Belt Killer. Dean felt a tug from one of his belt loops.

"Have you heard of this belt killer before?" she asked.

"I listened to a series of reports on the car radio while you slept," Dean said, inching into the opening as if he was entering a dark cave. "Some psychopath is on a rampage, strangling men with their own black belts. They don't seem to have a handle on who the guy is, what he looks like, why he's killing other men, or when he'll strike next."

"Hate to break this to you, Sherlock, but you're a man wearing a black belt."

"Didn't you come along on this venture to protect me from murderous males?"

"Very funny," she said. "How do you know the psycho they're referring to is a man? Maybe the killer is an avenging woman, repeatedly abused or beaten by a man with his black belt."

"I assume the killer is a male because most women can't physically overwhelm men by strangling them to death." Dean lifted the lantern higher. "But you do raise an interesting take on why he strangles his victims with their black belts."

The space between the closet wall and the outside wall spanned about four feet. In the middle, a cabinet held toiletries, folded clothes, and supplies. A stepladder leaned against the cabinet's side. Dean stretched to reach the top shelf. Whoever inhabited this cabin was shorter than his five-eleven. He drifted to the right side of the closet. His image grew larger in a mirror hanging on the side wall. Underneath the mirror was a dainty vanity table with various tubes and bottles of facial makeup. The first sign that a female could be living here.

Marti hummed a happy tune while she searched through outfits hanging from a wood clothes rod. Fear and doubt about whether this cabin belonged to K.A. from The Billy Orphan Foundation had disappeared. It was obvious she enjoyed rummaging through other people's property looking for nuggets of information. Witness her success in scavenging through Aunt Maddy's junk room.

The wardrobe included men's fashions straight out of *Esquire Magazine*, along with casual clothing, blue collar work pants and shirts, military uniforms, even shit-kicker western wear. Dozens of pairs of shoes, including five types of boots, lined the floor below.

Dean placed the lantern on the vanity table. The top shelf of the wardrobe held men's hats and wigs. Beards, mustaches, false teeth, glasses, fake eyelashes, and a women's brassiere with cups filled with sponge rubber falsies lined the shelf below. His eyes traveled back to focus on a black wig.

"Halloween must be his favorite day of the year," Marti said, shifting hangers. "Or maybe he has one of those multiple personalities." Her brown eyes grew larger. She removed a white nurse's uniform on a hanger and pressed it against herself. "Crackers told us about a man impersonating a nurse in Aunt Madeline's room. This dress is too large for me and too small for you. But it's a perfect size for the person Crackers described with long black hair."

"Good catch, Marti. Peggy portrayed K.A. as a man with short brown hair and a beard. There's a good chance that Crackers and Peggy were talking about the same person. Wherever K.A. goes he wears a different disguise. We're looking for a guy with dozens of faces, not counting what he looks like without camouflage."

"Crackers said the nurse's face was pretty," Marti said.

"Right. And Peggy referred to K.A. as the best looking male she had ever seen. Is he attractive enough to double as a woman, minus the beard?"

"It all fits, Dean. We have enough evidence now to show the police that K.A. killed Aunt Madeline. They can match his fingerprints. Put him in a lineup. Question him until he confesses."

"We have no proof yet that this is K.A.'s cabin." Dean touched her arm. "We need to find something definitive to give to the authorities besides a nurse's uniform, wig, and an old man's testimony. If the police can't arrest him, K.A. will just disappear."

"There has to be something in here that will incriminate K.A." She re-hung the uniform and moved to the other side of the closet. "If it's in here, I will find it for sure."

"Marti, there's not enough time to do a thorough search." He chased after her pointing at his watch. "It's five twenty-five. The Gumption Gap Post Office closes at six. Today is Saturday. We won't be able to question the postmaster until Monday if we're late. Marti? Are you listening to me? Marti?"

* * * * *

K.A. tugged both ends of the black leather belt around the young hitchhiker's neck, choking out what little life was left in him. Spending limited time to kill a man was no different than purchasing a *National Enquirer* at a market with money earmarked for food. Just substitute dollars for wasted time.

The rain sounded like a cattle stampede. Soon, the isolated area, where K.A. had chosen to strangle the hitchhiker would be a lake-sized puddle. The orange-haired young man struggled, splattering mud on K.A. with thrashing legs, but he was fast losing air and strength. Unintelligible words leaked from his throat. His bulging eyeballs appeared on the verge of popping out. That would be a first for the Black Belt Killer.

Color drained from the man's glistening cheeks. K.A. never felt remorse after a taking a person's life. But something was wrong. The intense wave of anticipated gratification from watching his prey die did not come. The Urge was still present, and unsatisfied. What was happening to him?

The hitchhiker landed face first in the puddle after K.A. released pressure. The belt remained wrapped around the neck – the Black Belt Killer's signature. K.A. had one more task to perform. The man's thin wallet revealed a sorry life story. No driver's license. No pictures or mementos. Just one lonely five-dollar bill, a free milkshake coupon, and a Social Security card. K.A. returned the wallet to the man's pocket, minus the Social Security card. Wildlife would probably take care of this body before it was discovered. The police might have trouble identifying him if his fingerprints were not in their bureaucratic files. The man's identity wasn't important as long as the Black Belt Killer received credit for the kill.

K.A. straightened up, out of breath. He ran for cover in his Jeep. Once inside, he removed a soggy, misshaped wig and peeled off the fake beard dripping with water. A few swipes with a rag eliminated all remaining makeup. Postmaster Fuzzy would not recognize him.

His real face would be the ultimate disguise.

The Jeep's back tires spewed out streams of mud when his foot hit the gas pedal. The front end drifted into a curve. He was pressed for time now to contact the Gumption Gap postmaster before the post office closed.

* * * * *

Dean followed Marti to the opposite side of the closet. She placed her lantern on a small desk personalized with nicks, scratches, and stains then sat down on a wobbly stool. A forefinger pointed first to a shelf above the desk lined neatly with books then to newspapers and magazines piled next to the desk.

"It looks like our mysterious K.A. is a reader," she said.

Dean thumbed through the stack far enough to realize the themes were crime and police. Police study the methods and minds of criminals. And vice versa. He noticed slivers of paper on the floor. K.A. must clip newspaper and magazine items of interest and paste them . . . where? What items did K.A. cut out, and why?

"The books feature famous murderers and criminals," she said. "Fascinating, huh?"

"Marti!" Dean tapped the face of his watch. "Gumption Gap. Post office. Six o'clock."

Marti pulled out the side drawer, revealing a magnifying glass, pens, pencils, glue, and scissors. She slid open the middle drawer, unveiling bundles of driver's licenses, Social Security cards, a ledger, three keys on a ring, and a lighter. She reached inside.

"Stop!" Dean felt his ass clinch. "Don't touch a thing."

She jerked her hand away as if there was a nest of black widow spiders in the drawer.

"What's wrong?"

Dean removed a handkerchief from his back pocket, using the linen to pluck a Zippo lighter from the drawer. He held it out in his palm for her to see.

"The person who lives here killed my friend Beals Becker," he said. "Read the inscription on the cover.

"To Beals – A big leaguer in my book. Regards, Dean." Marti's

168

eyes clouded with tears. "I'm so sorry, Dean. Why would K.A. kill Beals?"

"Beals was nosing around the charity, asking questions. He probably wasn't very subtle about it either. Ida, the store owner, is terrified of K.A., just like everyone else around here. She told K.A. about Beals. K.A. must have befriended Beals before murdering him, making it look like an accident."

Dean stuffed the hanky and lighter into his front pants pocket. K.A. killed his aunt, his friend, and almost got him too. If K.A. was here right now, Dean would be tempted to return the favor. A feeling he had never experienced before.

Dean held the ledger in his hand and emptied the remaining drawer contents into his coat pocket. He would examine everything later. It was time for them to leave.

"Now we have proof that the person who lives here is a murderer," she said. "We should go straight to the police as soon as we finish searching the closet."

"Marti, the postmaster in Gumption Gap can lead us to Billy Orphan's doorstep."

"How do you know that Billy Orphan isn't the person inhabiting this cabin? Think about it, Dean. The person who resides here was clever enough to devise a secret space—a space that would conceal more than just costumes and reading material. We can't leave now. This closet is the pot at the end of a rainbow."

Dean's stomach jumped, sending a late breaking news flash to his head. Did Marti want to stay here to find more incriminating evidence? Maybe evidence wasn't really what she sought. Maybe Marti had forced him to take her to Charity to seek a pot filled with gold at the end of The Billy Orphan Foundation rainbow. Or was Marti afraid he would discover a bag full of cash and wouldn't share it with her? He needed to know.

"We can come back later," he said. "It's too dangerous to leave you here alone."

"I'm staying," she said, crossing her arms in rebellion. "You go. Do what you have to do at the post office. Then pick me up."

"That's crazy talk, lady. What if K.A. comes back?"

"Peggy told you K.A. would be gone for a week." Marti put a finger on his lips to stop his rebuttal. "Besides, this way we can cover two places at the same time. We may not get another chance here." She pressed harder on his lips. "You have to admit, I have the talent and patience for discovering things, like Aunt Madeline's diaries. Please, Dean. Let me prove to you that I am worthy of your trust."

Dean removed her finger, but didn't let go. Had she just read his mind? Her plea to stay here made sense, but his instinct itched like a mosquito bite. What stopped him from lifting Marti up, throwing her over his shoulder, and carrying her kicking and screaming to the car? With all of his heart he wanted to trust Marti and erase all doubt.

"An hour," he said. "If I'm not back in an hour, whether you find anything or not, you have to promise to leave the cabin and wait for me by the oak tree where we parked."

"How about an hour and a half?"

"If only I'd had the good sense to leave you at Freddy's bar." He took Marti by the elbow, pulling her to the closet opening. "No deal, lady."

"Wait." She held her ground. "One hour. I promise. But I don't have a watch."

"Now you do." He slid the expandable band of his wristwatch up Marti's arm.

"Gee, does this mean we are going steady?" She ran her fingers over the gold band.

"You need to be asked first. Just make sure you keep your promise."

Dean left the cabin. If Marti violated his trust, he would lose a lot more than his watch.

CHAPTER THIRTY-FOUR

WELCOME TO GUMPTION GAP, POPULATION 3,999—MORE OR LESS. Dean's car raced past the pock-marked wooden sign and into the town of Gumption Gap.

Late afternoon rain and a gray gloom darkened one long block of business storefronts. The closest available parking space was across the street from the post office. 5:57 on the Ford's clock. Dean had three minutes before the postmaster locked his door for the rest of the weekend.

Heavy wind-driven rain greeted Dean when he left the protection of his car. The sidewalks were vacant. He sprinted into the street. The post office front was a blur. Raising his jacket above his head did little to keep him dry. How receptive would the postmaster be to a stranger asking questions at quitting time while dripping puddles on his floor?

Across the street, a car shot away from its parking space. The scent of burning rubber caught Dean's nose. The engine's roar trumped the sound of pounding rain. The vehicle snaked towards the center of the road without slowing down. Idle windshield wipers left a vague impression of a blond haired man inside the Jeep.

"Hey!" Dean yelled. Did the driver even see him? "Hey!"

The Jeep's speed shifted into the next gear as if Dean wasn't there. His desert boots skidded on the wet pavement as he tried to stop his momentum. A piercing jolt of pain buckled his knee into submission. He crashed down to the asphalt. The Jeep didn't change course or slow down. There was no time for Dean to rise to his feet and avoid the charging mass of metal.

* * * * *

K.A. didn't have the patience to turn off the Jeep's inner light after he peeled away from his parking spot near the post office. He yanked so hard on the windshield wiper lever that the knob came

171

off in his hand. The wipers leapt into action, pushing water away from the glass at a hyperactive rate. Without slowing down, both hands left the steering wheel to jam the knob back onto its metal rod.

A steady leak from the convertible top bounced off the dashboard, annoying K.A. all the more. An image of a man appeared in the middle of the street. The impression vanished as quickly as it appeared. A real person or just another ghost from K.A.'s past?

* * * * *

The Jeep's back tire grazed the heel of Dean's boot as he rolled towards the curb to avoid being run over. He struggled to his feet on the sidewalk in front of the post office. His hands swiped at road muck clinging to his clothes then stopped. The pouring rain would wash him off soon enough. He glanced in the direction the green Jeep had traveled. The tail lights never illuminated, leaving Dean in the dark. Had the blond male driver even seen him? He turned back to the post office.

"Damn it." The door was locked and the windows dark. The postmaster had closed early. With his fist Dean hammered the town seal attached to the wood door, hoping the postmaster was still inside. Was coming to Gumption Gap a wasted trip? He never should have left Marti alone in the cabin. "Damn! Damn! Damn!"

* * * * *

The Jeep plowed through a massive puddle, streaming water from both sides like a motorboat. K.A. slammed a palm down on the dashboard. The front end drifted from one side of the road to the other. If he had ignored the hitchhiker, Gumption Gap would have been minus one postmaster. In spite of his lack of discipline, he still managed to arrive at the post office seven minutes before closing time, only to discover Fuzzy had left minutes earlier. K.A. often smelled liquor on Fuzzy's breath. No doubt Fuzzy was frequenting one of the many bars in town. How many drinks and hours would it take to satisfy Fuzzy? Too many for K.A. to wait, especially when he wore no disguise. Some people say alcohol consumption can be bad for one's health. In Fuzzy's case, his thirst for firewater saved his ass. This time.

K.A. shook his fist in frustration. Soon, but not soon enough, one of life's quirky fatal accidents would befall the postmaster. With K.A.'s assistance, Fuzzy would stumble on the spike of a cast iron receipt holder, impaling himself clean through the heart—a realistic scenario for an old boozer like Fuzzy.

The speedometer crept past sixty. K.A. could sense walls closing in on him. Who had sent the Becker kid to play scout before the cavalry came? They were after him, only he couldn't identify who. How ironic. The invisible man was now sought by an invisible prey. His shoe pressed harder on the gas pedal. All of his ties with The Billy Orphan Foundation had to be eliminated, starting with final visits first to the charity building then to his cabin.

* * * * *

Dean peered through the post office's darkened window. Then he went back and knocked on the door until his knuckles hurt.

"You can keep pounding on that door until your hands bleed, son," a man said in a scratchy voice. "There isn't anyone inside to answer."

A thin man with stooped shoulders stood on the sidewalk holding an umbrella over his head. He wore a red hunter's hat with flaps covering his ears. The tobacco in the pipe sandwiched between his teeth glowed like a live volcano, emitting a cherry fragrance that smelled better than it could ever taste.

"It's not six o'clock yet." Dean pointed at the office hours painted on the door. "I need to speak to the postmaster. It's urgent. Maybe life and death urgent."

"Then follow me," said the Pipe Man in a calm tone. He blew out a puff of smoke. "Fuzzy's at the B of A. That's where I'm heading."

"The bank is open this late?" Dean soon matched Pipe Man's gait with some effort. The pain in his knee had not receded. "On a Saturday?"

"In Gumption Gap, B of A stands for Bar of America. Best watering hole in town. Fuzzy never misses happy hour—or the free-eats table."

The Bar of America was lively, loud, and packed. Smoke as thick as early morning fog obscuring the Golden Gate Bridge hung in the air. Dean shook his head. Fuzzy could be any of the sixty-odd people inside the tavern. He would have to wait for the Pipe Man's lead. Dean had been in more than enough bars in his life, especially small town bars, to know how counterproductive a stranger asking questions could be.

Pipe Man nodded to several people as he eased his way into the room. The wooden floor was thinly layered with sawdust and peanut shells. At a leisurely pace, he hung his coat and hat on a brass hook and leaned his collapsed umbrella against the wall underneath. Then he found an unoccupied table and sat down.

"My name is Dean. What the hell did you not understand about the urgency of my speaking with Fuzzy?"

"I'm Harlan." He pointed his pipe stem at a crowd surrounding the food table. "Hold your water, Dean. Fuzzy's the bearded, bald guy piling food onto his plate. It will benefit your urgent cause to have a drink waiting for him. He is a rye whiskey man and as cheap as Jack Benny. Just so happens to be my drink too."

Harlan stood up, reserving the table by laying down his pipe. He moseyed towards the food. Dean fought his way to the bar. Two bartenders were on duty: one with a handlebar mustache, the other without but whiskers might have enhanced her looks. She acknowledged him with a toothy smile.

Asses in blue jeans occupied each stool. To Dean's right, dice cups pounded the bar top. Beyond the dice throwers a round table in the corner accommodated poker players and chips. Men threw darts at wall targets attached to the opposite corner. Not long ago, he would have enjoyed a raucous, fun joint like this.

"Didn't your mama teach you to get inside when it rains?" the female bartender asked.

"Nope." Dean combed fingers through his wet hair. His body trembled from the cold. "But Mom did warn me to not to wear tight pants because she wanted grandchildren."

She giggled and asked, "What'll it be, handsome?"

"Bottle of rye, two glasses." Dean peered at the labels behind the bar, evoking a longing. "Make it three glasses. The third being Jack Daniel's over, two shots."

CHAPTER THIRTY-FIVE

The gas gauge fell to the wrong side of empty. K.A. backed off on the accelerator. He was anxious to reach his cabin then the charity building, but not at the expense of running out of gas. Ida's store was less than a half mile away.

K.A. pulled into the Ida's parking lot next to a gas pump. Elbie often left the station before seven, which could be a problem. K.A. would have to wait for Ida to man the pumps. He had purposely lied to Ida when he told her he'd be gone for a week, a move meant to keep her and her family in the dark about his whereabouts.

When Elbie poked his big head out from the garage, K.A. grinned. Elbie ventured into the rain wearing a yellow slicker. Water dripped from the wide brim of his straw cowboy hat like a leaky gutter. Rain or shine, his walking pace never changed.

Elbie pumped gas without being told. K.A.'s rear view mirror reflected a queer expression on Elbie's face when he stared at the back license plate. Wait until Elbie sees the driver of K.A's jeep is blond with no beard? If Elbie is confused now, he'll be downright mystified tomorrow.

* * * * *

Dean headed for Harlan's table carrying two glasses and a bottle of rye whiskey in one hand. The other hand held a glass filled with two shots of Jack Daniel's. Seated next to Harlan was a bald, red-bearded man with a full plate of food in front of him. Dean navigated through a mass of rowdy patrons without spilling a drop of Jack, an accomplishment more difficult than making an improbable diving catch without dropping the ball. He placed the bottle and glasses on the table.

Harlan took his cue and left with a glass full of rye without making introductions. Smart man. Dean set Jack down on the table and poured a shot of rye into Fuzzy's glass. His mouth watered for a reunion with his old friend. One glass of Jack would help take the chill away and stimulate his mind. He caressed the polished curves of the stubby glass.

"You must want to talk to me real bad," Fuzzy said, raising his glass. "You a G-man? Private dick? My old lady's lawyer?"

"Relax, Fuzzy. I don't work for the government or a law firm. But I am investigating The Billy Orphan Foundation."

Fuzzy choked in mid-swallow. Dean waited for the coughing fit to end. Fuzzy's pudgy cheeks turned crimson as he gulped for air. This man was dirty. Just how dirty?

"I don't have much time, Fuzzy, so we're going to cut right to the nitty-gritty." Dean's eyes left Fuzzy to ogle Jack then back to Fuzzy. "Here are the ground rules. If you play ball with me, meaning you tell me everything you know, I will keep your name out of my report. However, if you screw with me, I will make sure you lose your job and acquire a permanent number for the back of your shirt. It's your call, but make it now."

"I haven't done nothing bad." Fuzzy drained the color from his glass. "Maybe I bend the rules a bit, that's all."

"Who do you bend the rules for, beside yourself?"

"Don't know the man's name. Said he represents the charity."

Jack's aroma made Dean's hands tremble. He peeked at his naked wrist. Damn. Marti had his watch. How long had he been gone? The walls were crowded with mirrors and mementos: stuffed animal heads, advertisements, pictures, old rifles – everything but a clock.

"Give me a description of the guy from the charity," Dean said.

"Beard. Brown hair. 'Bout my height, 'cept much thinner. Mean disposition. Drive's a green Jeep. That's about all I can tell you."

"You just described a man known as K.A. When was the last time you saw him?"

"'Bout a week ago, I guess. Maybe longer."

"How much does he pay you, Fuzzy?"

"He don't pay...How'd you know?" Fuzzy reached for the rye.

"Hold on, partner." Dean quick-handed the rye bottle from

Fuzzy's reach, leaving Jack unattended. He knew exactly how the demons inside tormented the old man. Dean's head was spinning. Watching Fuzzy made him ache even more for just one sip. His left hand formed a fist to stop the shake. One alky denying the other. "No more happy water until I get answers. Then you can get as blotto as you want. How much does K.A. pay you?"

"Two-hundred dollars a month, cash," Fuzzy whispered, turning his head to see if anyone else could hear his confession.

"Two-hundred a month under the table to do what?"

"I put all the mail posted to The Billy Orphan Foundation into postal sacks for his inspection. Ain't nothing against the law there. He would bring the sacks back to me. I then transferred the contents of the sacks into cardboard boxes and send them to two post office boxes. Honest to trigger, that's it."

"Are any of the letters he returns to you open?" Dean asked.

"Sure. All of the envelopes are slit open. What's wrong with that? He works for The Billy Orphan Foundation. He also includes loose checks and forms people must have dropped off at the charity."

Dean poured an eighth of an inch of rye into Fuzzy's glass. One quick swallow and the drink was gone. The postmaster had earned a liquid reward for explaining the arrangement he had with K.A. Most of it made sense now. K.A. didn't have the authority to cash checks written to the charity, but he kept all the cash—a whole shitload of it. And the mail-trail to The Billy Orphan Foundation vanished at the post office in Gumption Gap. A system, albeit illegal, that was efficient as hell. Fuzzy sent untraceable boxes of opened Billy Orphan Foundation envelopes, checks and forms at the expense of the US Mail. Where do the checks go? Who cashes or deposits those checks?

"You're doing great, Fuzzy." Dean's poured more generously. "Now I need names and addresses for those post office boxes."

"That K.A. guy warned me to never divulge any information to no one about the charity. Said he'd hurt me, real bad, if he ever found out I talked. I believe he would do more than that."

"Hate to break this to you, Fuzzy," Dean said, "but K.A. is going to kill you whether or not you give me the names and addresses. He has murdered a number of people already and he won't hesitate to eliminate you. No bullshit, your only chance to survive is for K.A. to be caught, and caught real quick."

Fuzzy's features bunched like he had a sour stomach. He knocked his drink over into his plate of food. His staccato breaths sounded like a thirsty hound.

"Again, where do you send K.A.'s boxes?" Dean had raised his voice a notch. "Remember, Fuzzy. Time is of the essence. And your time is running out, literally."

"Billy Orphan Foundation. Care of Billy Orphan. P. O. Box 143, Reno."

"Box 143 in Reno," Dean repeated. "What's the other address, Fuz—"

The room suddenly rained poker chips and cards. One of the players had upended the poker table, accusing another player of cheating. A chair went flying into the wall. The on-tilt player threw a beer mug at the accused. The mug whizzed past the player's ear and smashed into Fuzzy's forehead. Fuzzy hit the floor like he had been shot.

Dean kneeled over the postmaster to protect him from the brawlers. Fuzzy's eyes rolled back and forth trying to focus. Damn. He wasn't out, but he certainly wasn't all there either. Blood seeped from a gash in his forehead. He mumbled incoherently.

"Stay with me, Fuzzy." Dean cradled the postmaster's head. "Don't pass out."

"What happened to him?" Harlan asked, with a hand on Dean's shoulder.

"A flying beer mug dimmed his lights. Get some water to throw on him."

Dean heard the smack of a punch landing, followed by shouts and glass breaking. Another man went down. Dean had never been in a bar fight sober before. And he didn't intend to start now.

Harlan returned with a half pitcher of beer. Dean poured the suds into Fuzzy's face. Fuzzy's head moved from side to side with blinking eyelids.

"Fuzzy," Dean shouted. "Tell me the name and other box number?"

"Name?" Fuzzy muttered.

"Where do you send K.A.'s other boxes? The name."

"Nah...nah...pro."

"Nahnahpro. What the hell is a nahnahpro?"

"Corp..."

"You mean corporation?"

"Caps. N-A-H-P-R-O Corp . . ." Fuzzy's eyelids sprang open revealing glassy, lifeless eyes. "Oak..."

"Oak? Oak what?"

"Oakland. Box..."

"The number, damn it. What's the box number?"

Dean pulled at Fuzzy's hairy cheeks. Fuzzy's eyelids closed.

"Did this dude punch out old Fuzzy?" a strange voice asked.

Dean released the postmaster. Before he could gather himself to stand, two strong hands lifted Dean to his feet. A fist was poised ready to launch at his nose.

"Hold on, Vern." Harlan threw an arm between them. "This guy didn't hit Fuzzy. If you want to help, separate the poker players."

"I don't give a rat's ass about fightin' no poker players," Vern spit out. "I'm defending the town's mailman. He's the only one we got. And I hate strangers taking up room in my favorite bar."

Dean floored Vern with a hard shot to the chin. Vern shook his head and smiled. He leaned to the side to rise. Harlan kicked Vern's jaw, sending him to the same state Fuzzy was visiting.

"Thanks for the help, Harlan." Dean eyed his untouched drink. "I owe you one."

"Vern doesn't even like Fuzzy. He just likes to fight strangers. It seems like old Fuzzy is the most popular person in Gumption Gap tonight."

"What do you mean?" Dean said, lifting his glass of Jack from the table.

"A couple of minutes before you showed up, another man banged on the post office door just like you. About your age. Blond."

"Have you seen this guy before?" Dean asked.

"Never. His face was strange to these parts."

"Where's the nearest phone, Harlan?"

"Over there." Harlan pointed to a hallway with his pipe. "But it won't do you any good. All the phone lines are down in Gumption Gap 'cause of the storm. The closest working phone might be at Ida's store in Charity."

"Ho, shit." Dean handed his glass of Jack to Harlan and darted for the exit.

CHAPTER THIRTY-SIX

Shadows on The Billy Orphan Foundation porch concealed Dean. He looked at his bare wrist. The clock in his head guessed that he had twenty minutes to pick up Marti.

Ida's store lights shone through the rain. Both parking lots were empty, bad news for business and a nice break for Dean. No sign of Elbie, another good sign. Maybe he was off duty and gone for the day. A confrontation with Ida's massive brother would seriously inhibit Dean's investigation and life expectancy.

Harlan, the pipe smoker from Gumption Gap, had been wrong. The nearest telephone was not at Ida's store. The phone inside the charity was closer and more private. But the phone would not do Dean a bit of good unless one of the three keys he had taken from K.A.'s cabin unlocked the front door and the charity's secrets.

He examined the keys. Two were similar in size, the third smaller. He inserted one of the larger ones into the lock's cylinder. It fit, but wouldn't turn. The second key entered like its brother then clanked the lock's tang into the cylinder when he twisted. He glanced at the store and waited several beats before removing the key.

A hard push on the handle slid the heavy door inward into the building several inches before meeting resistance. Dean forced it far enough for him to sidle inside, but he couldn't see a thing. The light switch might be close by, but turning on the lights would draw unwanted attention. He closed the door and removed Beals' lighter from his pocket, still wrapped in the handkerchief. Faint whiffs of lighter fluid caught Dean's nose. As he flicked the Zippo into action, Dean found himself amidst a lode of envelopes, checks, cash, and coins that had piled up behind the door.

The room was stuffy. He held the lighter above his head, exposing a chair and desk at the far end. These interior walls were devoid of donation propaganda or the sad face of that orphan boy on the billboards outside. Obviously, the inside of The Billy Orphan Foundation in Charity, Nevada was not intended for the public. The building, mail slot, desk, and phone were meant to meet the minimum IRS specifications for a nonprofit.

"Too hot to handle", a baseball term used when a hitter smashed a catchable ball that went unfielded. Even with the handkerchief, the metal lighter had gone from warm to scorching hot in an instant. Dean rushed to the desk and plunked the lighter down next to the telephone, still lit. How many minutes worth of fuel did the Zippo lantern have left?

Seams appeared in the rear wall. A closed door. An electric fan was plugged into a wall socket near the door. Dean reached for the doorknob then backed off. He touched his sore chest, a reminder of K.A.'s killer cat hiding behind a closed door. Jiggling the handle didn't produce any tell-tale sounds. He opened the door an inch at a time, revealing a small bathroom with a shower. He shut the door. At least this building had indoor plumbing and electricity, amenities missing from K.A.'s cabin.

When Dean sat down at the desk and slid open the only drawer, he found pads of paper, several pencils, a metal letter opener, five state maps, and bundles of donation slips. Similar to the cabin, nothing inside the charity identified K.A. Not even a wastepaper basket. Meticulous K.A. left nothing to incriminate him, covering his existence like a sandstorm.

Dean removed the top pad of paper and examined it near the flame. Indentations of what had been written on the previous page showed in the paper. He lightly ran a lead pencil back and forth over the recessed grooves. White letters and numbers appeared against the grey background. K.A. had penciled two names and their addresses on the previous sheet. Accomplices? Or K.A.'s next victims? Dean lifted the phone receiver and dialed 0.

"Operator," he said in a low tone, while pointing a finger at the second name printed on the paper. "I would like to make a long distance call to a Sarah Henderson in the state of Oregon. The number is. . ."

While waiting for the operator to make the connection, Dean removed K.A.'s ledger from underneath his jacket and scanned the names and addresses on the first page. Nothing recognizable jumped out at him, except all the people listed were from Oregon, California, Nevada, Utah, and Idaho – four out of five states surrounding the hub of Nevada. Page two was more of the same.

"Sorry, sir," the operator said after seven rings. "But your party does not answer."

"I'd like to make another long distance call, operator. This one is to Harold Meade in Petaluma, California. . ."

Dean closed the ledger when a man answered after the fifth ring.

"Is this Harold Meade?" Dean asked.

"Who's calling?"

"My name is Dean. I'm calling from Nevada."

"I'm Harold's neighbor, Clark Burack. Could you speak up? I can barely hear you."

"Mr. Burack," Dean said notching up the volume, worrying in case someone outside could hear him, "is Harold Meade there?"

"Are you a relative?"

"No, sir. I'm calling from The Billy Orphan Foundation."

"Harold told me he invested a bunch of dough in your organization," Burack said. "You're too late to get any more of his money. He died four days ago. I've been going through his stuff here trying to figure out if he had any family left. Doesn't seem like he does. Man, I warned him. You charity leeches are all the same. Every time someone gives you something, you always come back wanting more. In fact, a cousin of mine in Idaho invested with you Billy Orphan people. When he died, his stepson got nothing."

"How long ago did this happen to your cousin, Mr. Burack."

"About three years ago. Maybe more. I kind of lose track of time nowadays."

"How did your cousin die?" Dean asked.

"The old coot fell down a flight of stairs." Burack snorted in a breath. "Listen...I don't remember what your name is. The only reason I answered Harold's phone was I was hoping you were a relative of his. Would have made my life a hell of lot easier."

"What was your cousin's name?" Dean flipped back to page one.

"You've got a hell of a lot of Goddamn nerve asking me these—"

"Please bear with me, Mr. Burack. I told you I was calling from The Billy Orphan Foundation but I'm only in their building. I'm not affiliated with the foundation. On the contrary, we're investigating the charity for fraud and murder. It's vital that you answer my questions. If my suspicions are correct, your cousin's family, along with a number of other families, have been victimized by this charity. If I can prove what I just stated, perhaps all the wronged families can get some or all of their money returned to them."

"Well, when you put it that way, my cousin's name was Ronald Washington Kirk."

Dean found the name Ronald Washington Kirk from Boise, Idaho six lines from the bottom of page one. The Billy Orphan Foundation had been killing investors for at least four years, probably longer.

"How did your neighbor Harold Meade pass?"

"It's the craziest thing," Burack said. "Apparently Harold mistakenly used a box of rat poison as sugar for his cereal and coffee. The man was as blind as Mr. Magoo without his bifocals. Killed himself and his dog. Looked to me like one of those freaky accidents people have, especially older folk."

"Was Mr. Meade having problems with mice?" Dean asked.

"Now that you mention it, I kind of wondered about the rat poison when I discovered Harold in his kitchen. We have more feline mousers around this area than Carter has little liver pills and he had a terrier. They're good ratters." He paused to blow his nose. "Besides, Harold loved Parky, that's his dog, better than any human. He wouldn't even spray his weeds with weed killer because he was afraid Parky might get poisoned."

"Mr. Burack," Dean said, ogling the lighter's diminishing flame. "I don't have time to explain, but Harold Meade may have been murdered by someone from The Billy Orphan Foundation. Same as your cousin. Please call the police and have them investigate."

Dean disconnected the call. A homicidal maniac with the

initials K.A. was killing old people for their investment money and getting away with it. The Billy Orphan Foundation was a money-producing machine that most likely had little or nothing to do with charity. Wealthy, innocent, good hearted old people – like Harold Meade, like Aunt Maddy – were dying prematurely because of someone's pure greed.

The lighter's flame was burning at half mast. Dean, eager to exit the charity and rescue Marti from K.A.'s cabin, had one more call to make. A noise outside stopped him from picking up the receiver. Footsteps. Someone was on the front porch.

CHAPTER THIRTY-SEVEN

Dean killed the lighter's flame with a silent breath of air. He stared at the door. His body was tense, ready to spring into action. The person on the porch had either left or was standing still waiting for him to make a noise. Maybe the silence of being in a strange, dark room was getting to him. Maybe...

The mail slot opened, followed by an envelope making contact with the paper pile on the floor. Dean relit the lighter after footsteps ebbed away. He dialed O again.

"Operator, I'd like to make a person-to-person collect call to Harry Spitari in San Francisco California. My name is Dean Mason..."

After a minute of silence, Harry growled, "I'll accept the charges, operator. But if I'm not satisfied with what the caller has to say, I want a refund." The operator giggled before disconnecting. "This had better be important, Dream. My phone bill is—"

"Damn it, Harry, I have no time to listen to your bitching. I called collect because I don't want the bill for this phone to show a call made to you. I'm in Charity, Nevada, about ten miles off Highway 80 on Lonesome Pass Road. It's not a town. Hell it's not even big enough to stable all those losing nags you bet on. The Billy Orphan Foundation is nothing more than a dummy office with a desk, phone, and mail slot in the front door for donations. Their trail stops here, intentionally as you know. However, we were able to find a ledger with names and addresses—"

"We?" Harry queried.

"Marti and I."

"You took the goddaughter with you. I knew you had the hots for her. Obviously, you trust her. Then again, you trusted your ex-wife Dede and look where that got you."

"If I wanted advice to the lovelorn, Harry, I would've called Dear Abby." Dean winced when the lighter's flame flickered lower. "Literally, everything is about to go dark. I believe The Billy Orphan

Foundation building and the grocery store next door are owned by a corporation called NAHPRO. Let me spell that for you."

"You don't have to, Dream. NAHPRO is orphan spelled backwards."

"Good catch, Harry. I wondered what the acronym stood for. They have a P. O. Box in Oakland. I don't know the number, but their office must be located in Oakland or the East Bay. Find out how NAHPRO is involved with The Billy Orphan Foundation."

"Shouldn't be a problem. NAHPRO is probably part of a network of corporations— easier to hide whatever a company wants hidden. But I will pull some strings and get the name or names you are looking for."

"There's more." Dean turned to page five in the ledger. "Grab your detective notebook and sharpen a yellow number two. I have a list of names and addresses for you to check out. All the names in the ledger include a checkmark, except for the last person listed. I believe the checkmark means these people are dead. For the sake of time, I'm only going to dictate the names on the last page. They may be the most recent victims, but there is a common thread. These people were old with little or no family. They invested substantial amounts of money with The Billy Orphan Foundation. And they all may have expired from an accident or suicide."

Dean read each name to Harry starting from the top of the page. Harry repeated back as he wrote. Dean's forefinger stopped at the name on line nine. His breath caught.

"Is that it, Dream. Hello. Hello. Are you still there?"

"H-Harry. The next name is Madeline Principal." Dean exhaled a deep, pained breath. For Dean the ninth line on any page would forever be like the number thirteen. "The name after Aunt Maddy, the second to last name on the list, is Harold Meade from Petaluma. I just got off the phone with Mr. Meade's neighbor. Mr. Meade is dead. He died the day after my aunt from accidental poisoning. I also called a Sarah Henderson in Riley, Oregon, the last name on the list, but got no answer. She was the person who did not have a check mark by her name. If she's not dead yet, she will be soon."

"A brilliant scam," Harry said. "So good, wish I had thought of it. Why would the police consider foul play? Sick, frail, or

incapacitated elders are prone to self-destruction and harmful mis-
haps. The donation money received by The Billy Orphan Foundation
is just peanuts compared to the investment principal they garner
from dead investors. Why wait for investors to die a slow, natural
death when the charity can speed up the process? Your detective
work is impressive. You must have had a great mentor."

"Harry, I think there's a Northern California connection to The
Billy Orphan Foundation, but I haven't been able to put it together.
Find out how many patients from Twin Rose Nursing Home and
other City nursing facilities have died due to suicide or an accident
in the last five years. We can compare their names to the ledger
later. Also, can you sniff around to see if my ex, Dede, is somehow
involved? She made an unexpected visit to the nursing home to see
my aunt. I still can't figure out why."

"I can answer that question now, Dream. You were away playing baseball when Dede asked Madeline's forgiveness for taking
advantage of you. She wanted to make amends before it was too
late. Dede died two days ago from an incurable disease."

"Ho, man." Dean blew out a troubled breath. Samantha knew
Dede was in poor health by her appearance. "I'm sorry Dede's life
had to end that way."

"I agree, but that file is now closed. Your sexy friend Samantha
from the nursing home, however, is another story. I believe she's
involved in something."

"At this point, Harry, I suspect everyone. Including you."

"That hurt, Dream." Harry cranked out a series of coughs. "In
spite of your last insult, I'll find out about NAHPRO, Samantha, and
if anyone else has died in a nursing home under dubious circumstances. Do you have any idea who is doing the killing?"

"More than an idea," Dean said. "The killer goes by the name of
K.A. I doubt those are his real initials. He could be Billy Orphan. He
also murdered my friend Beals Becker. K.A. is either a hired assassin or part of The Billy Orphan organization. His network of kills is
in at least five states. The guy has more disguises than a chameleon.
No one knows what he really looks like. Marti found his ledger of
kills in a dilapidated cabin he uses near the charity."

"Your partner didn't find a bundle of money along with the

ledger, did she?"

"Sorry, Harry. It looks like we'll be coming home without hitting a big jackpot."

"Damn."

"Ever consider how much easier your life would be if you quit betting the ponies?"

"You are one to preach. Talk to me when you break up with your pal Jack Daniel's."

"Touché." Their afflictions were similar and neither wanted to quit. Harry had been in a slump at the track for a long time. One could get rich by betting on Harry to lose. He owed a number of people. A share of Dean's inheritance would save his addictive ass. Was Harry so far in the arrears that he had involved himself in a scam and murder?

"Are you calling me from the cabin?" Harry asked.

"Hardly. The cabin doesn't have running water, let alone electricity. I just broke into The Billy Orphan Foundation to use their phone. Marti is rummaging through K.A.'s secret closet looking for more incriminating evidence."

"If you don't know K.A.'s whereabouts, aren't you rolling the dice with Marti's life?"

"Have you ever tried to talk a woman out of something when she's dead set against what you're trying to talk her out of?"

"Good point, Dream."

"Shopkeeper here said K.A. will be traveling for a week."

"You will find this K.A. cat when he finds you," Harry said. "At least he doesn't know that you're related to Madeline. Hmm. Or does he? Either my ulcer is acting up, or you haven't told me everything."

"K.A. tried to run me down the night I returned to San Francisco."

"I'm not going to ask you why you didn't inform me of that tidbit, Dream. Get Marti's pretty little caboose out of that cabin and get the hell out of the town of Charity."

"Exactly what I plan to do."

The room went dark. Beal's lighter had finally run out of fluid. Dean burned his fingers when he touched it.

"Give me a number where I can reach you," Harry said.

"You can't reach me. I'll call you back as soon as I can."

"It better not be person-to-person collect, you son of a—"

Dean hung up the phone. He tucked the ledger under his zipped jacket, grabbed the lighter with the handkerchief and darted for the door. In the dark, the envelopes on the floor served as a path to the only exit out of The Billy Orphan Foundation's office. He yanked open the door and ran into a wall. A human wall named Elbie.

CHAPTER THIRTY-EIGHT

Dean bounced off Elbie's bulky body and landed on The Billy Orphan Foundation's paper-cushioned floor. Without entering the charity, Ida's brother blindly ran one hand up and down the inside wall until his fingers connected with the light switch. The other hand carried a rifle, not that Elbie needed a weapon.

"I remember you and the good-lookin' gal in the car," Elbie said. "Asking all them questions about the charity. Tryin' to pump me for information. You waited until you thought no one was looking to break into the foundation to steal money from the orphans, didn't you?"

"I didn't break in." Dean stood up and pointed down at the loose envelopes, checks, and green bills on the floor. "Nor did I steal any money."

"This door is always locked, partner. Only one person has the key and it ain't you."

"Think about it, Elbie. There is only one way in and one way out of here. How do you think I got in?"

Elbie's eye's narrowed in thought. His lips puckered, shortening the scar on his cheek. He tilted the rifle barrel to push his wet hat back.

Dean smiled at the confused big man. Elbie's boots remained glued to the porch. Peggy had told Dean the truth about Elbie's reluctance to mess with K.A.

"What are you afraid of, Elbie? You can come inside. Obviously, K.A. isn't here."

"K.A. is meaner than a skunk with a hair-trigger stink." Elbie took a brief look over his shoulder. "Wait. How do you know about K.A.?"

"You really don't know who I am, do you?" Dean said.

"No. Can't say that I do." Elbie pointed the rifle barrel at Dean's chest. "Just who the hell are you?"

"I'm Billy Orphan, the principal owner of this charity. K.A. works for me."

Dean's heart felt like it would jump into his throat. He had just thrown Elbie a changeup. But if Peggy did not know what Billy Orphan looked like, why would Elbie?

"How do I know that you're really Mr. Orphan?" Elbie asked in a softer tone. "I've never seen you around here before today."

Good question. A question that deserved a good answer, not that Dean had one. Elbie was not as dumb as his exterior advertised. Then again, Elbie was also in a quandary. If Dean was the real Billy Orphan, Elbie would not want to say or do anything that would jeopardize his sister's sweet deal and Elbie's employment.

"As you can see," Dean jingled the keys, "I didn't break in. How else would I have known about K.A.? I hired him to manage my Nevada branch of The Billy Orphan Foundation. We have satellite charity buildings like this in five states. Traveling the countryside to help orphans is rather time consuming." Dean stepped towards Elbie. "Now I have a question for you. Why did you come over here carrying a gun?"

"Ida makes me look out for your place when K.A. ain't around." Elbie lowered the gun. "In fact, I always kind of thought K.A. was you."

Dean nodded. What Elbie just said made sense. K.A. was the only person they saw representing The Billy Orphan Foundation. Keeping an eye on the charity was a condition in Ida's agreement with K.A. What other information was Elbie privy to?"

"You did right by checking me out, Elbie." Dean stuffed the keys back into his pocket. "Quite frankly, I'm not pleased with the way things are being handled around here. Someone has been stealing money from my foundation."

Elbie's eyelids blinked several times then he looked away. Innocent people often react as if they are guilty when presented with that kind of charge. On the other hand, maybe Elbie was not so innocent. If a gas customer gave him extra money for a donation to The Billy Orphan Foundation, would Elbie slip the contribution through the charity's door slot? Or did he pocket it?

"Honest injun, Mr. Orphan. I've never taken a dime."

"Relax, Elbie. I know you're not the thief. K.A. is the person in question here. Be honest with me now. Have you ever seen K.A. take money intended for the charity?"

"Well," Elbie puffed out a relieved breath, "K.A. sometimes brings filled mailbags into the charity. Then brings the same bags out and packs them back into his Jeep. I don't know what's in them bags or where he takes 'em."

Dean ran a hand across his lips. The bags must be stuffed with checks written out to The Billy Orphan Foundation that K.A. returned to Fuzzy at the post office. From there, Fuzzy boxed the checks and sent them to Reno and/or Oakland. Fuzzy said he didn't see cash. Was that how K.A. paid the postmaster two hundred dollars a month of hush money? Or maybe Fuzzy pocketed some or all of the cash K. A. sent with the checks. Dean glanced at the paper pile. The short search of K.A.'s secret closet didn't reveal a cash reserve. Was that the reason Marti insisted on staying, to hunt for cash?

"It has been brought to my attention that K.A. travels a lot," Dean said. "Do you know where he goes?"

"Nope. The only thing folks around here know about K.A. is not to piss him off."

"You seem like a real trustworthy fellow, Elbie. There might be an opening for the manager's position here real soon. You interested in the job?"

"Do bears like honey? You bet, Mr. Orphan." Elbie rested the butt of the rifle on the wood porch and grinned. "Wouldn't that just fry Ida's big butt? Then maybe I could bring in some real dough like my sister. Plus I wouldn't have to fret none about being hard-assed by a prick like K.A."

Dean slid a loose check back into the pile with his shoe. Thus far, it seemed that Elbie and Peggy were not mixed up in the charity's illegal transgressions.

"Is your sister Ida involved in any way with K.A. or the charity?"

"Ida hates K.A. more than I do. She takes his shit 'cause she doesn't want to lose her store."

"When was the last time you saw K.A.?"

"Funny you should ask. A clean-shaven blond-haired guy the same size as K.A. came in for gas, driving K.A.'s Jeep. I recognized the license plate. It's a little game I play to keep my brain exercised. It could have been K.A.'s brother. Or a cousin. You just missed him by about thirty minutes."

"Holy shit!" That must have been K.A. out of disguise. Dean pushed Elbie out of the doorway like he was the size of a batboy. If Marti reneged on her promise to wait for him at the oak tree by the road, and K.A. caught her alone in his cabin . . . "Holy shit!"

* * * * *

Sheets of rain battered the Ford's windshield. The headlight beams could not penetrate more than ten feet in the downpour. Dean's jaw gyrated back and forth. He leaned forward in the driver's seat, concentrating on a road that played like an LP record stuck in the same groove.

The ink map Peggy had drawn on his hand was smudged and useless. He navigated by memory. Throwing darts blindfolded at a moving target might be easier than trying to find K.A.'s cabin in these conditions.

The defroster had quit working. Dean wiped the windshield with his hand. The road was still difficult to follow. It took restraint not to press harder on the gas pedal. If he drove off the road and disabled his car, his chances of getting to Marti in time would be eliminated. He had risked Marti's life so she could prove herself to him, and justify his reluctant trust in her. His first inclination had been correct. He should have hauled her out of the cabin when he had the chance. The heavy rain that pounded his car was nothing compared to the guilt pelting him.

A lightning bolt lit up the sky, followed by a distant thunderclap that sounded like a gunshot. A furry animal scurried for cover across the road. Dean's foot instinctively lifted off the gas pedal. The little critter's life would have been shorter without the aid of illumination by lightning. How ironic. Yet when he had sprinted across the main street in Gumption Gap, the Jeep driver who almost hit him never even seemed to try to stop. . .

Good God! That blond driver was K.A.

A distorted image of a road appeared. Dean slowed to a stop. Nothing looked familiar, but the road to K.A.'s cabin had connected to a three-corner intersection similar to this. He turned onto a muddy road driving faster than he should, but not fast enough. The hood ornament pointed towards the center of the road, but the sloppy conditions caused his car to drift from one shoulder to the other. He notched down his speed. The slightest curve would send the Ford sliding off the road.

He shook his head. Peggy had told him the cabin was about a mile away. It seemed like he had driven much more than a mile. A front tire hit a pothole, splashing a wave of blinding water across the windshield. Dean bounced up, hitting his head on the ceiling before the car frame slammed down. He managed to keep both hands on the steering wheel, avoiding the urge to rub the new bump on his head.

The driving storm lessened, as if someone had turned the rain faucet a notch to the left. The drops were softer, more manageable. A lucky break.

Dean ratcheted up his car's speed. K.A. may not have had a sense of urgency to return to his cabin. He had no way of knowing someone was chasing him or rummaging through his stuff. Maybe K.A. hadn't gone back to his cabin after all.

"Damn, why didn't I think to ask Elbie which direction K.A. headed after getting gas?"

Dean pressed down harder on the gas pedal. K.A. could have been on his way to Highway 80. Or maybe the Jeep had a flat tire...

"What the hell?"

A mountain of rock and dirt appeared before Dean. He hammered his shoe down on the brake. The tires hydroplaned on the mucky surface. His car skidded to a stop before hitting a rocky dead end. He had taken the wrong road.

CHAPTER THIRTY-NINE

Faint light emanated from the cabin's open front door, prompting K.A. to turn the Jeep off the road into a puddle of weeds. His covert sanctuary had been invaded. How many intruders were inside violating his space? No one had ever come this close to him before. The hunter had become the prey.

He slammed the Jeep's gear into four-wheel drive to propel it back on the road. Then he twisted his upper body around and peered through the Jeep's windows at the area around his cabin. No other vehicle visible. How did someone discover his hidden lair?

A hawk flew in and out of K.A.'s line of vision. Perhaps the situation was not as dire as it seemed. Untamed growth surrounding the cabin glistened with moisture. He noticed a blazed trail of broken weeds that led to the front door then disappeared around the structure's left side. Two or more people created that path. Hiker's seeking shelter from the rain? A plausible scenario, but his instincts screamed a different story. The people inside his cabin were not seeking cover. They were pursuing him. What if they discovered his hidden closet?

He snatched a revolver from underneath the driver's seat and shoved open the Jeep's door. His heart pounded with emotions he had not experienced since childhood. At least he still had surprise on his side. But this time he would kill for survival. He had every right to defend himself against intruding strangers. What an odd twist of events for him to be on the proper side of the law.

The Smith & Wesson .38 Special felt heavy in his hand. And for good reason. He had never fired a gun before. How ironic for a master killer to abhor a device meant to kill. His prejudice against firearms had nothing to do with a conscience burdened by taking a human or animal's life. He detested gunpowder's foul odor and the penetrating noise a discharged bullet produced. However, under the circumstances, a gun might be necessary.

He stepped into the rain and closed the Jeep's door without making a sound. His thumb pulled the hammer back, like he had seen movie actors do. Just how difficult could it be to aim at someone and pull the trigger? He might soon find out.

The revolver had been swiped from a World War I vet after K.A. had pushed him down a flight of stairs. Twice. The tough old bird hadn't died the first time. Before the man had his "accident," he bragged about his marksmanship with the double-action .38, a gun used by cops, soldiers, and crooks alike. The old guy even told K.A. his gun was loaded with special rounds. K.A. had found the gun in the pocket of the man's old army uniform in the bedroom closet, along with two leather sacks full of diamonds.

The special ammo meant nothing to K.A. His only concern was how many bullets were at his disposal. He fought the urge to explore the guts of the gun, fearing it could go off by accident. In cowboy movies they used six shooters. But some of the guns never seemed to run out of ammunition. He guessed he had at least six bullets, enough to eliminate a handful of cabin invaders.

The gun's bluish-gray barrel led the way as he dashed into the sopping weeds. Precipitation was still in the air, but nothing like the hard downpour from before. He pushed the safety switch to the off position. Or did he just switch it on? He would find out after he pulled the trigger. The route he took to the cabin's door had a slight downward slope. The footing was treacherous and slowed his progress. He almost fell twice. Still, he quickened his pace, anxious to carry out this mission.

From his vantage point, the cabin appeared to be nothing more than an abandoned structure ready to keel over. The sickly grey wood frame was blistered, warped, and had long given way to abusive sun, wind, and rain. A perfect hideout—until now.

A grating, high-pitched noise froze him in a stop. Cheetah, the cabin's cat screeched again then darted off into the tall weeds. The cabin's bedroom door must have been opened, releasing the cat. Hopefully, Cheetah had responded with a vicious reprisal.

K.A. was out of breath. Who could be inside his cabin and why? Were they looking for the Black Belt Killer? Without discovery of the dummy wall, the break-in would be a wasted effort. But not for K.A. As far as he was concerned, each and everyone in there was dead meat.

A flicker of movement inside the cabin caught his eye. His hand tightened on the gun handle. Was he seeing things again, or did he glimpse a person with dark hair? He rushed forward for a better angle. His left shoe sunk up to his ankle in a muck hole. He fought to stay upright. He tried to plant his right foot for leverage, but slid across the mud instead and fell forward. His gun hand struck a brick and fired towards the cabin.

His ears rang. He wriggled his foot loose from the mud hole, minus his shoe. Had he heard a human voice cry out? Awkwardly, he managed to stand. A shock of dark hair surfaced in the doorway again. K.A. aimed the short barrel at the predator and fired until the gun's chamber emptied. No mistaking the sharp shriek that followed. A sound only a woman could produce.

* * * * *

Dean's car plowed up a stream of water and mud as he sped away from the dead end. In a fit of temper, his driving had become more reckless. He had turned down the wrong road, a turn that may have cost Marti her life.

The windshield wipers still labored at a feverish pace, but the defroster was still on strike. Dean rolled down the window to defog the windshield. Rain peppered his left side. He smelled fire.

He tapped the brake, anticipating a turn onto the connecting road up ahead. A green Jeep zoomed before him speeding towards Charity. It was too dark inside the Jeep for Dean to see who sat behind the steering wheel, but he had no doubt that K.A. was the driver. Did K.A. spot Dean's car?

Without stopping Dean turned in the direction the Jeep had come from. Pursuing the killer wasn't an option. He only cared about Marti.

The gas pedal was close to the floorboard. Another right turn appeared up ahead. He sped into the turn too fast. The Ford snaked in the mud, and a rear tire found the mucky shoulder. Dean managed to keep his car on the road and raced towards the cabin. The odor of fire became more prevalent.

"For God's sake, no!"

Dean's worst nightmare was no dream. Clouds of white smoke billowed upward into an early evening background, hovering above the area where the cabin should be located. He drove faster. When he blasted past the cabin, flames were shooting up from the roof. He laid on the horn to alert Marti. His foot jammed down on the brake pedal. The Ford slid to a stop by the designated oak tree. Marti wasn't there. That bastard K.A. had left her in the cabin to burn.

"Marti!" Dean left the car door open and sprinted into the sea of weeds towards the cabin door, running as if his knee had never been damaged. Yellowish orange flames lit up a portion of the inside. Smoke spewed upward into the night air like an Indian signal. He fell, face-first, into the weeds, gliding on the wild grass like he was stealing a base. His wet shirt pasted hard against his smarting chest. "Marti!"

He bounced back up, running in a crouch like a soldier facing enemy fire. Burning wood crackled louder with each plodding step. The rain he had cursed earlier was now a Godsend, somewhat retarding the fire's progress. But for how long?

"Marti!" Panic dripped from his voice. The reek of charred wood nauseated him. He entered into K.A.'s smoky hideout and slipped on the wet floor, but managed to stay upright. The kitchen area was aflame. Thankfully, Marti wasn't in the room. Fire had eaten a hole in the ceiling, funneling smoke up into the exposed sky. Soon the whole cabin would be an inferno.

Dean darted into the bedroom, the only room Marti could be in. His stinging eyes teared. He kicked something soft across the room—Aunt Maddy's first aid bag that Marti had brought from the car when she patched him up after the cat attack.

"Marti!" he choked out. He dropped to his knees, lowered his face to the floor, and crawled to the cat's wall. His hand blindly reached for the space underneath the middle boards. The door swung open. A whoosh of smoke and heat jumped out at him. He fell hard on his back.

Dean forced his way inside the closet. Hot tears streamed from his eyes. He couldn't see, but Marti had to be somewhere in this space between the walls. He crab walked towards the desk.

Heat from the kitchen penetrated the wall. His air supply was near empty.

"Marti!" he gasped then went into a spasm of throaty hacks.

He raised the collar of his shirt over his nose and mouth. Still on his knees, he hurried to the opposite side of the closet. The top shelf housing K.A.'s wigs and paraphernalia collapsed on top of him. Using the makeup table, he pulled himself up. Marti was not in the closet or the cabin. Where the hell was she? Oh no. Was she being held captive in the Jeep he saw a few minutes earlier?

Dean stumbled out of the closet coughing and gagging. The only window in the bedroom was boarded up. He rushed towards the door. A loud crack sounded, followed by a crash that stopped him cold. The doorway was filled with fire from a burning beam. Flames clawed at Dean like a pissed off panther. He jumped back, trapped.

CHAPTER FORTY

Crackling wood hissed an ominous noise from the fire-engulfed doorway. Dean backed further into the bedroom. His air supply was nearly exhausted.

The cabin's foundation rumbled like a San Francisco earthquake. Dean lifted K.A.'s clumsy, single mattress from the floor and hoisted it over his head. He closed his eyes and visualized the route to the front door. On a baseball diamond, he experienced countless crucial moments, but this was a real life do-or-die. If he failed to perform in the clutch, there would be no tomorrow.

Dean charged into the burning beam blocking the doorway. The collision jolted him off balance. He managed to stay on his feet. His bearings were guided only by his directional sense.

Intense heat permeated the thin mattress. A flame licked his ankle. He shoved at what seemed to be an immovable obstruction. The beam shifted slightly. His legs kept churning. With a grunt, he pushed with all he had. The last smidgen of air gushed from his mouth. The beam gave way, sending him into the next room. He had to keep moving. Where was the damn front door? He blindly surged onward. The mattress connected with something solid, pushing back into his shoulder. Boards gave way. His body fell forward into an abyss of darkness. He landed on top of the mattress then bounced into a puddle of muddy water that extinguished fire clinging to his pant cuff.

Steam emanated from his hot body. He choked out inhaled smoke and gasped for more air, followed by an uncontrollable coughing jag. It felt like he might hack up a lung, but he was alive and free from the fire. He peered up at the burning cabin. Flames stretched high into the night. He wiped away soot from his face with wet hands and sucked in more precious mouthfuls of oxygen.

The cabin groaned. A deep rolling sound came next. Dean scuttled into the dense weeds. The structure wobbled before collapsing like a house of playing cards. Orange sparks danced up into the moist night. The mattress that had saved his life disappeared in the burning debris before him. The cabin's walls and roof were now memories, charred into oblivion, along with any remaining evidence linking K.A. to the murders of Aunt Maddy and Beals Becker. At least Marti had not been inside. . .

"K.A.'s got Marti."

Dean scrambled to his feet. He fought through the weeds. The fire provided light to guide his way. The more effort he exerted to speed up, the more slowly he seemed to move. He hit the muddy road in full stride heading towards his car, yet it still felt like he was running in place. His mouth hung open to draw in as much air as possible. A bend in the road appeared as a dark outline. He leaned into the turn without slowing down. His shoes skidded in the slippery muck. The muscles in his burning legs worked hard to regain lost speed. How many minutes had elapsed since he saw the Jeep race towards Charity?

A fireball burst into the sky like fireworks, followed by a deafening explosion. The blast had come from the direction of The Billy Orphan Foundation and Ida's store. K.A. must have set fire to the gas pumps to incinerate all trails leading to him.

Dean sprinted towards the giant oak tree. Without warning, his knee locked up. He plunged into the sludge. His damaged joint never played favorites, breaking down anywhere at anytime. He managed to rise to his feet after twice slipping back into sludge. Precious seconds ticked away. Seconds that could make the difference between finding Marti or . . .

A pair of bouncing high beam headlights blinded him. He shielded his eyes with a hand. Churning tires created a wake of mud and water.

Dean lifted his shoes up and down in the suctioning mud, ready to react if the car zeroed in on him. The front of the vehicle veered away, the rear fishtailing as it passed. Brake lights lit up. The driver had lost control. The car skidded part way off the road before stopping. Tail lights shone again. The chassis rocked back and forth from reverse to drive, trying to dislodge spinning tires from their muddy trap. The car finally jockeyed all four tires back onto the road and rolled towards Dean. He grabbed a base-ball-sized stone. One good throw through the windshield or side window could incapacitate whoever was driving. Even if the rock missed its mark, the shattered glass might give Dean enough time to pull the driver from the car.

Dean's hand angled back to make his throw when the car stopped moving. He lowered his arm. He had almost thrown the rock at his own Ford Crestline Victoria. The driver's door flew open. Marti dashed to him shouting his name. The rock fell from his hand, plopping down into the mud. She jumped into his waiting arms.

"Why did you go back into the cabin when it was on fire?" Marti said, interlocking her fingers around his neck.

"I thought you were trapped inside."

"Oh my God, Dean. I almost got you killed twice." Marti's words shot out in rapid fire. "Your car's windshield defogger didn't work. Everything was so blurry. I thought you were K.A. When I realized it was you, I lost control of the—"

Dean kissed her. He didn't kiss Marti to prevent her from talking. He simply could not help himself. The internal governor damming his emotions had broken wide open. A flood of unabashed passion gushed through him. Marti didn't resist. Quite the opposite, in fact. Her yielding lips responded in like hunger.

The cabin's massive flames served as a romantic backdrop for two people meshed in harmony. All sense of time and proximity vanished. Dean's myriad hurts disappeared, healed by the weight-less woman in his arms. They were both reluctant to let go. If their embrace had taken place on the pitcher's mound in Yankee Stadium in front of sixty-thousand raucous fans, it wouldn't have mattered. Their bodies had melted into one, producing a lover's rhythm. Yet, as hard as they tried, they couldn't quite get close enough to each other.

A flash of light illuminated the sky above them, followed by another thunderous explosion. The high voltage chemistry charging through them would pale in comparison to being struck by lightning. Dean reluctantly pulled his lips away. Disappointment creased Marti's features.

He seized her hand and ran to the car. Inside, she sat snuggled next to him as if they were teenagers on a date. The Ford slithered in the mud like a scared sidewinder when Dean pressed down on the gas pedal. She clutched his leg above the knee to keep from sliding on the bench seat.

"I got the impression you were happy to see me," Marti said softly into his ear.

"I have never been so glad to see anyone in my whole life."

"It took you long enough to let me know how you really feel." She kissed his cheek. "Does this mean I get to keep your watch?"

"That is negotiable. Why weren't you waiting for me at the oak tree like we agreed?"

He tried to sound angry, but anger was not the emotion he was feeling. How could he be mad – Marti was sitting next to him, unharmed and safe.

"I never got a chance," she said. "For some reason, K.A. fired his gun while he was sneaking up on the cabin. Since I had never actually heard a gunshot before, I thought it was your car backfiring. I went to the front door. He shot a volley of bullets into the cabin. Frightened, like never before, I ran back to the closet then to the kitchen. K.A. entered the cabin screaming obscenities. I turned around and threw the lantern down to the kitchen floor. Fire spread immediately. Then I went through the broken window and ran for my life. I think K.A. went to the closet rather than venturing through the fire to chase after me."

"K.A. is a master at surprising others. He must have been thrown off his game when he saw someone in his cabin." Dean took her hand into his. "Well, at least now we know he has a gun and is not a very good shot. Did you get a clear look at him?"

"Not really," she said. "He's blond. If I heard his voice again, I would recognize it."

Dean turned onto the road leading back to Charity. If Marti couldn't identify K.A. then there was a good chance that K.A. only saw a strange woman with dark hair inside his cabin. Plus, K.A. had no way of knowing that Marti was with Dean, the man he tried to kill in front of Aunt Maddy's house and in Gumption Gap. But now K.A. knew his hidden closet had been breached and someone might be pursuing him.

Dean rolled his window down all the way to defog the windshield. A distant siren blared, most likely from a fire truck. No doubt the town of Charity was now minus its only two buildings. Hopefully, Ida and her family had gone home before K.A. set fire to the gas pumps.

Dean stopped at the crossroads, then turned left.

How wrong he had been about Marti. She was the antithesis of women like his ex-wife Dede or Sam from the nursing home. Marti had not reneged on their agreement. To the contrary, she had risked her life to protect him.

"I never should have left you alone." He wrapped an arm around Marti's shoulder and squeezed tight. "I could have lost you. I won't let that happen again."

"Is that a promise, Mr. Mason?" She fondled his watch on her forearm.

"Is this another negotiation, Miss Cooper?"

"You bet. In return for my being your partner for say . . . the next hundred years, I will share with you what I discovered in K.A.'s secret closet. You will not believe what I found, Dean."

"What happens after a hundred years?" he asked.

"We can renegotiate."

"Deal. What did you find?"

"Not so fast, slick," she said. "I think you should find a nice cozy place where we can consummate this agreement."

CHAPTER FORTY-ONE

Marti cuddled into Dean, using his arm and chest as her pillow. The bed's commercial mattress was no different than what most motel rooms provided, but Dean could not remember ever feeling this comfortable or aware of his partner. A woman's heartfelt sigh could articulate more than a cluster of meaningful words. When was the last time he had been intimate with a woman without being under the influence? Hell, when was the last time he had gone this long without a drink?

This cabin's rustic log exterior had made it look like a cozy hideaway. A wood stove in the corner removed the chill from the room until unleashed body heat took over. Each cabin unit was separated by ten feet of privacy for lovers.

Dean's hair was still damp from a shower and two rounds of lovemaking. The first time was frantic and greedy, followed by a slow, tender union of exploration that satisfied in a whole different way.

Marti sighed again. Her eyes remained closed. Their love nest provided a temporary haven from any evils that may have been lurking outside.

"Dean," she murmured in a sleepy voice. "Do you remember being in Aunt Madeline's kitchen when you recited, with great amusement I might add, my hangover rants that morning after?"

"How could I forget? You accused me of slipping you a Mickey, implying I was after the cherished bloom you were saving for Mr. Wonderful."

"That is when I fell in love with you all over again."

"What do you mean, again?" he asked.

Marti's eyes opened. She played with a tuft of his chest hair, careful not to touch the cuts and scratches created by K.A's attack cat. Her cheeks reddened.

"I know this may sound silly," she said, "but you have always been my Mr. Wonderful. I have been in love with you for as long as I can remember—something my diary can verify. It was like Christmas when a new letter from Aunt Madeline would arrive. Mother would read it out loud to me. Your aunt complained a lot about this and that. No surprise there, right? But she always boasted about all of your sports honors and what a great young man you were."

"A little girl's crush." He massaged the small of her smooth back. "That's not love."

"Your aunt was much wiser than you give her credit for," Marti said. "She somehow knew we were right for each other. That's why she created a will that forced us to interact after she was gone."

"Aunt Maddy despised my ex-wife and most of the girls I dated. To my aunt, your mother's biased letters about her pretty and virtuous daughter probably painted a picture of the last nice young girl in all forty-eight states. Your fascination was no different than a young boy idolizing a star baseball player."

"Except my infatuation matured as I grew up. Oh, I didn't allow my secret romantic attraction for you to stop me from dating or having boyfriends. I knew the odds of the two of us meeting were about as good as sending a rocket ship to mars. I guess you were the Sir Galahad of my Camelot dream world. Why else would I carry a photo of a boy who only knew me as 'the goddaughter'?"

Marti stretched across his body and snatched a wallet from her purse on the nightstand. She removed a black and white picture of Dean in his high school baseball uniform. Dean grimaced at the kid starring back at him. The hat covered an outdated flattop haircut. But it did not hide the teenage pimple outbreak. How could Marti have fallen in love with such a spazzy looking guy?

"How could you recognize me from this picture after smashing into my car in the parking lot?" he said.

"I didn't smash into you." She pinched his bicep. "Our bumpers . . . touched. Aunt Madeline kept mother and I up to date by sending current pictures of you. Our little accident really shook me up, though. But it was nothing like seeing you in person. It was like a surreal scene with the vision of my dream man shattered when you were so nasty to me."

"I guess I was a little rough on you," he said, smiling.

"Yes, you were. And for good reason I later found out. You had just lost your career and only living relative. Then this ditzy-female bumps into your car, offering you nothing but excuses. Less than an hour after that, you lost an inheritance that would have made you wealthy beyond belief."

"Are you saying that you changed your opinion because you felt sorry for me?"

"Just the opposite, Dean. I also lost my inheritance, not that I ever expected to receive one. But I discovered an even greater treasure." She eyed his muddy, soot- covered clothes piled on the floor. "The shining armor may be a bit tarnished, but my Sir Galahad is more wonderful than I ever could have imagined. Although you took every opportunity to express your dislike for me, you never failed to be my protector or a gentleman. Which meant you cared about me, but didn't want to show it. When I literally had no other place to stay, you took me into your home. Even if you may not acknowledge it, I believe you would have done so even without the negotiation. Your creativity got me my teaching job back and put my principal, Mr. Timmons in his place. God only knows what would have happened if you had not rescued me from Jimbo at my apartment. Also, I notice that you have been ignoring your former friend Jack Daniel's. And why."

Dean closed his eyes. Marti was as sharp as Ty Cobb's chiseled metal spikes. She had realized how he felt about her long before he could even admit it to himself. She was willing to wait for him to come around, with one major exception. Her sobering it's-me-or-Jack declaration in Aunt Maddy's kitchen after he learned about Beals' death was her deal breaker. He was an alcoholic, just like Aunt Maddy. Just like Marti's father. An addiction he would have to battle for the rest of his life. Right now, he only craved Marti. Yet history told him his need for Jack would re-surface to wage ongoing battles with his self-discipline. Marti did not have the power to stop him from drinking. Only he did. Yet, for the first time since he was introduced to Jack, Marti's love strengthened a steely resolve to stop. But for how long?

"It looked like you were a million miles away just now," she said. "Where were you? What were you thinking about?"

"How nice it would be for this moment to never end."

"I feel the same way, Dean. Could we go back to Aunt Madeline's house? Give the police all the information we have. Let them chase after that psycho K.A. and Billy Orphan, if there really is a Billy Orphan. Do you realize there are only three days left to refurbish your aunt's floors? Otherwise you will lose the house."

"We're so close, Marti, to finding the lead person behind all of these bizarre murders. We can't just quit now."

"I was afraid you would say that." Marti planted several soft kisses on his cheek. "I was also afraid that your ex-wife Dede permanently ruined your ability to trust another woman."

"You're not the only female to throw that line at me."

"Yet, you went against your phobic distrust and left me alone in the cabin. Why?"

"I wanted to justify being in love with you," he said, looking deep into her eyes.

"Well, sir. Your trust in me shall not go unrewarded."

Marti got up and scooted away from the bed. Dean's toothy grin of pleasure vanished when she donned the long sleeve shirt he had loaned her when her jacket and skirt were at the cleaners. Most of Marti's glorious naked body was now covered. Some reward.

Marti returned to the bed carrying a scrapbook and small suitcase. She lowered the case onto the floor and propped her pillow against the headboard. Leaning back into the pillow, she held the scrapbook like it was the Holy Grail.

"We don't have time to play *This is Your Life*," Dean said, shaking his head.

"What if we take a peek into K.A.'s life then? I found this scrapbook and suitcase behind K.A.'s desk in the closet." She rubbed her cheek against his shoulder. "See, good things happen when you trust in me."

Dean was instantly ready for round three. Marti placed the musty-scented scrapbook in his hands instead, flipping pages of glued newspaper articles towards the leather front cover. Some of the clippings had yellowed with age.

"I've read most of the articles." Marti stopped at the first page, pointing at one of two clippings with an accompanying photo of a grossly charred house. The headline read, **COUPLE DIES IN FIRE**. "For the sake of time, I'll give you a synopsis. Jesse and Alma Wilkes perished in the blaze. The fire was blamed on the couple smoking in bed after having too much to drink. Miraculously, their eleven year old son, Tyler Wilkes, escaped." Marti moved her finger to the second article. "This is a follow up report on Tyler. Since there were no family members to take him in, the authorities placed him to an orphanage after his release from the hospital."

Dean squinted to read K.A.'s pencil printing next to a burned match glued between the two articles: Father and Mother, I bet it's even hotter in hell!

"Let's see if we are on the same page," he said. "This is where all the killing started for K.A. His real identity is Tyler Wilkes. He murdered his parents by setting fire to their bed. The match and the articles are mementos."

"Right-o. When and where do you think the initials K.A. came into play?"

"Your guess is as good as mine," he said. "Maybe they are from a person he killed. Or the initials represent someone or something he admires."

"Why do think he murdered his mother and father?"

"Perhaps Tyler just snapped after years of being abused," he said. "Setting fire to their bed could have been his way of stopping the mistreatment. Maybe he enjoyed the experience so much, it inspired him to continue killing."

"Or maybe Tyler was just a bad seed." Marti turned the page. "This article is about a boy who died at Tyler's orphanage. The boy fell out of an upstairs window. There were no witnesses. They called it an unfortunate accident. Or a possible suicide."

Next to the article, Tyler printed in pencil: "With my help, the little son of a bitch tried to imitate the flying Wright Brothers— minus the plane."

"The articles about Tyler's parents and the orphan boy are telling," Dean said. "Even more telling are his penciled remarks. The

Billy Orphan Foundation investors listed in K.A.'s ledger all expired by way of accident or suicide. Sounds like K.A.'s killing style formed at an early age."

"They moved Tyler to another orphanage after the accident," Marti said, turning a few pages forward. "Maybe they suspected he was responsible, but couldn't prove it. The new place was for wayward boys called Uncle Pete's Orphan Sanctuary, or as you can see in Tyler's pencil print: The Hell House."

Dean smoothed the wrinkled newsprint with a fingertip. The paper felt cushioned, as if there was another article underneath. He ripped the newsprint away from the glued corners. A black and white photograph of two boys slid out. He studied the scruffy looking teenagers wearing dirty T-shirts and holes in their pants. The dark-haired boy with a squinty-eyed, shy expression looked like he had a shadow or a splotch of paint on his forehead. The fair-haired boy, who seemed several years older than the other boy, held an axe pick and glowered at the camera.

"That's him," Marti cried out.

"That's who?"

"The blond boy is a younger version of the man who fired bullets at the cabin. That's K.A. Look how good looking he was even as a youngster."

Dean took a closer look at the blond boy's features then he turned the photo over, unsure. Printed in pen on a piece of masking tape were the words: Billy and me after I nailed Uncle Pete with a pickax to save Chub's fat ass from another beating. Dean turned the photo over again. In the background, there was a fuzzy image of a body and shovel lying on the front porch of a two story house.

"Any ideas who took this picture?" he asked, still gazing at the photo.

"Not a clue, but Uncle Pete's name is mentioned in the next article. His orphanage burned to the ground, killing all the boys and the overseer Peter Tolbert. The sheriff's department determined arson was the cause of the blaze. Fourteen bodies were found burned beyond recognition, making identification impossible. County records accounted for sixteen orphans. It's possible two or three orphans escaped the fire."

"Uncle Pete finally got the point" was written in pencil under the article.

"K.A. killed the overseer before he torched the house," Dean said.

"But why would he kill the other orphans?"

"To eliminate witnesses, I guess. And by setting fire to the orphanage, he erased his identity and the identity of the other boy in the photo. They were the boys who escaped."

"Hey, Dean," she snatched the photo from his hand. "If that's a blue birthmark on the brunette boy's forehead, he could be the baby found in the bus depot. Harry told Aunt Madeline her son died in a fire at an orphanage. Does that mean her son is still alive?"

"Good call, Marti. K.A. referred to the dark-haired boy as Billy, as in Billy Orphan. What if this Billy is my cousin and he's in cahoots with K.A. to bilk investors out of their money and lives?" Dean cleared his throat. "And if that's the case, he may have helped kill his own mother without even knowing it."

"Then it is possible Billy Orphan is also involved in the Black Belt Killer murders."

"Whoa." The back of Dean's head fell back against the brass headboard. "Where did that come from?"

CHAPTER FORTY-TWO

Marti fanned K.A.'s scrapbook pages of deadly accomplishments, sending puffs of air Dean's way. She stopped at the page she was looking for. Accumulating clues to solve a crime was like assembling interlocking jigsaw puzzle pieces together until a revealing picture formed, without the aid of a box-top depiction.

"From this point on," Marti said, using her finger as a bookmark, "the articles are about the Black Belt Killer and his victims. I didn't count, but there have to be dozens of items about men strangled with their own black belts. What is really amazing is that none of the articles provides clues to the killer's identity or description." She handed the book to Dean. "No clues until now. Either K.A. is an ardent admirer of the Black Belt Killer, or he is the Black Belt Killer."

Dean turned the pages, scanning the headlines. The Black Belt Killer moniker stuck after the third killing. If possible, K.A. was even more dangerous than they thought.

"I wonder if K.A.'s partner knows that he's the Black Belt Killer." Marti turned the page. "Remember, that movie that came out a couple of years ago? *The Three Faces of Eve.* It was based on a true story about a woman with multiple personalities. They were all veiled from each other. What if K.A., the killer for hire, doesn't know about K.A., the psychological murderer? Or...what if K.A. killed Billy and assumed his identity?"

"Interesting takes. If Dr. Freud was here right now, I don't think he could answer any of your questions."

"Okay," Marti said, "here's something out of the realm of logic. K.A. is a master at disguising who he really is. He leaves no clues, and simply vanishes. Without this scrapbook, no one would know anything about his childhood history, his obvious infatuation with killing people, or the Black Belt Killer's highlights. Why would he keep such an incriminating book that could lead to him getting caught?"

"These pages are his resume of kills." Dean held up the scrapbook. "K.A.'s autobiography, a vehicle to give him fame and notoriety after he dies. What if, deep down, K.A. knows he's eventually going to get caught? Even deeper in his subconscious, he wants to get caught. The scrapbook is his most prized possession, not unlike an Oscar to an actor or a Most Valuable Player award to an athlete."

Marti shuddered. "At least he doesn't know how to find us."

Dean flicked a fingernail against the scrapbook cover as if it was worthless then gave Marti a reassuring squeeze. K.A. knew damn well that Dean was staying at Aunt Maddy's house. And now, the killer knew that a dark-haired woman swiped his most valued possessions. If K.A. had not figured out that Dean and Marti were a team, he would soon. K.A. wouldn't hesitate to return to San Francisco and finish the job. Unless K.A. was caught, they would be in danger for the rest of their lives.

"Marti, the scrapbook and ledger of The Billy Orphan Foundation victims are worth more than a mountain of gold to K.A. In contrast, these scrapbooks have no monetary value to us, but they represent power over K.A. that no one else has ever had. He would do anything to get them back. Maybe even negotiate."

"How do you negotiate with someone we can't even find?"

"I have a hunch where K.A. may be heading next."

"Is this a baseball thing?" She curled a finger under his chin. "A competition for you? You're treating this just like a game, Dean. The man is a murderer—a murderer of many people. The prudent and safest thing to do now is to contact the police, give them the books and information, and let them track this maniac down."

"K.A. is on a mission to erase everybody and everything connected to him and the charity. By the time the police get their act together, K.A. will be long gone and his cronies dead. I'll call the police after we track him down."

"Aunt Madeline never mentioned you were so hardheaded." Marti leaned forward ready to spring from the bed. "What are we waiting for? Where is our next stop?"

"Hold on. What's inside the suitcase you brought from his closet?"

"I have no idea," she said. "It's locked."

"I may have a remedy for that."

* * * * *

Sitting before Dean and Marti was K.A.'s undersized suitcase. Dean inserted the small key from K.A.'s key ring into the centered lock and twisted a half turn. Then his thumb touched the latch pushbutton.

"Wait," Marti said, jumping off the bed. "What if this is another K.A. trick, like that vicious cat? Maybe there is a bomb inside. Or poisonous gas."

"You found this suitcase hidden with the scrapbook, which means the contents are valuable. At least they have value to K.A. Maybe it holds a bunch of money."

"What if it is a human head?" Marti flinched when the latch clicked opened. "Bones. Or a collection of bloody belts..."

Dean lifted the lid in slow increments, just in case Marti's first instinct was correct. Neither one of them was prepared for the shock of the contents revealed.

"Holy sparkling greenbacks!" Marti grabbed a handful of loose diamonds and rare coins sitting on top of sectioned bundles of hundreds, fifties, and twenties. "This is not a suitcase, it's a bank vault. Your inheritance, Dean. And then some."

"Maybe a small portion of it. This money also belongs to the other families duped by The Billy Orphan Foundation, starting with the people listed in K.A.'s ledger."

"You're right, of course." She held a diamond up to the light. "K.A. likely stole the diamonds from someone he killed. At least your share should be enough to refurbish the floors and get Aunt Madeline's house out of hock. That is if we get back in time."

"I'm willing to roll the dice that we will. Are you?"

"There is no talking you out of going after K.A., is there?" she said. "And you accused me of never listening to your sage advice. Okay, I go where you go. Which is where?"

"We are heading to the biggest little city in the world," Dean said. "But this time, we'll take a page from K.A's playbook."

CHAPTER FORTY-THREE

The whirling ceiling fan in the post office lobby did little to stifle Reno's afternoon summer heat. Dean leaned a shoulder into the wall to ease the strain on his legs from standing for so long. He yawned behind his *Reno Gazette* held up to hide his face. Rows of metal boxes ran from one end to the other of the opposite wall. He had been monitoring P.O. Box 143 through pinholes in the paper. To spy on an inanimate object was more draining than playing defense behind a wild pitcher who couldn't find home plate with a map.

He turned back to the front page and re-read the article about last night's gas tank explosion in Charity. The Billy Orphan Foundation and Ida's Grocery Store had disappeared in the blast, along with Ida, daughter Peggy, and brother Elbie. The poor family never knew what hit them. Until K.A. was apprehended, anyone linked to The Billy Orphan Foundation was in peril, including Dean and Marti.

The newspaper shielding Dean's face wasn't his only disguise. A crusty old baseball hat from the Ford's trunk covered his head. A fake Clark Gable-like mustache irritated his upper lip. The masquerade was not for Billy Orphan's benefit, or whoever showed up to collect the mail. His veiled appearance provided a form of protection. Better to spot K.A. first before the assassin recognized him.

Twice, K.A. had missed killing Dean by inches and K.A. had shot a barrage of bullets, albeit poorly, at Marti. The killer's motivation to eliminate them would intensify if he knew they possessed his ledger of kills, scrapbook, and money from the cabin closet.

A car horn toot caught Dean's attention. He turned the paper towards the front door then relaxed. False alarm. Marti had positioned the Ford to view the post office entrance. They had agreed that two consecutive beeps would warn Dean that someone K.A.'s height and build, male or female, was entering the post office.

Dean turned his attention back to the P.O. Box and smiled.

Marti's disguise consisted of sunglasses and a cheap blonde wig purchased from a five and dime store. Her scarf held down the wig, with only flaxen bangs showing.

Dean rotated his head to stay loose, just like he would on a ball field. So far, none of the postal clerks had paid attention to his presence. The edges of the newspaper were wet from his sweaty fingertips. Five people were visible including one clerk. If K.A. entered the building, Dean would have no choice but to pounce on him. Yet he had to be mindful not to put others in danger. K.A. had killed dozens of people for The Billy Orphan Foundation and dozens more as The Black Belt Killer. The psychopath would not hesitate to slaughter every person in the building.

At the counter, an attractive young woman in a Harold's Club dealer's outfit paid her postage fee with a silver dollar. Several Reno casinos used silver dollars in lieu of one-dollar chips. Gambling, along with prostitution, was legal in some parts of Nevada. Little did the individuals inside this post office realize they were gambling with their lives just by being here.

Two beeps sounded. Dean recognized the Ford's horn. His muscles tensed. He removed his shoulder from the wall and turned towards the front entrance again.

The door swung open. A man hurried into the lobby and went directly to the wall of P.O. boxes. He wore a brown suit, tie, and a wide-brimmed fedora pulled low over his forehead. He was beyond skinny. Pasty white cheeks enhanced the frail look. Thick glasses straddled a needle nose that stood out like a hood ornament. The man's face could have been a Halloween mask, except that all the parts were genuine. Would K.A.'s masquerade mastery ever have drawn this much attention to himself?

Dean lowered the paper. Marti had double-honked for another reason. Even with the hat covering most of the man's forehead, Dean recognized an older version of one of the boys in the picture from K.A.'s scrapbook—the one referred to as Billy, as in Billy Orphan.

Billy turned the knob of the combination lock on P. O. Box 143 back and forth, pulled open the door, and removed a handful of mail and yellow postal slips. After closing the door and giving the knob a final twist, he moved swiftly to a waiting clerk behind the counter.

Dean edged closer behind Billy Orphan. Billy nodded when the clerk said hello. The clerk received the notices without saying another word then disappeared through a back door. How many times per week, for how many years, had these two men met like this? It seemed odd that they did not exchange verbal pleasantries.

Billy examined envelopes before stuffing them into the inner left pocket of his coat. With his left hand, he pulled from his right pocket an addressed envelope that had a blue four cent stamp highlighting the fifty year Arctic Explorations of 1909—the same stamp advertised on a wall poster.

Dean couldn't make out the handwritten name or address on the envelope. The contents intrigued him just as much. The clerk returned and placed two boxes on the counter without much exertion. Were the boxes filled with checks and Billy Orphan Foundation forms from the Gumption Gap Post Office? Billy slid the letter to the clerk and lifted the boxes.

Dean started for the counter. He stopped halfway. Interfering with United States mail was a punishable offense—unless you were the postmaster in the town of Gumption Gap. Billy was having trouble holding the stacked boxes with one hand and opening the front door. Dean sidled past him and held the door open for him.

"T-t-thank you," Billy offered in an alto voice, without looking at Dean.

Dean acknowledged him with a nod. Ah, so Billy didn't converse with the clerk because of his stutter. Dean once had a teammate who stuttered. He was a highly intelligent kid who never stammered when calling for a fly ball or singing along to a song in a bar.

Dean tailed Billy to a blue Buick with whitewall tires. Billy placed the boxes in a huge trunk then headed to the driver's side door. Marti straightened up from behind the steering wheel when she saw Dean hustling back to the Ford. He settled into the passenger seat and pointed at the Buick.

"Follow that car," he said, placing both hands on the dashboard.

"Just like in the movies." Marti fired up the Ford's engine. "Next you are supposed to say that you'll pay for all of my tickets."

"That will be a bus ticket if you don't get going."

Marti tailed Billy's Buick, lagging behind by about ten car lengths. Dean turned to look through the back window. No one was following them. Once again, K.A. had pulled the unexpected by not showing up.

CHAPTER FORTY-FOUR

ean pushed the doorbell and took one step back on the cement front porch to stand next to Marti. He stared at Billy Orphan's black rubber doormat while his fingertips touched his upper lip minus the fake mustache. The mat offered no word of "Welcome".

Marti had followed Billy's Buick LeSabre to his Nevada home in a suburban neighborhood of scattered houses and vacant lots west of downtown Reno. The window drapes of the gray, A-frame house were drawn tight as if it was night time, yet several hours of daylight remained. The front yard, landscaped with small round rocks surrounded hardy plant life that could withstand extreme weather. A black mailbox with painted white address numbers was attached to a post embedded in dirt close to the road.

Dean pivoted to face the street, expecting to catch someone spying—specifically K.A. Unless K.A. had turned himself into a tree, they were not being observed. Dean shook his head and focused on the front door again. He had guessed wrong about K.A. resurfacing at the Reno Post Office and now at Billy Orphan's home.

A twinge of discomfort settled in Dean's stomach. The pangs in his gut were from instinct, not hunger, as the lingering fear that K.A. would launch an attack wouldn't go away.

Hard soled footsteps sounded inside. Dean stared in silence at the solid wood door's peephole. Obviously, Billy had heard the doorbell ring. If he looked out he would see two strangers on his porch.

Marti patted her dark hair. She switched the ledger to her left hand and reached for the doorbell. Dean corralled her slim right wrist before her forefinger made contact.

"Wait," he whispered. "He knows we're here. Let's see what he does."

They heard metal scraping metal from inside. Had Billy latched the chain lock? A not-so-subtle message. His footsteps faded to the right. Was he moving to the other room to sneak a peek through the closed curtains? If so, it wouldn't do him any good. The porch was hidden from the window and Marti had parked the car two blocks away. Billy's sightline would be limited to a portion of the front yard and scattered trees in an otherwise empty lot across the street.

"Plan B." Dean took Marti's hand and moved past a closed garage door to the side gate. He reached over the top to unlatch the bolt. "If Billy has an attack dog, run back through the gate opening and close it."

"What about you?"

"I've always had good rapport with man's best friend," he said.

"I like it better when we do things together."

"Will there ever be a time that you will just listen to me?"

"I always listen to you," she said. "Listening and doing are two different things."

Dean pushed open the gate. Backyard treetops towered over the roof. He stopped at the side door leading to the garage. If Billy had a guard dog, the mutt was either hard of hearing, in the one-car garage, or in the house. The doorknob wouldn't budge. He removed a plastic Texaco gas credit card from his wallet and slid it between the door and latch until the doorknob turned.

"A little trick Harry taught me," Dean whispered. "He probably learned it from watching *Richard Diamond, Private Detective* on television."

They left the side door open to provide light into the garage. Billy's Buick was centered in the middle. Dean found the door to the house unlocked. They entered a semi-dark kitchen. The stuffy house needed a good airing out. Faint music came from another room. Marti followed him through a dining room big enough for only a four-person table. He stopped at the front door entryway overlooking a sparsely furnished living room. A black and white cat lying on the couch lifted its head then continued its nap.

The hallway to their left probably led to bedrooms where the classical music played. They took slow, cautious steps down the hall. Dean stopped at a door and inched it open far enough to see into the unoccupied, brightly lit room.

Marti held onto his arm as they entered the room. Covering the wall behind a metal desk hung plaques and framed award certificates honoring The Billy Orphan Foundation for its philanthropic efforts. Two binders were stacked on the desktop between scattered accounting papers, a phone, and an adding machine. File cabinets lined the wall, along with a bookcase containing labeled binders. Both boxes from the post office were open and on the floor next to the desk chair.

A small table behind the desk held a hi-fi record player. Dean turned it off. Billy's home doubled as his office.

"Who are you?" Billy demanded from the doorway brandishing a large pistol pointed at Dean's chest. "And why d-d-did you break into my house?"

Dean stepped in front of Marti, shielding her from the long barrel. The gun looked too big for Billy's small hand. Billy had shed his brown coat, tie, and hat. Without the coat his white-shirted torso appeared even more emaciated. Overhead lights drew attention to his forehead and its blue birthmark the shape of Lake Tahoe's lake.

"We've traveled a long way to meet you, Billy," Dean said. "Put your Wyatt Earp six-shooter down so we can talk."

"No," Billy said. "T-tell me what you want? You've broken into the wrong place if you are looking for money."

"We're not after money, Billy." Marti moved towards him offering a sweet smile.

Billy's features bunched further in confusion. He inched back. Marti's smile could make a store mannequin whistle, but with Billy it had the reverse effect. His reaction was understandable. How many attractive women had ever responded that way to him?

"My name is Dean Mason. This pretty lady is Marti Cooper. Your birth mother was my aunt and Marti's godmother. Her name was Madeline Principal."

"Bunk." The gun barrel bobbed up and down. "We are not related. I am an orphan for criminy sakes. I'll shoot you if you don't t-t-tell me why you're here."

Dean's eyes zeroed in on the shaky gun. Billy was left-handed just like Aunt Maddy. Was the gun loaded? Most likely not, but Dean was reluctant to test his assumption.

"In the hospital," Dean said, "before you were named Billy Orphan, the staff referred to you as The Birthmark Baby after you were found in a Reno bus station bathroom."

Billy glared at Dean through thick lenses. He rubbed a finger under his nose then pushed the gun in Dean's direction again.

"Billy, you also have a blue birthmark on your stomach," Marti said. "We know this because it was written in your mother's diary. To the day she died, your mother regretted giving you up."

No words came out of Billy's open mouth. He lowered the gun. Tears fell underneath his glasses. He wiped his cheeks and nose with a shirt sleeve, fighting to catch his breath.

"What else did she write in her d-d-diary? Please. I need to know."

CHAPTER FORTY-FIVE

A leafy tree across the street from Billy Orphan's house had camouflaged K.A.—a perfect vantage point to monitor Billy's porch. He watched the ballplayer and dark-haired female accomplice carry his ledger. Unknowingly, they had done him a great favor.

A portion of the front curtain had inched open for a few seconds, exposing part of the ugly little bastard's face. The couple had waited several minutes before venturing past the gate to the side door to the garage. Would a surprised Billy yell "hel...hel...help" when he discovered two strangers in his house? Then again, what if Billy saw them first and called the sheriff? That would foil K.A.'s plan.

"First they tracked me down," K.A. muttered. "Now, they're after Billy. Why?"

K.A. lowered his binoculars. The stuttering nerd was as much of a recluse as K.A. How did the ballplayer and that woman know to come to Reno? And how did they discover where Billy lived?

"Fuzzy, the postmaster in Gumption Gap," he whispered, making a snapping sound with his fingers. "Then they must have staked out the post office in downtown Reno. They're good, but not good enough."

A sharp twig poking K.A.'s side began to hurt. He repositioned himself on the branch. The dark-haired woman had stolen everything he valued most in life: The Billy Orphan Foundation ledger of kills, a suitcase full of money, and a scrapbook that would be as good as a confession identifying K.A. as the Black Belt Killer. They would probably keep the cash and diamonds for themselves and turn over the books to the G-men. Who would the feds believe—a man who does not exist or the do-gooder couple?

Gusts of wind fluttered the tree's outer branches, producing massive clapping from thousands of nature's little hands. K.A. plucked a dry leaf from a branch and squished it in his hand. His fingers spread open allowing the dead foliage to fall. He had failed to eliminate the postmaster by a few lousy minutes. His Jeep had barely missed hitting the ballplayer in San Francisco by mere inches. And none of the wild bullets he had fired at the woman connected. His timing had been off, or maybe it was bad luck. But now his fortune and timing were about to change for the better. He could not only kill Billy, he could eliminate all three. Most hick deputy sheriffs would have a difficult time figuring out a "who-killed-who-first" crime scene of dead bodies when a fourth person simply disappeared without leaving evidence, or was never there. A good plan. But first he would have to wait and see if a deputy's car showed up.

A bird landed on an upper branch. K.A. removed the gun from his pocket and spun a replenished chamber full of bullets. The Reno gun store owner had demonstrated how to load the gun and work the safety. K.A. repaid the owner's kindness by shooting him dead with his own bullets. What choice did he have? The owner could have identified him.

K.A. snapped the gun's chamber back into place. The slight noise caused the bird to fly away. Unlike the bird, Billy and his visitors would not hear K.A.'s advance.

* * * * *

Dean's Adam's apple jutted in and out as Billy opened a drawer to his desk and withdrew a fifth of Old Grand-Dad. Dean gritted his teeth, craving something he could no longer have. Not now, not ever. His hands trembled.

Billy poured several shots into a glass. He gulped down most of the whiskey then nodded to Marti to continue her summary of his mother's diary.

The distinct aroma of Billy's drink, real or imagined, found Dean's nose. He closed his eyes for a moment, and felt a burning sensation from throat to chest. His hands formed tight fists. Marti slipped her arm through his. Maybe she had seen her father go through similar spasms. The shakes would eventually go away, but the urge to inject alcohol into his system would always be there.

"Why would she abandon me?" Billy said.

"After you were born, Billy," Marti said, still holding Dean's arm, "your mother believed you would have a better chance in life with someone else. She knew she was an alcoholic who, at times, could not give proper care to a baby."

"By the way, you are not the only orphan in this room," Dean said. "When my parents were killed, your mother took me in. I realize now, Aunt Maddy assumed responsibility for me because of you. I never understood what drove her to drink until Marti found the diary. I watched her fight a losing battle. No matter how hard she tried, she couldn't get off the booze. Our family, meaning your mother, me, and obviously you, too, Billy were born with a weakness for alcohol."

"You t-too?" Billy's eyes questioned Dean.

"Big time, cuz."

"But you're normal looking. Why—"

"A weakness is a weakness," Marti said. "There aren't any beauty contest winners for alcoholism. Just losers."

"Easy for you t-to say. You are pretty. I look in the mirror and see ugliness like everyone else sees. No one wanted me as a child. Nothing changed as an adult. T-that's why my office is in my home. The less I go out, the better. People stare. Or look away, repulsed."

"Your mother hired a private detective to find you." Marti said. "The detective's report ended with you perishing in an orphanage fire. She didn't believe the report. She knew, in her heart, that you were still alive, Billy. Only a mother would have that feeling."

Billy plopped down onto the chair behind the desk, his gaze glued to the floor like a ballplayer who just made a bonehead play to lose a game. His fingers sneaked beneath his glasses to rub his eyes.

Dean swiped a hand over dry lips. They had just unloaded a whole lot of shit on Billy. Unfortunately, his cousin's compost pile was about to become much larger.

"How did you find me?" Billy looked up at Dean.

"By investigating The Billy Orphan Foundation."

"Are you the police?"

"No, we are not the police."

"Th-then why were you investigating the charity?"

"For starters, try fraud, grand theft, murder—"

"Murder? Fraud?" He shook his head. "You're crazy. The foundation is legitimate. Bunk. A bunch of bunk. I was starting to believe you."

"Who is the person responsible for the operation of The Billy Orphan Foundation?" Dean asked, peering down at the open cardboard boxes by Billy's feet.

"I am, of course." Billy lifted the glass to his lips, shifted his view to Marti and placed the glass on the desk.

"We are aware a man named K.A. sends you donation checks from Charity."

"Who? No, no, you are wrong. Tyler Wilkes sends me the donations. You have the wrong guy."

"Tyler Wilkes goes by a pseudonym of K.A," Marti said. "We don't know what the initials stand for. Or what Tyler's role is in the foundation."

"Tyler oversees the office in Charity, as well as other d-donation sites. I can't be in all places at once. Is Tyler in some kind of t-trouble?"

"What do you do with the donation checks that you receive from Tyler?" Dean asked.

"Deposit each check into the charity's bank account here in Reno." Billy pointed to the binders and folders. "Every penny is accounted for. I'm a numbers person. D-do the work of five people. Ninety-seven percent of the money I receive goes proportionally to almost every orphanage in the United States. T-t-three per-percent is for overhead – my salary and expenses. The charity is my life. No one knows more about how d-difficult it is to be an orphan than me."

Dean studied Billy's expression. No giveaways like a wrinkled brow, hesitation, facial tics, blinking, lip or hand movement. Yet, Billy had lied. Perhaps, it was someone else's lie.

"How does Tyler get paid?

"Ohhhh." Billy's pale cheeks reddened. "Is that what this is about? Tyler keeps all the cash we receive to pay for the work he does for the charity. He'd steal most of it anyway. But I don't t-think

Tyler cares much about money."

"Why would you employ someone who would steal from you?" Marti asked.

"We made a pact."

"You keep saying we," Dean said. "Does that mean you and Tyler? No one else?"

"Chub. He's like an older brother; the only person who could ever control Tyler. Chub created the concept of sending d-d-donations to one organization to benefit a number of the orphanages. And it was Chub's idea to attract d-donors by combining my name with Tyler's boyhood picture. Chub said naming the charity The Billy Orphan Foundation was so hokey, people would t-think it had to be legitimate. Chub was right. It worked like magic. Money poured in right from the start."

Dean's shakes were stabilized by unleashed adrenaline. He put his palms flat on the desk and leaned towards his cousin.

"What was in the envelope you mailed today at the post office?" Dean asked.

"How did you know...Oh, of course. You were spying on me at the post office. I sent a list of names and addresses of the d-donors to Chub, along with an accounting of how all the money is distributed. Their bookkeepers can audit what I do that way. It's all on the up and up. Legitimate."

"Billy, we've got some bad news for you," Dean said, stabbing a ledger sheet with his finger.

CHAPTER FORTY-SIX

Billy scowled at the photograph taken out of K.A.'s scrapbook then sent it skidding across the desk back towards Dean as if it was tainted. Marti corralled the picture before it stopped moving.

"Do you remember having that picture taken, Billy?" Dean asked.

"You d-d-don't do me any favors by showing me old pictures of myself. They gave me the last name of Orphan because I was too ugly for any mother to k-k-keep."

Marti bit her lower lip. Dean touched a callus on his palm with a fingertip. He also felt sorry for Billy, but with reservations. Billy might have grimaced at the photo of himself and K.A. for another reason. What if the picture brought back orphanage memories Billy wanted to block out? Just how involved or clueless was Dean's cousin in the transgressions K.A. committed before and after the founding of The Billy Orphan Foundation?

"Do you recall posing with K.A., ah Tyler Wilkes, for that photo?" Dean repeated.

"Of course. It was t-t-taken at Uncle Pete's Orphan Sanctuary for Boys. Uncle Pete was a sadistic man. He abused the boys, especially Chub. That picture was t-taken after Tyler smashed Uncle Pete's head with an ax. It was gruesome, blood all over the porch, but Pete d-deserved it. The boys cheered Tyler like a hero."

"Did you know Tyler was going to kill Uncle Pete?" Dean studied Billy's face.

"No one knew what Tyler was ever going to do. Not even Chub."

"Who took the picture?"

"Chub. With Uncle Pete's camera. The camera Uncle Pete used to t-take filthy pictures of the boys. Where d-did you get that photo?"

"We found it in Tyler's scrapbook. What happened after you posed with Tyler?"

"Chub and I took off after he snapped more shots. Tyler stayed to t-t-take care of the boys. He caught up with us later."

"Tyler took care of them, all right," Marti said. "He set fire to the orphanage with the orphans locked inside."

"Tyler would not do that. Tyler's mean, but he would not k-kill the other boys."

An outside noise made Dean's limbs stiffen. He turned to the window expecting to catch sight of K.A. A tree rustled against Billy's window. The breeze outside had picked up. Dean relaxed. Any unexpected sound readied him for action.

"Brace yourself, Billy," Dean said. "Tyler not only murdered Uncle Pete and the orphan boys, he has been killing people who invested millions of dollars in The Billy Orphan Foundation. That's why we are investigating your charity."

"Investing? K-killing? Billy jumped up from his chair. "You can't prove it."

"Not only can we prove it, you can help us."

Marti placed K.A.'s ledger in front of Billy. She opened the cover to page one and aimed a polished fingernail at the first name. Billy peered up at her with deep lines of confusion on his face.

"We found this ledger hidden in Tyler's cabin," Dean said. "Each person on this list donated money to The Billy Orphan Foundation. Then they were persuaded to invest much larger amounts in the foundation. If you are as good as you say you are with facts and figures, your accounting files will verify the names, dates, and how much money they donated. The first name is Doris Edelstein. Look up her donation history in your records."

Billy brought the binder labeled E back to the desk. It didn't take him long to find Doris Edelstein's name. The page was half full of twenty-dollar contributions. Her last donation was dated May 17, 1955.

"Over four years since she donated money to the charity," Dean said. "The reason? K.A. murdered her on the third of August of the same year."

"T-that doesn't prove anything. If she died, it's a coincidence. She was old."

"Look up the rest of the names. You will discover the pattern is more than a coincidence. Most, if not all, of these donors stopped sending money to the foundation after a history of mailing in payments. Instead, they became investors in The Billy Orphan Foundation."

The stack of binders on the desk grew as Billy compared investor names from K.A.'s ledger to the binders full of donor names. He nodded as if he knew them personally. Finally, he pushed the binder aside and blew out a bothered breath.

"What d-do the check marks by the names mean?" Billy asked.

"The check marks indicate the investor is dead at the hands of Tyler Wilkes," Dean said. "Tyler is a creative, insane killer with no conscience. He made the investor deaths appear to be accidents or suicides."

"I just can't believe t-that."

"Unfortunately, the facts we're presenting to you get worse." Marti flipped through the ledger pages until she found the right one. Her finger moved to line nine. "Madeline Principal was your mother and Dean's aunt. I'm sorry, Billy."

"Tyler ki-ki-killed my mother?" Billy choked out.

"Tyler didn't know Madeline Principal was your mother," Dean said. "If you don't believe us, call the San Francisco Police Department and ask for Detective Lynch. He will tell you Madeline Principal either committed suicide by jumping off her third floor nursing home balcony or she accidentally fell. You will get a similar story with each name check marked in the ledger, but the common thread is they are all dead."

Billy's fingertips traced his mother's printed name. Dean could only imagine what thoughts were bouncing around in Billy's head after learning the truth about his mother and Tyler Wilkes. Billy looked as if he was in extreme pain.

"My Aunt Maddy also donated money to other orphan organizations," Dean said. "Maybe it was her way of trying to reach you. Last January, someone from The Billy Orphan Foundation persuaded her to invest almost nine hundred thousand dollars in your charity. She was led to believe the interest from investment principal would go to me after she passed. In truth, once she died, the money stayed in the charity coffers. Your mother was duped, Billy. She was promised one thing, but the small print in the contract said something different. Were you the person who persuaded Madeline to invest her life's savings with The Billy Orphan Foundation?"

"Me?" Billy shook a fist at Dean. "You are d-d-daft. I want people to contribute to orphan welfare, not to make money for d-donors. We give away almost every red cent of the contributions we receive. My records prove it."

"Whether you realize it or not," Dean said, "The Billy Orphan Foundation has two different divisions. One is for donations. The other is an investment program."

"Bunk." Billy peered down at the ledger. "I would know if people invested in my foundation."

"You may run a reputable business helping orphans, Billy, but you are connected to fraud and murder whether you know it or not. Someone from The Billy Orphan Foundation ingeniously preys on the elderly for their life's savings. If you're not the person who convinced the people in this ledger to invest in your charity, then who did?"

"D-don't know."

"Sure you do," Dean said. "Is it Tyler Wilkes?"

"No," Billy said in a weak voice.

"Then who is it?"

"It could only be Chub." Billy shook his head.

"What is Chub's real name?"

"Quincy Nash. He has a brilliant mind."

"Brilliant in a dastardly way," Dean said. "Quincy Nash had the foresight to incorporate the killing talents of Tyler Wilkes, first with Uncle Pete, then with the charity's investors. Nash manipulated you to run a legitimate foundation. On the surface it seems like a perfect plan: You devote all of your time and energy to assist orphans and orphanages while Nash takes care of all the sticky government red tape and public interaction. You probably thought Nash was doing you a service by handling the foundation phone calls because of your stutter."

Billy nodded.

"Quincy Nash used you to shield the foundation's corrupt corporate component. He used the lists of donor names you mailed to him to create an inventory of potential investors. Once a donor became an investor, they weren't long for this world."

Billy gazed at his drink before slugging it down. He ogled the bottle, but picked up the ledger instead and waved it at Dean.

"I helped k-kill my own mother." Billy placed his gun in the Jim Beam drawer.

"Tyler Wilkes and Quincy Nash killed your mother, Billy," Marti said. "Not you."

"Marti's right. You have devoted your life to helping other orphans. Aunt Maddy would have been proud of her son." Dean moved to the side of the desk and picked up the phone receiver. "Borrow your phone, cousin?"

"Who are you calling?" Marti asked, after Billy nodded his consent.

"A woman from my past." Dean dialed '0' under Marti's watchful eye. "But first I need to speak to Harry. In the meantime, enlighten Billy as to the real identity of the notorious Black Belt Killer."

Harry Spitari answered the operator's call on the first ring with a cheery hello.

"Been waiting for your call, Dream. I have most of the answers to your questions, and then some. For starters, Samantha from the nursing home is dirty. Did you ever wonder how a nursing home general manager could afford to drive a brand new Cadillac, shop at Saks Fifth Avenue, and have a house in the Marina district?"

"She told me her parents were wealthy," Dean said.

"Actually, Samantha is an orphan. She has her hands in a number of cookie jars filled with green dough. She hustles her vendors for cash on the side so they can keep their accounts. Samantha is also involved in the Billy Orphan scam, but indirectly. She provides NAHPRO CORPORATION confidential background information on her patients under the guise of potential client lists for insurance companies. Most likely, other nursing home managers make the same data available for a price."

Dean shook his head in disgust. Samantha was one shady lady. He recalled the night she had phoned him at Aunt Maddy's house after he had seen her earlier at the nursing home. Sam's lure of seduction hadn't been a ploy meant to negotiate a refund for the unused months on Aunt Madeline's one year advance room payment. Sam didn't want him investigating the crooked dealings she was involved in.

"Sam will be looking for a new job when I get back to The City," Dean said.

"When will that be?" Harry asked. "And where the hell are you this time?"

"26 Yosemite Drive in Reno, Nevada. Standing next to me is Billy Orphan, Aunt Maddy's son and my cousin. You may have come to that conclusion already."

"I figured Madeline's bastard baby could still be alive since two or three boys escaped the orphanage fire," Harry said, after a throaty cough. "But the odds were that he didn't. Just so you know, the surname Orphan is not that uncommon throughout the continental United States."

"Thanks for the census lesson, Harry. You should have told me about your investigation."

"It was for your own good, kid. Listen, life is too short to stew over the small stuff."

"You are in too good a mood, Harry. And you didn't complain about my person-to-person phone call. Did you hit a big one at the track?"

Harry's silence was serenaded by soft static over the line.

"Daily double," Harry said. "Long shots."

"Congratulations. Now you can pay for our trip to Nevada."

"In your dreams, Dream. You still owe me a percentage of your inheritance."

"A percentage of nothing is...well, you do the math, Harry. I need Valerie Dotson's phone number. Dotson is her maiden name. You will have to look up her married name."

"Way ahead of you," Harry said. "She now goes by Valerie Johnson. Will give you her number in a second. First, let me hit you with the lowdown on NAHPRO. As I originally suspected, NAHPRO is part of a conglomerate of businesses."

"Is there one principal's name linked to NAHPRO and the other businesses?"

"Quincy Nash. On paper, Mr. Nash is worth big, as in enormous, bucks."

"Quincy Nash is the third orphan along with my cousin Billy, and Tyler Wilkes. Tyler torched the orphanage and is now the assassin who kills The Billy Orphan Foundation investors."

"Are you saying Cousin Billy is part of the corruption?" Harry asked.

"No, just the opposite. Cousin Billy is a fine humanitarian. But Nash is so dirty no self-respecting pig would allow him into his sty."

"Here's what you don't know about Quincy Nash, Dream. He is also—"

"Dean!" Panic permeated Marti's voice.

Dean clapped a hand over his free ear. Holy shit. Did he hear Harry correctly?

"Can you repeat what you just said, Harry? It sounded like—"

"Dean!" Marti pointed to the doorway.

K.A. had a short-barreled gun aimed at Billy.

"Hang up the phone, ballplayer," K.A. ordered. "This game is over."

CHAPTER FORTY-SEVEN

Dean followed K.A.'s command and returned the phone to its base, cradling the receiver without disconnecting the call. K.A. stepped inside the room. His gun sights shifted from Billy to Dean, the person he probably deemed most equal to taking him on. Marti moved to stand next to Dean. Three against one, the numbers were in the good team's favor, except K.A. was the one with the gun.

K.A.'s handsome, choirboy face belied his madness. He wore Levi's and a white T-shirt that revealed a sculpted but brawny physique like a gymnast. His short blond hair was neatly combed to the side. He wore nothing to camouflage his appearance. No wig, facial hair, glasses or makeup to hide his real image—a sign he had no intention of leaving witnesses. The son of a bitch was enjoying the moment like a cat playing with its prey before the kill. How long would the cat stay entertained before losing interest in his game?

Dean leaned into Marti's side trying to move her out of harm's way. She wouldn't budge. K.A. produced a tight-lipped smile. Was he amused? Or annoyed?

Dean's eyes followed K.A.'s every move. How had K.A. known they would visit Billy? Dean was positive his car had not been followed from the post office. A coincidence? K.A. always seemed to be one step ahead.

"Long time no see, Billy," K.A. said with a nod. "Actually, I've been watching you for years, not that you ever noticed me."

"Why d-did you come here, Tyler?"

"Have you been listening? I go by K.A. now. Your two new friends stole that ledger from me, along with a suitcase and scrapbook. I want everything back."

"Can you believe this guy, Billy?" Dean's voice was louder than normal. "A murdering thief is accusing us of stealing from him. There's only one reason we are still alive. K.A. doesn't know where we put the scrapbook that highlights the history of his kills.

Or the suitcase filled with cash and diamonds stolen from people he murdered."

"Don't look so smug," K.A. said to Dean. "Everything is in your car trunk."

Years of baseball's highs and lows had taught Dean to maintain a stoic expression. Inside, however, he berated himself. How did K.A. know where he stored the scrapbook and money? Had it been a lucky guess? Their lives may depend on the answer to that question.

Dean resisted the urge to look at Billy's phone on the desk. If Harry could decipher the dialogue from his end of the line, he would call the police from his other phone. If not, they were sinking faster into a pit of deep shit quicksand.

"Losing your touch, K.A.?" Marti squared her shoulders. "Or maybe you are not as sharp as we thought you were. We knew you would come here to kill Billy. That is why we hid your scrapbook and money in places you would never find. Otherwise, there would be no room for negotiation."

Dean swallowed hard. Marti was one clever and ballsy lady. But K.A. was not a coward like the greaser-hood Boyd Weber at Freddy's bar. K.A. killed without conscience. If she pushed him too hard with her bluff, the results could become more ugly quickly.

"I don't negotiate." K.A. re-aimed his gun at Billy. "I eliminate."

Ho shit. Dean's heart thumped like a tom-tom. Billy thrust his hands out in front of him as if they could deflect a bullet. Marti had miscalculated in trying to bargain with an assassin.

"Not a smart move, K.A." Dean snatched the ledger from the desk. "The lady called it right. You're predictable. You see, only Marti knows where the money is hidden. And I'm the only one privy to the location of your scrapbook that reveals your murderous activities. We also wrote a letter describing your real appearance along with your disguises. If you harm one of us, the letter, money, and scrapbook will be soon be public knowledge. You won't be able to show your face anywhere, altered or otherwise."

"Listen to him, Tyler," Billy pleaded.

"Shut up, stammer mouth," K.A. responded.

BOOM. K.A. fired his gun. The bullet hit one of The Billy Orphan Foundation wall plaques behind Billy. Stunned, no one moved. Dean couldn't tell if K.A. missed Billy on purpose. Or maybe K.A. was a bad shot like had Marti had said. How could Dean stop K.A. from pulling the trigger again?

"We're at a Mexican standoff," Dean said. "Meaning, no one wins. Think about it, K.A. By killing us, you would actually be hurting yourself. We're offering you a way out if you're willing to compromise."

"Compromise?" Puzzled lines wrinkled K.A.'s face. "A way out? I'm holding the gun, spaz brain."

Dean released a silent breath. He suppressed another urge to peek at the phone. Did Harry call the police? If so, how long would it take for a squad car to arrive? Stalling was not a strategy often practiced in baseball, a sport that doesn't use a clock. But in this game, he was playing for time.

"Which item is more important to you?" Dean said, knowing the answer to his question. "The money or the scrapbook? We aren't going to give you both."

"You're in no position to bargain." K.A.'s idle hand formed a fist.

"Wrong," Marti said. "The items we removed from your cabin are insurance."

"Like life insurance?" K.A. grunted out a laugh. "There's a flaw in your policy. Life insurance doesn't extend life. It kicks in when you're dead. I'm running out of patience." He aimed the barrel at Marti. "I want the letter, scrapbook, and money."

"All right," Dean said. "I'll take you to the scrapbook. Then we'll telephone Marti and Billy to get the money location." He waited a beat. "On two conditions. That Marti and Billy will not be harmed. . ."

"You're willing to sacrifice your life for theirs?"

"Yes," Dean said without hesitation. "I care enough about both of them to risk my life. Feelings you would never be able to understand, K.A."

"What's the other condition?" K.A. shifted the gun from his

right hand to his left.

"I want you to answer a few questions for me."

"Answers won't do you much good if you're dead," K.A. said. "I'll grant you one question. Take your best shot."

"Who else is involved in the charity's investment sham besides Quincy Nash?" Dean asked, noting Billy's splotchy black and white cat peeking his head into the doorway. "The boy at the orphanage who you called Chub."

"You've done your homework. Nash is the mastermind. No one else is involved, if that is what you're asking. Don't worry about Nash, though, he's as good as dead."

"You're going to kill him too?" Marti asked.

"That shouldn't come as a surprise to you after reading my scrapbook."

"How could you and Chub betray the orphans and d-d-donors?" Billy slapped his palm on the desk. "And me?"

"If they ever give out an award for being naïve, Billy, it would have a depiction of your ugly mug on it. You got your answer, ballplayer. Now take me to the scrapbook."

"Don't do it, Dean." Marti's voice edged frantic. "He'll kill you as soon as he gets his hands on the scrapbook."

Dean strained to hear non-existent sirens. The silence meant he was out of options. The gun was back in K.A.'s right hand.

"You win, K.A." Dean wiggled his fingers by his thigh to catch the cat's attention. "I'll drive you to the scrapbook. Then you can make your phone call to get the location of the money from Marti."

"Are your nerves getting the better of you, ballplayer? I enjoy looking into the eyes of a person who knows he's going to die, and there's absolutely no chance for—"

The cat rubbed against K.A.'s leg on his way to Dean. K.A. jumped, eyeballing the floor. With a backhanded wrist-flip, Dean sent the ledger rocketing at K.A.'s gun like one of those new plastic Frisbees. The book missed the gun, hitting K.A.'s wrist instead. The gun fell to the floor, causing the cat to skitter from the room.

Dean charged at K.A. With cat-like reflexes, K.A. avoided the full impact of Dean's attack. The wall stopped their momentum.

K.A. landed a lightning-quick punch packed with more power than Dean expected. Dean managed to keep his balance. He blocked the next blow with his left arm and knocked K.A. to the floor with a vicious right. K.A. bounced up like he was on a trampoline.

Good God. Dean had given him a hard shot. Was this guy human? The fierceness in K.A.'s eyes told him otherwise. K.A. kicked Dean in the right kneecap—his good knee. Dean ignored the pain. If K.A. had known about his bum knee he probably would have aimed for the damaged joint.

Dean glimpsed Marti edging up on K.A. He shook his head for her to back off. She kept coming. K.A. threw a violent elbow into Marti's stomach, sending her to the floor gasping for breath. K.A.'s move offered Dean an opening. He threw a fist with everything he had. K.A. deftly evaded the blow. Shit. They circled each other like wrestlers. K.A. produced another kick that nicked the side of Dean's bad knee, but didn't do any damage. Lucky. They circled each other in the opposite direction. K.A. landed a sharp punch to Dean's chin. Dean feigned falling then countered by smashing a fist into K.A.'s nose. Dean felt the crunch of breaking bone. Blood splattered as K.A. hit the floor.

Dean turned to Marti. She had a hand cradling her stomach. Her eyes widened in terror. She pointed to the floor. K.A. had rolled to his gun. He managed to stand. His forefinger encircled the trigger while he aimed the barrel at Dean's heart.

"No!" Marti screamed.

BOOM. Deafening gunfire exploded in the room. Then another explosion. Its force pushed K.A. against the wall. Unintelligible sounds leaked from his mouth. Red spots grew larger on his chest and stomach. His lifeless eyes remained open.

"T-t-that was for my mother." Smoke wafted upward from the long barrel of Billy's gun. "And for my cousin, Dean."

CHAPTER FORTY-EIGHT

The scent of gun powder and death lingered in Billy's home office. Dean hung up on Harry while he was in a mid-sentence rant about his share of the money found in K.A.'s suitcase, but not before that wily detective conveyed the missing link of information about The Billy Orphan Foundation. Now it all made sense.

Dean put his arm around Marti. She clung to him tighter than a catcher's chest protector, burying her cheek in his shirt. He shielded her view from the sheet now covering K.A.'s dead body. Dean flashed back to the anguish that had gripped him after running into K.A.'s burning cabin thinking he had lost Marti forever, only to experience euphoria when he found her alive on the muddy road. He squeezed her shoulder. Was Marti replaying a similar scene in her mind? K.A. had been less than a second away from drilling a bullet into Dean's chest when Billy pulled his trigger.

Sitting behind the desk, Billy shook his head. He turned another page in K.A.'s scrapbook that Dean had retrieved from the trunk of his car. His interest was in the damning pages, not the open suitcase of accumulated green bills and sparkling diamonds on the desktop.

"How could I have been so blind?" Billy slammed the scrapbook shut and tossed it on top of K.A.'s ledger of kills. He peered up at Dean and Marti with disgust plastered on his face. "What are you planning to d-do with all this money?"

"You could give it to the police," Dean said.

"Then again," Marti said, "you could keep it and proportionately share the money with the relatives of the deceased investors and your orphanages." Her smile lit up the room. "We think it should be your call, Billy."

"You could have k-k-kept the money for yourselves, and no one would have known."

"You would have known," Dean said, placing a hand on Billy's shoulder.

A distant siren's whine filtered into the room. Three heads turned towards the window. Harry had called the Reno Police. Were Reno's finest finally on their way? A shudder crept up Dean's spine. His great strategy to save them from being assassinated by K.A. had been a colossal failure.

"Aunt Maddy left her home to me, Billy," Dean said. "But it's really your house. Come back to San Francisco with us. We can share it together."

"No. No. The house is yours." Billy placed the cash and diamonds into the suitcase and closed the lid. "My mother wanted you to have it. I need to stay here. D-deal with the sheriff. And pay back the families. But you guys should leave as soon as possible. Stop Chub before he hurts more innocent people."

Dean and Billy shook hands. Marti kissed Billy's cheek, making him blush redder than K.A.'s blood on the white sheet.

"Would it be possible t-to visit both of you someday?"

"You bet, cuz," Dean said. "We have a lot of catching up to do."

CHAPTER FORTY-NINE

Dean studied the photograph hanging on the wall above the credenza in NAHPRO CORPORATION's Oakland California office. A similar picture had mystified him the first time he had noticed it. Now he understood the photo's significance, leaving him with a powerful urge to rip it apart, frame and all.

The walls in the voluminous one-room suite were bare with the exception of the photo. A massive desk held four telephones and a nameplate of finished wood with QUINCY NASH carved into it. Office equipment included an IBM typewriter on a metal stand next to the desk, a hand-cranked adding machine, and a Dictaphone on the credenza. Against the back wall stood tall metal storage cabinets and an A. B. Dick Mimeograph stencil maker on a six foot table. Missing from the suite were visitor chairs.

Marti sat on the credenza, allowing her curvy nylon-clad legs to dangle. She wore a brown double-breasted wool jacket and a matching pleated skirt hiked above her knees. The pointed toe of a stiletto flirted with Dean's pant cuff while her fingers played with one of the office machines. He responded by taking her free hand into his. Their lovers' play was inappropriate for a business suite, but nowhere near as unacceptable as the behavior that had taken place inside the pictured house—the one with windows covered by iron bars.

A key inserted into the outside lock caught their attention. The door slid open over the carpeting. Dean released Marti's hand. A man removed the key from the lock, reached down to retrieve his briefcase from the hallway floor then peered up in surprise.

"What are you two doing here?" Franklyn Edwards stuffed the key into his pocket.

Edwards moved into the office, leaving the door half open. He wore a grey suit, narrow striped tie, familiar aftershave, and a concerned expression on his puffy face.

"We could ask you the same question," Dean said.

"I work on retainer for Mr. Nash, so I have my own key." Edwards shifted his eyes to different sections of the office. "How did you get in?"

"Your secretary, Valerie, opened the door for us." Dean revealed the key.

"Valerie? She doesn't have a key."

"She used the spare key from your office desk," Marti said. "Apparently you once had her deliver that key to you here when you locked yourself out. By the way, Valerie quit. You'll find her resignation letter at the reception desk."

"Quit?" Edwards said, with a concerned expression. "I don't understand. Was she having difficulties with her pregnancy?"

"More like she was having a major problem with her shyster boss," Dean said in a serious tone, "once we informed her how you conduct your business."

Dean made himself comfortable on a desk corner. He flipped the office key in the air then caught it. Edwards frowned at him.

"Mr. Mason, it is understandable that you are still distressed about the loss of your aunt and inheritance. But you have no right to spew unwarranted defamatory words at me or bother my employee. Nor should you be occupying this office without permission." Edwards pushed the door open wider. "Vacate immediately or I will call the police."

"I seriously doubt you want the police involved." Dean stuffed the key into his pocket.

"Why is that, Mr. Mason?" Edwards said, picking up his briefcase.

Marti answered Edwards' question by holding up handwritten pages. Her finger traced each name she said aloud, as if she was reading a story book to her second graders.

"You may stop, Miss Cooper," Edwards said. "None of those names mean anything to me."

"If we were in court right now," Dean said, "you would be perjuring yourself. The people listed on these pages have four things in common: They were old; they invested multi-millions in The Billy

Orphan Foundation; they died prematurely from assumed suicide or accident by the hands of a man called K.A., and a good percentage of them were your *pro bono* clients, including my aunt, Madeline Principal."

Edwards blinked at Dean twice. His swallow was noticeable. He moved to the desk and placed his briefcase on top, then turned to catch Dean's eye.

"Pure conjecture on your part," Edwards said. "For all I know, you copied those names from newspaper obituaries. I am not aware of anyone who goes by the name of K.A. Nor am I affiliated with that particular charity, or any other charity for that matter. And I certainly did not kill anyone."

"K.A.'s real name is Tyler Wilkes," Dean said. "Quincy Nash ordered him to kill all of those people. He is just as responsible for their deaths as K.A."

"How dare you." Edwards pointed to the name plate by Dean's thigh. "Mr. Nash is a pillar of the Oakland business community."

Dean nodded to Marti. She held out the picture from K.A.'s scrapbook for Edwards to see. His eyes widened in recognition. He caught himself, shrugging his shoulders in mock indifference.

"Why are you showing me an old picture of two scruffy boys?" Edwards asked.

"We discovered that Quincy Nash took this photo of Billy Orphan and Tyler Wilkes at Uncle Pete's Sanctuary for Orphan Boys in Nevada," Dean said. "Three orphans celebrating their independence. Wilkes had just killed Uncle Pete with a pickax. The house pictured on the wall here is the same building in the background of this photo."

Dean's stare connected with Edwards' glare. Edwards round face reddened. Sweat glistened from his cheeks.

"This is absurd." Edwards said. "How the devil can you prove Mr. Nash, or anyone else, took that picture? Or prove those houses are the same?"

"There's more," Dean said. "Quincy Nash, Chub to the other orphan boys, uses the alias of Franklyn Edwards. You have lived your whole adult life as two people: Franklyn Edwards the attorney, and Quincy Nash the multi-millionaire entrepreneur and master-mind behind The Billy Orphan Foundation."

Edwards removed a white handkerchief from his coat pocket and dabbed his face. He exhaled loudly and pointed a shaky finger towards San Francisco.

"The names on the diplomas in my law office say Franklyn Edwards. Proof that I –"

"There is no Silver State University or law school," Dean said. "Those diplomas are just as phony as the name Franklyn Edwards, meaning you are not really an attorney. Instead you are just a big fake, killing people for money. Did you order Tyler to burn down the orphanage with the orphan boys trapped inside?"

"No, asshole, I didn't tell Tyler to torch the orphanage." Edwards' voice had changed to a deeper, rougher tone. He lifted his bangs, exposing the hideous scar on his forehead and looked past Dean to stare at the picture on the wall. "Tyler killed Uncle Pete of his own volition after that perverted son of a bitch did this to me with a shovel blade."

Dean winked at Marti. Edwards' demeanor had also changed. He puffed his chest out the same way a hood would before a fight. In their lovers hideaway, Marti had mentioned the movie "Three Faces of Eve." Did Franklyn Edwards, or Quincy Nash, have multiple personalities? Or was he just playing a different role?

"Why do you keep the photograph of the orphanage on your wall?" Dean asked. "Isn't the scar enough of a reminder of what Uncle Pete did to you?"

"I keep that picture to never forget the indignity of being an orphan," Edwards spit out. "Or for being abused by scumbags like Uncle Pete." He sat behind his desk, punishing the springs in his chair. "Being a homeless orphan is like being a stray mutt snared by a dogcatcher. The only difference is that the pound humanely puts unwanted dogs to sleep when no one will adopt them."

Dean peered at the Window when a siren sounded then ebbed away. Edwards didn't react to it. Minutes ago, he had been sweaty and shaky. Now he was cockier than a single rooster in a hen house. Why?

of care for a loyal accountant who had put him on a proverbial pedestal for all these years.

Dean blew out a troubled breath. What was Edwards' game? He wasn't acting like a man who had just been caught red-handed. On the contrary, he was sitting smug like he had an advantage they didn't know about.

"You are just as certifiable as Tyler," Dean said.

"Am I, Mason?" Edwards said. "A headshrinker will tell you I am the sanest person in this room. But the goddaughter touched on my ultimate stratagem. The government should have a holiday honoring me. I have done society a great service by eliminating old, worthless people who in turn provide money for homeless waifs. Money, more often than not, that ended up lining the pockets of predators like Uncle Pete. There are literally hundreds of thousands of donors like Madeline Principal. They think they're helping. The guilty little secret – the act of giving makes them feel less culpable about past sins. Their donations don't help. They hurt. They hurt orphans in ways you can't possibly imagine. Your godmother deserved to die just like all the others."

"The law will have a different perspective," Dean said.

"You're not going to contact the police." Edwards smiled again. "I knew this day would eventually come, just not this soon. And definitely not from you. My failsafe is Tyler. I'm the only person Tyler won't harm. Tyler will eliminate anyone who tries to hurt me. At my command, not even an army of hired bodyguards will stop Tyler from killing the two of you. In other words, if anything happens to me, you might as well add your names to that long list of dead people you read to me earlier. If I go, you go."

"I believe he's serious about ordering Tyler to come after us," Marti said to Dean.

"I don't doubt him for second," Dean countered.

"But I'm willing to give you and Miss Cooper a *quid pro quo*." Edwards said, smirking.

Dean felt adrenalin rushing through his veins. Edwards was finally about to reveal his ace in the hole.

"We're listening," Dean said.

"You forget everything you know about me, Tyler, and The Billy Orphan Foundation, and I will double your inheritance and return it to you year by year."

"What about Tyler?" Marti asked.

"You have my word he will not harm you. In essence, we are creating wills of trust."

"What do you think, Dean?" Marti said. "Mr. Edwards is offering you $1,740,000. I bet you could buy the San Francisco Giants with that amount."

"Tempting," Dean said. "But there are three major flaws in Edwards' deal."

Edwards cocked his head and threw Dean a queer look. "Do tell, Mason."

"First:" Dean said, "I can't be bribed, no matter what amount money you offer. Second: Tyler Wilkes was on his way to murder Quincy Nash after he killed Billy. Third: Tyler Wilkes is dead."

"Come on, Mason." Edwards cranked out a sharp laugh, making his soft body jiggle. "You can do better than that."

"There's no need to," Detective Lynch said, entering through the open door, "Mr. Edwards or Nash or whoever you are at this moment." A second detective and Harry Spitari followed. "Billy Orphan shot Tyler Wilkes dead yesterday in his Reno home, saving Miss Cooper and Mason from a similar fate. By the way, you're under arrest."

Color drained from Edwards' face. He glanced at the open door then back to Lynch.

"On what grounds are you arresting me?" Edwards asked his voice catching.

"Murder, grand theft, fraud, money laundering, doing business without proper certification. You've probably broken enough laws to put Franklyn Edwards and Quincy Nash away for ninety-nine years each."

"You can't prove I murdered anyone. Or I had any affiliation with Tyler Wilkes."

"This will give them all the proof that's needed." Marti pressed rewind on the Dictaphone then played back a portion of their earlier dialogue.

"Told you she was a keeper, Dream," Harry said.

"Harry has information," Dean said to Detective Lynch, "on Quincy Nash's network of corporations starting with NAHPRO here in Oakland. If you trace backwards, the money trail will end with The Billy Orphan Foundation's dead investors."

Edwards slipped a small pill bottle from his pocket. Harry's hand chopped the plastic bottle to the floor. Edwards looked longingly at the vial, then tore at his top shirt button and tie, gasping. Suicide was favorable to being locked in a jail with a gang of Uncle Petes. He looked up at Dean.

"Damn you, Mason," Edwards growled. "Damn You."

Dean pointed to the wall.

"I think you will find that prison is very similar to an orphanage with iron bars," Dean said, ushering Marti to the door.

CHAPTER FIFTY

Dean's knees dug into the hardwood floor of his former bedroom. He stopped working, peered up at the ceiling, and smiled. The brilliance of certain people often goes undetected until they pass on. Aunt Maddy had been a master strategist. Even Harry would have admired how she planned a life for the two young people she cared for most.

A cry of pain from the backyard was followed by hysterical barking. Dean dropped the hammer and chisel, rose to his feet, and moved to the room's only window. The early sunlight unveiled a comedic scene. Mrs. Butera's doberman pinscher, Darko, had a tall man with greasy black hair and long sideburns trapped up a backyard tree. The man's ripped Levi's pant leg exposed a nasty bite wound oozing blood. Darko continued with a steady stream of fierce growls and barks. This was better than an episode of *I Love Lucy*.

Dean phoned the police from the kitchen then went back to his bedroom window. Marti pushed open the door. He turned to face her. One of her hands knotted both ends of the white bedspread concealing a luscious bare body that had snuggled against Dean two hours earlier. Her disheveled dark hair reminded him of her hangover morning in Aunt Maddy's kitchen. She fixed her eyes on the portion of torn up hardwood floor before her feet pitter-pattered to the window.

"Why is Darko so upset?" she asked, leaning a shivering shoulder into him until he wrapped a warm arm around her. "Oh my God. Is that Boyd Weber, that hood from Freddy's bar, up in Aunt Madeline's tree?"

"Either Boyd or a new species of bird called the Greaser."

"Should we call the police?"

"I already did," Dean said. "Good thing Mrs. Butera loaned us Darko while she's visiting her son in Modesto. Boyd isn't going anywhere. That's for sure."

Each time Boyd moved, Darko reacted with a vicious growl and raised his front paws on the tree trunk. Marti put her arm around Dean's waist and nuzzled her cheek into his chest.

"You knew Boyd would come here, didn't you?" she said.

"Boyd is predictable. He probably drove by the house every morning after his night shift at the graveyard while we were in Nevada. When he saw my car in the driveway this morning, he made his move."

"If Darko hadn't stopped him, what kind of move do you think he would have made?"

"Probably some kind of high school harassment."

"I don't see toilet paper hanging from the tree limbs, Dean."

"It's nothing to worry about, Marti."

He gave her shoulder a reassuring squeeze. A necessary fib. She hadn't noticed the gasoline can in the dirt by the tree trunk. Boyd had intended to torch the house with them in it. With his dirty fingerprints all over the gas can as evidence, an attempted arson conviction should keep him locked up for a long time.

"I doubt we will have to worry about Boyd again," he said. "However, just to be on the safe side, maybe our first financial investment should be a relative of Darko's."

"Good idea. But we won't have much investment money until I start my teaching job in the fall."

"What are you saying?" he quizzed. "Are you going to support me?"

"Why not?" She said. "You supported me."

"We could always hock my watch for a doberman or German shepherd."

"No dice, Bryce," she said. "I negotiated fair and square for that watch. There is significant sentimental value in that timepiece. Still, I could trade the watch back to you if it is replaced with a smaller band . . . say for my ring finger."

"I suppose this smaller band you are referring to includes a diamond?"

"That would be nice. However, due to the current state of our finances, I think a gold or silver ring would suffice."

"The person who taught you how to negotiate did one hell of a good job. And to think I didn't trust you."

"The question is, can I trust you?" Marti turned and pointed to the hole in the floor. "Ripping out hardwood slats is not what Aunt Madeline had in mind when she wanted you to refurbish the floors."

"Actually, I did exactly what Aunt Maddy guided me to do."

"Help me understand," she said. "The will indicated your aunt wanted her floors maintained. A will, may I remind you, that is not even legal. Mr. Edwards or Nash was not a legitimate lawyer. You don't have to do anything to the floors to keep this house. Nor do you have to give me a thousand dollars a year. But we still have to worry about the back taxes and interest on the house."

"My aunt never wanted the floors refurbished. Believe me, if she did, those floors would have been stripped and lacquered many times over before she died. That clause in the will was a clue. Aunt Maddy's intention had always been for me to discover her diary and the loose boards underneath the carpet."

Dean led Marti to the area he had been working on. He kneeled to the floor, pulling her down with him. The bedspread opened. She didn't bother to close it, which didn't bother him one bit. He reached into the floor opening with both hands and withdrew a portion of the contents. Marti's eyes widened. Then he flipped the handful of green bills to the ceiling. Bills that had multiple zeros.

"Ten-thousand dollar bills, just like mother talked about." Marti stared at the face on one of the bills. "I have never heard of Salmon P. Chase, but he is the second handsomest man in this room. You will never have to worry about money again, Dean."

"The money is half yours, Marti." He co-mingled bills of different denominations and stacked them like a deck of cards. Aunt Maddy had a vision of the two of us sharing her fortune as a couple."

"Aunt Madeline's vision and my dream came true," Marti said.

Dean reached into his shirt pocket and extracted a polished rock. He dropped the diamond into her soft hand. Her sightline bounced from his face to her palm.

"But you were so vehement about not keeping K.A.'s stolen stash."

"I figured we deserved a finder's fee for all of our hard work," he said.

"No argument from me. Does this mean what I think it means?"

"If you accept this diamond as part of a lifetime partnership, it means half of the money found in this room will also be legally yours." Dean cradled her face with both hands. "Aunt Maddy left me the greatest gift of all by bringing you into my life."

Two knocks at the front door interrupted an embrace that was prelude to another round of love making. Marti pulled away, out of breath, placing both hands on his chest.

"One of us should answer the door," she said.

"A knock this early in the morning is often a harbinger of bad news."

Marti rose to her feet in one swift move, knotting the bedspread with a hand. Dean managed to rise with her, cranky knee and all. He held her back.

"Don't answer it," he said.

"It is probably the police or a neighbor complaining about Darko's barking." She gave Dean a big smooch and left him alone with Salmon P. Chase, James Madison, and Grover Cleveland.

"Why the hell did I think she would start listening to me now?" he mumbled.

Marti came back holding a yellow Western Union telegram. She handed it to him. He pushed the envelope back and asked her to read it to him.

"Mr. Mason, Walter Finley passed away August 11. He bequeathed the Billings Mustangs to you. Please respond immediately."

"Damn," he said. "Here we go again."

"More than you know. It says here that the will is being contested by Mr. Finley's three sons."

"Mr. Finley left the Mustangs to me because he knew I would oversee it the way he wanted. More to the point, he did not want his sons ruining the team."

"You had the same expression on your face when you told Franklyn Edwards that Aunt Madeline did not commit suicide or have an accident."

"There is a good chance Mr. Finley didn't die of natural causes." Dean took her hand into his. "Are you up for another road trip?"

"I go where you go, slugger."

"Wouldn't want it any other way. Neither would Aunt Maddy."

ACKNOWLEDGEMENTS

Heartfelt thanks to the following people for contributing, in a myriad of ways, to my novels *Bum!*, *The Ticker*, and **Will To Kill**.

Allison Anson, Bill Archibald, Bob Archibald, Julie Archibald, Frank Baldwin, Scott Benner, Jesse Bloom, Robin Brooks, Donna Smith Brown, Frank & Barbara Butera, Dennis Cacace, Carole Carl, Sharyl Carter, Whitney Cicero, Shiela Cockshott, Mary Ruth Conley, Ryan & Racquel Cosare, Clarence Cravalho, Pat Cuendet, Brian Davis, Darryl Davis, Gary Davis, David Drotar, Louise Englehart, Carolyn Flohr, Steve & Joni Gimnicher, Sue Goldman, Margi Grant, Barbara Hembey, Valerie Huber, Warren Joiner, Mark Jones, Jason Kawamoto, Marie Kennedy, Jennifer Lindsey, Serena Ludovico, Laura Lugan, Jacqueline Machada, Jimbo Manansala, Mike Marshall, Allison Martindale, Sharen McConnell, Lorraine McGrath, Rockin' Roy McKinney, Princess Kristina Merlini, Virginia Messer, Kristal Miles, Gus Milon, Jeff Morena, Colleen Navarro, Alicia Robertson, Ken & Lora Rolandelli, Laura Senderov, Seton Hospital's Wonderful Wound Care staff Helen Dolan, Cesena Coleman, Lauren Jones, and Randall Varilla, Jack Smallwood, Dr. Kalpanu Srinivasan, Steve Stahl, Kelli Jo Stratinsky, Rick and Scherrie Taylor, Catherine Teitelbaum, Gail Tesi, Elisabeth Tuck, Bill Tyler, James F. Whitehead, Donnalyn Zarzeczny.

Special thanks to Optometrist **Dr. Howard Rose** (my words are more readable to his literary patients) and daughter **Debby Rose** for their super support, **Gin Geraldi**—who blooms radiance wherever she goes, **Jeannie Graham**—a most gracious hostess, **Karin Marshall** —always there to help nurse a rough draft, **Alicia Mazzoni**—a supporter from day one, **Tracy McNamara**—my corner would be lacking without her, **Claire McVay**—an inspiration to all, **Scott Taylor**—a tenacious businessman and good friend, **Pat Vitucci**—"Don't Invest And Forget," **Nancy Archibald**—who relishes the book's words almost as much as the cover, **Leslie Walsh**—a budding editor and nice person, **Laurel Ann Hill**—award winning author and clutch friend.

Without my four literary and crafty amigas, **Barbara Drotar, Jana McBurney-Lin, Caroline Nelson**, and **Martha Clark Scala**, I'd still be writing on public bathroom walls. The best support group any author could ever have.

To my wife, **Joanne**, who serves as Creative Special Effects Manager, Sales Manager, Typo Editor, and Head Cheerleader, THANK YOU for your selfless help.

CPSIA information can be obtained
at www.ICGtesting.com
Printed in the USA
FSOW02n2134271014
3328FS